A GHOUL'S GUIDE TO LOVE AND MURDER

A GHOST HUNTER MYSTERY

Victoria Laurie

AN OBSIDIAN MYSTERY

OBSIDIAN
Published by New American Library,
an imprint of Penguin Random House LLC
375 Hudson Street, New York, New York 10014

This book is an original publication of New American Library.

First Printing, January 2016

Copyright © Victoria Laurie, 2016
Excerpt from *Abby Cooper, Psychic Eye* copyright © Victoria Laurie, 2004
Penguin Random House supports copyright. Copyright fuels creativity, encourages
diverse voices, promotes free speech, and creates a vibrant culture. Thank you for
buying an authorized edition of this book and for complying with copyright laws
by not reproducing, scanning, or distributing any part of it in any form without
permission. You are supporting writers and allowing Penguin Random House to
continue to publish books for every reader.

Obsidian and the Obsidian colophon are trademarks of
Penguin Random House LLC.

For more information about Penguin Random House, visit penguin.com.

ISBN 978-0-451-47012-6

Printed in the United States of America
10 9 8 7 6 5 4 3 2 1

PUBLISHER'S NOTE
This is a work of fiction. Names, characters, places, and incidents either are the
product of the author's imagination or are used fictitiously, and any resemblance
to actual persons, living or dead, business establishments, events, or locales is
entirely coincidental.

Penguin
Random
House

To all you glorious Ghost Hunter Mysteries fans.

M.J., Heath, Gilley, and I thank you
for ten amazing years.

Acknowledgments

I've been sitting here for the past hour trying to find the right words to let all of you who read the Ghost Hunter Mysteries know how very much I have appreciated the gift of your support for these past ten years, and I'm not thinking that this will be the most eloquent of speeches, but I hope the sentiment of that gratitude at least comes through. I started M.J. on a whim way back in 2004—maybe '05. I had lunch in Manhattan with my amazing agent, Jim McCarthy, and my pitch went as follows: "So, there's this character that I've introduced in *A Vision of Murder* and her name is M. J. Holliday. She's a descendant of Doc Holliday, her BFF is a flamboyantly fun boy named Gilley, and she has a parrot named Doc. M.J. is a ghostbuster, and she's a badass, and I kiiiiiiinda want to do a spinoff series featuring her."

His response? "How fast can you write it?" ☺

I never expected M.J.'s story to turn into the successful series it has. I figured she'd last about four, maybe five books, and I'd move on to something else. But she remained strong and consistent, and that is due mostly to you, my wonderful fans. And I know that some of you reading this will be surprised that this is the last installment in the series, and I also know that it might make you a little sad. . . . I'm sad too. I've loved working on her stories. I've loved watching her grow and evolve and fall in love—twice—and mature into something less badass and something more . . . nurturing. I think I knew about three years ago that her story arc was coming to an end. It just felt right to end the series at number ten. But it's also heartbreaking in a way, because I love these characters and I've loved hearing about how you've loved them too. So, thank you for that. Sincerely. It's meant the world to me to have so many devoted fans, and I promise you that while this may be the end of hearing about M.J. and Heath, it's not the end of my storytelling. There will be more from me. Much more. (Hinty, hinty . . .) And I pinkie swear you'll like it. ☺

And now, if you'll indulge me, I'd like to take a moment to thank everyone who's supported me and encouraged me professionally these past ten years with the series. In particular I'd like to begin by thanking Jim McCarthy, my agent and one of the very best people I've ever had the sincere pleasure to call a friend. Early in the crafting of the very first book, I knew that I wanted to have a character inspired by Jim, and he has so generously allowed me that license. Gilley never would've been the truly fabulous, flamboyant, witty, fun, and hilarious character that he is without Jim's influence. In fact, I doubt Gil ever would've existed without Jim. I owe him for that, and maybe also for being the very best agent on the planet. Thank you, honey. You and Gilley will hold a very special place in my heart for the rest of my life, and there aren't words to express how truly grateful I am for that.

I'd also like to take a moment to thank Sandra Harding-Hull, my editor for more than seven years, who was so integral to the longevity of the series. If not for Sandy, I'm quite convinced I would've ended the series much sooner, but I loved working with her, so I kept going. She's moved on from being my editor, and it still makes me cry to think she won't be lending her sage advice to my books, but her legacy is deeply entrenched in both M.J. and Abby, and I'll always remember the lessons she taught me. Thank you, Sandy. I miss you, I adore you, and hope you're still reading my stuff and that you know how very much you have contributed to my success.

Thanks also go to Jessica Wade, who jumped in and assisted with the edits on this book, and who is now taking over for Sandy. I liked you immensely in the first ten seconds we spoke, Jessica, and I knew that I'd be in the very best of hands at second eleven. ☺

Also, thank you to my amazing publicist, Danielle Dill, who's just, like, *awesome*! It's been so much fun sharing puppy pics with you, Danielle. Thanks for being so fantastic and so personable. You rock!

Finally, I'd like to thank the people in my personal life who constantly support me even when I'm running myself ragged trying to make that deadline. Brian Gorzynski (I love you, honey. I'm the luckiest woman in the world with you at my side), my amazing sister, Sandy

Upham, Steve McGrory, Matt and Mike Morrill, Katie Coppedge, Leanne Tierney, Karen Ditmars, Nicole Gray, Jennifer Melkonian, Terry Gilman, Catherine Ong Kane, Drue Rowean, Sally Woods, John Kwaitkowski, Matt McDougal, Dean James, Anne Kimbol, McKenna Jordan, Hilary Laurie, Shannon Anderson, Thomas Robinson, Juliet Blackwell, Gigi Pandian, Martha Bushko and Suzanne Parsons.

Chapter 1

It was a drizzly spring late afternoon in Boston when Heath and I walked into my office off Mass Ave, holding hands and smiling wickedly. Who's Heath, you ask? Well . . . that's where things get a little complicated.

In order to tell you who Heath is, I need to swear you to secrecy. Not the "Oh, I will only tell my eleventy million friends on Facebook—pinkie swear" kind of secret.

An. Actual. Secret.

See, the last time I checked in with you all, Heath was simply my boyfriend. My love. My partner in both the business and domestic sense, and yes, sometimes our domestic stuff is all about the "bidness," but I digress. Or first, perhaps I must explain.

About eight months ago "the call" came in . . . and by that I mean that myself, Heath, Gilley, and respective members of our *Ghoul Getters* cast were made rich, I tell you . . . *rich*!

The call was from a major motion picture studio, which had agreed to distribute a movie we'd made a few years back while on location for our TV ghostbusting show, *Ghoul Getters*. The individual episode and all of the extra footage from one particular ghostbust we'd done in Scotland had been purchased by a production company—Prescott Productions—but the production company had needed the backing of a major motion picture studio to green-light the distribution before the movie actually got funded and any of us got paid. For several years all that extra footage just sat on the shelf, but just when we'd all given up the dream, the call had come in that the movie was a go.

In fact, *The Haunting of the Grim Widow* was set to release in theaters everywhere a week after Heath and I got back from our trip. I hadn't actually seen the completed film yet, mostly because I'd barely lived through my encounter with the Widow and had no urge to relive it.

Still, we had captured some stuff on film that would make your hair curl, and luckily for us, some studio execs finally took notice. They were now all over the idea of promoting a "real" horror flick that was as creepy as *The Conjuring*, without all the special effects.

What that had meant for us, specifically, was a *considerable* signing bonus, with an additional amount due later in the form of a portion of the box office in royalties. In other words, the second we stopped taping our last *Ghoul Getters* episode, none of us—the talent and our small crew—ever really had to work again if we were careful and invested wisely, of course.

Anyway, it'd taken about seven months to finish that last location shoot for *GG*, but at the end of the week, we each received our first big check.

Now, money will motivate you in a way that you might not think. It makes you do things impulsively, the way finding out you have only a short time to live does. Most of us did things that we might not otherwise have done if not afforded the freedom that a big pile of moolah gave us.

Gilley (my BFF and our tech expert on the shoots) proposed to Michel, our cameraman and Gilley's boyfriend, on the same day that Michel proposed to him. It was insanely cute to see the recap of the two flash mobs brought together at the same restaurant, not having any knowledge of each other, and have it dissolve into something resembling the Sharks and the Jets. In the end there were a *lot* of tired dancers and nearly a million hits on YouTube, and Gil and Michel were engaged, so it worked out okay.

Our director, Peter Gopher, funded a documentary he'd been trying to get off the ground and set off to Nepal to begin filming.

John and Kim, our sound guy and production assistant, booked a trip to Asia and were slowly making their way across the region, keeping us updated through Facebook posts and the like.

Meg, our adorable hair and makeup assistant, had promptly gone back to college up in Montreal, and she'd also paid off her parents' mortgage.

And Heath and I got married. (You read that right. We got hitched.) By the way, *that's* the part y'all need to keep on the down low, because if Gilley finds out that I got married before him, well, I'm likely never to hear the end of it.

Our wedding was truly impulsive. Heath surprised me at the end of March with a three-week trip to St. Thomas. Have you ever been to St. Thomas? It's gorgeous. *Gorgeous!* Think aqua blue water, white sandy beaches, drinks in coconuts, genuinely lovely people, and romantic ambiance out the yin-yang.

On our second day there he left me a note asking me to be his for the day and to meet him for a romantic walk along the beach. From our cabana I traveled down a bamboo walkway and around a little bend to find my beautiful man, standing there with a rose in his hand. As I approached he got down on bended knee and said, "Em, will you be mine, not just for today, but forever?"

He then presented me with the most beautiful ring you've ever seen. But I'd have said yes if it was carved from a puka shell. They don't make men like Heath in abundance. I'm lucky.

So, we spent the first week of our engagement talking about our future, and by the end of that beautiful week, we both knew we didn't feel like waiting to call each other husband and wife.

We were married by a local justice of the peace in the waning light of the setting sun, with purple, pink, and peach streaks coating the tropical sky and the sound of the rolling surf the only music to be had. I wore a soft peach sundress I found at a shop in town, and Heath wore a light blue shirt, white shorts, and a smile as wide as Texas. It was perfect.

The next week we had ourselves a proper honeymoon, and now we were back in Boston, wading through a steady drizzle and miserably cold temps, but our spirits were in no way diminished. "What time are we meeting Gil?" my husband asked as we came through the door shaking our umbrellas.

I nearly tripped over the small pile of mail that'd been shoved through the mail slot.

"Seven," I told him, flipping on the light before stooping to gather some of the mail and glancing at my watch. It was ten to five. Traffic had been horrible—given both the weather and the onset of rush hour, it'd taken more than an hour to get from the airport to my office, a commute that normally takes only about twenty minutes. "We're meeting for dinner before he heads to the opening of the exhibit." The studio was sponsoring an exhibit of items from the movie and our TV show to create some buzz for the actual premiere of the movie, which would be released the following week. The Boston premiere of the movie was going to be shown at the IMAX theater that was housed in a building adjacent to the Museum of Modern Science—and that was also the location for the *Ghoul Getters* exhibit.

Paranormal investigations weren't exactly considered "modern science" by the museum's standards, but the studio had thrown a *lot* of money at them, and they'd come around. (Surprise, surprise.)

"You still don't want to go?" Heath asked.

"Gilley will be there to represent us," I said to Heath. "And I'm way too tired to go to that thing. I'd much prefer a relaxing, low-key evening and a good meal."

"It's probably not gonna be very relaxing if we meet Gil for dinner," Heath muttered, but I'd heard him. And I could sympathize.

Gil had talked of little else but his wedding for months, and we were all well and truly sick of it. He was going big—as he had a nice big pile of money to play with—and no one could seem to rein him in. I'd decided early on to withhold any and all opinions, sage advice, judgmental looks, or mutterings on the matter. If my BFF wanted to be a diva, and a ginormous wedding would make him happy, then so be it.

"What's our plan?" Heath said, plopping into a chair in front of my desk.

"Well," I said, extending my left hand to smile again at the wedding and engagement rings. "I have to hide the evidence for a little while. Just until I'm sure he's not going to be upset by the news that we got married first."

"So, until after he gets married?" Heath asked.

I ducked my chin. "Maybe," I said, swiveling in the chair to move aside a cabinet door that hid a small safe.

"Em," Heath said, "he's not getting married until *September.*"

My shoulders sagged. This coming back to reality was a real bummer. "I know, honey, I know. But you've seen how he can be. He'll perceive it as our upstaging him, and he's in such an emotional state as it is—"

"Only because he's turned into a groomzilla," Heath interrupted.

I sighed, swiveling back to my husband with hands up in surrender. "Okay. How about we wait just a little while. Until we find a good moment to tell him."

"We could always tell Michel and have him spill the beans."

That made me laugh. "You are such a chicken," I told him. "And no way are we doing that to poor Michel. Gilley is fully capable of shooting the messenger."

Heath grimaced, but then he seemed to brighten. "You know, maybe it won't be so bad. Maybe he'll be happy for us instead of thinking we stole his spotlight."

My jaw dropped. "Excuse me, but have you *met* Gilley Gillespie?"

Heath's grimace returned. "If he's gonna freak out about our being married, what's he going say about the fact that we're moving to Santa Fe?"

That's another big change that I forgot to tell you about. Heath and I had decided to retire from Boston and move to Santa Fe to be closer to his family. It'd be a big adjustment for me, but in recent months I'd grown closer and closer to his mom and his cousins. They were such lovely, warm, and welcoming people, and now that they were also my family, I wanted to be near them.

"We'll cross that bridge when we come to it," I told him.

"Like when Gilley and Michel are off on their honeymoon?" Heath said hopefully.

I pointed at him. "Exactly." Then I turned away to bend over and fiddle with the dial on the safe. "Honey, could you hand over your ring?"

"I think I'm going to hold on to it, Em."

I looked over my shoulder at him. He was tugging on his wedding ring, about to take it off. "You sure you don't want me to put it in here where it'll be safe?" I asked, a bit worried he'd lose it.

"Yeah," he said, still tugging. "It's my good luck charm."

That made me smile, and I went back to focusing on the combination to the safe. After opening it up, I took off my rings and was about to place them on the bottom shelf when something inside the safe caught my eye.

Or rather, it was the absence of something that caught my eye. *"Ohmigod!"*

Heath came around the desk and over to me. "What?" he said. "What is it?"

I pointed inside. "The dagger! The dagger! It's gone!"

Heath stared first at me, then inside the safe, and the color drained from his face.

For the past few years we'd kept an extremely rare and incredibly dangerous relic in our safe: a dagger once owned by a particularly evil and quite deadly Turkish warlord named Oruç.

Heath and I had first met at a hotel in San Francisco, where we'd been hired as the talent on another cable TV show, a special called *Haunted Possessions*. We were two of the four mediums hired as the talent to assess various objects that were said to have been possessed by evil spirits. Of all the objects put in front of us, only Oruç's dagger had truly been possessed by something evil—and evil he was.

Oruç had lived several centuries earlier, and he'd

developed a lust for killing young women by stabbing them with his dagger.

After he was murdered by a woman he tried to kill—with the dagger—his ghost figured out a way to use the dagger as a portal, which is a sort of gateway between our world and the lower realms, where evil things lurk.

Oruç's ghost was a crazy powerful spook in his own right, and his ability to completely possess anyone who handled the dagger was a very scary thing. His spirit could completely overtake the person in question and force him or her to commit murder.

If that weren't reason enough to lock the dagger away, it came with an added terrifying bonus: The dagger was also the portal for a demon that I don't think was ever of this world.

Oruç's demon was truly a monster. I'd never actually seen it, but I'd sure as hell felt it, and I had the scars on my back to prove it.

Its presence was big, like . . . *big*, and it would strike by swiping at us with its three talons. We knew they were talons because everywhere the demon struck it left that distinctive three-line gouge—in walls, in furniture, in flesh. It had been somewhat neutralized back when we'd first encountered it, meaning that it hadn't been powerful enough to ever show its true form, but one of my biggest fears was that someday, that demon would figure out a way to escape the dagger again, and if it ever became powerful enough to do that, then there was no telling what harm it might cause.

After first encountering the dagger and its horrors,

we'd had a hell of a time putting those two genies back in their bottles, so to speak, and sadly, not before more than one person had been killed. Since then, however, we'd taken every precaution with it, securing it with powerful magnets that blocked the portal's gateway and wouldn't allow anything from the lower realms to come through.

Essentially, we'd sent Oruç and his demon back to the lower realms where they belonged, and as long as we had possession of the dagger, I knew with some certainty that the warlord and the demon were sufficiently shut down. But now the dagger was missing, and my first thought was one of panic, because in the wrong hands that thing was—at best—deadly. "Ohmigod," I whispered as I continued to stare at the inside of the safe. "It can't be gone. It can't!"

Heath moved a little closer to me and began pulling other things out of the safe. There was a wad of cash for emergencies, the lease for our office, and a few other odds and ends, but no dagger. No magnets either, but that hardly mattered with the dagger missing.

"What the hell, Em?" he said when he'd emptied the contents of the safe.

I stared wide-eyed at him. "It was there before we left for vacation," I swore. "I know it was because I had to move it to one side to get to our passports. Sometime in the last three weeks, somebody got into the safe and took it."

Heath stared at me; then he inspected the door to the safe, which showed no tampering. "Who the hell knew about the dagger and also knew the combination?"

A trickle of sweat slid down my back. "The only other person who knows the combination, besides you and me, is Gil, but he'd never take it. I mean, he's afraid to even look at this safe, knowing what's inside."

"So this had to be a professional job," Heath said quietly, his eyes roving around the room suspiciously. I looked about too, and I knew that both of us were worried that we'd been burglarized, but nothing else seemed to be missing. My laptop was on the desk, and my scanner/copier—an expensive one—was over to the right, both untouched. In the corner our camera equipment was piled on a table, along with two extra laptops that Gilley had as backups.

I got up and went over to my filing cabinet, where I kept the small box filled with petty cash, and the money was still there and also untouched.

"Someone came in here and took the dagger but left everything else alone," I said, a cold chill vibrating up my back.

Heath sat down in the chair I'd just vacated. "So, somebody with knowledge of that dagger came in here and robbed us?"

A second chill radiated down my spine and along my arms. "If that's true, then they'd only want the dagger for one purpose: to cause harm."

Heath ran a hand through his long black hair with trademark white streak along one temple. "We could be in serious trouble if that happened, babe."

I pulled out my phone and brought up a local news Web site. I scrolled through the stories from the past few weeks looking for any hint of unusual and violent deaths in the area, but it didn't look like anything involving the dagger had occurred. No strange or unexplainable stabbings or deaths. No rooms destroyed by an invisible demon. No telltale talon marks left behind to photograph. Nothing.

Which only meant that the magnets binding the dagger hadn't been removed. Yet.

"We have to find it!" I said, feeling myself starting to panic. That dagger had been our responsibility. We'd promised people that it was safe with us. That they could trust us with it. To find it missing was like discovering that a vial of anthrax was loose in the city. It could only bring about horrendously terrible things.

My phone rang as Heath and I were staring at each other, wondering how we were going to track it down before the spook Oruç and his demon had a chance to possess someone and kill someone else. Lifting the phone again I looked at the display. "Gil," I said, not even bothering with the niceties. "I can't talk right now. We have a situation."

"You're not the only one," he drawled. "The flower shop wants more money and the caterer is refusing my calls. Why are wedding people so difficult?" He nearly shouted. And then he did shout. *"Why, God, why?!"*

"Gilley!" I told him firmly. I had no patience for his antics just then. "I'm serious."

"And I'm not?"

My brow lowered and my fist clenched. "Heath and I just looked inside the safe in our office, and . . . Oruç's dagger is missing." On the other end of the line there was silence. I took it for shock. "Gil?" I called. "Honey, are you there?"

"What were you doing in the safe?" he replied, which was an awfully interesting question—given the circumstances.

"Putting away our passports," I lied before focusing on him again, my suspicions raised. "You don't sound surprised that Oruç's dagger is missing. Why?"

There was a long pause; then Gilley suddenly said, "Oh! It's the caterer. Thank God. Sorry, M.J.—gotta take this call." And the little bastard hung up on me.

I pulled my phone away from my ear to stare at it in shock before I connected the dots. *"Son of a bitch!"*

"Talk to me," Heath said.

I ignored him for a moment as I dialed Gilley right back. It rang three times before going to voice mail. "My left foot he was on the phone with the caterer!" I spat. Had he actually been on the phone, the call would've gone straight to voice mail. Three rings meant he was purposely ignoring me. I nearly threw my cell across the room I was so furious. Only the fact that the iPhone is a six-hundred-dollar piece of technology not easily replaced stopped me. But just barely. "That . . . weaselly . . . sneaky . . . manipulative . . . little . . ."

"Em," Heath said, coming over to me to grab my shoulders and get me to focus on him. "What. Happened?"

"Gil," I said through clenched teeth. "He took the dagger."

Heath blinked. "Why the *hell* would he do that?"

I called Gilley again. "I have no idea, but when I find out, you're going to need to stop me from stabbing him with it." Again the phone went to voice mail, so I clicked off his number and over to Michel's.

"M.J.!" he said when he answered the line. Michel is Scottish-born, but his mother was French. He's a gorgeous man, about five-ten, black hair, sharp features, and beautiful big brown eyes with the most lovely brogue that becomes heavier whenever he talks of home. He's very laid-back, patient, kind, well-spoken, and polite, and the absolutely perfect complement to Gilley, who is almost never any of those things. "How was your trip?"

"Michel," I said, bypassing the niceties to get right to the point. "*Where* is Gilley?"

"Where's . . . uh-oh, don't tell me he's gone off and done something stupid again."

"He's gone off and done something *insane* again," I said. "He's stolen an *extremely* dangerous relic from our safe here at the office, and, Michel, in the wrong hands, and by wrong hands I mean *anyone's* hands but ours, that thing is seriously scary. Deadly scary. I need to find Gilley and get it back asap."

There was a pause, then, "Might you be talking about that dusty dagger from the Turkish warlord, M.J.?"

I gasped. "That very one, Michel. He's shown it to you?"

"Yes, I'm afraid so," Michel said, a hint of worry in his voice. "And a few more people have likely seen it as well. But no one's been hurt or upset by it as far as I've heard. You're sure it's dangerous?"

My heart rate ticked up into the red zone. "What do you mean 'a few more people have seen it as well'?"

"Oh, has Gilley not told you about where he's taken it, then?" Michel asked.

I moved unsteadily over to one of my office chairs and gripped it hard as I sat down. Putting Michel on speaker so that Heath could listen, I said, "He hasn't told me squat, Michel, and as I said, that dagger is *deadly*, so please, if you know where it is, please tell me."

"Oh, M.J.," Michel said, "I'm so sorry. I made him promise me before he did anything to get your permission, but you know Gilley. He's a wee bit willful when it comes to money."

I put the phone on the desk and lowered my head nearly to my knees, on the verge of a panic attack. "Please, please, please tell me he hasn't sold the dagger!" I cried. If Gilley had put innocent bystanders in jeopardy I really would kill him.

"No!" Michel was quick to say. I felt Heath's steadying hand on my back. "He hasn't sold it. He's simply loaned it to the museum hosting the exhibit for the movie."

I glanced up at Heath and shook my head. I was unable to say anything more. I simply needed to focus on breathing. Heath took the cue. "Michel, Gilley hasn't mentioned anything about it. Please tell us what the hell is going on and start from the beginning."

We heard the faint sound of a creaking chair and I imagined Michel leaning back in his desk chair and swiping a hand through his hair, his own anxiety probably ratcheting up now that he was stuck in the middle and playing the role of messenger. "The studio called Gilley about two weeks after you two left for your trip. A producer from Prescott Productions said he'd heard about the dagger, and he told Gilley that a haunted relic like that would be the perfect thing to really draw in the crowds. He asked Gilley if he would consider loaning it to the museum for the length of the exhibit, and at first Gilley said no, but then the producer called back and offered Gilley a sum of money that my sweet fiancé simply couldn't refuse. So Gilley agreed to the loan, but he also demanded that he be in charge of securing the dagger for the exhibit. When I pressed him about it later, he insisted that the dagger was safe and there was no threat of its being stolen or any harm coming to it."

"The harm wouldn't be coming *to* the dagger, Michel," I said. "It would be coming *from* it."

"Yes, so you've said," Michel said soberly. "Had I known that, M.J., I never would've allowed him to take it from your office."

My hands were curled into fists. I'd never been more angry with Gilley in my life. "Michel?" I managed, my jaw still clenched.

"Yes, love?"

"Would you please call your fiancé and tell him to meet us at the museum in half an hour, and, Michel, let him know that if he doesn't meet us there in that time, then I will personally post to my Twitter feed and

Facebook pages all his deepest secrets, including his real height, age, and weight and why his last boyfriend broke up with him."

Gilley was very careful about controlling his online image. The mere suggestion that I'd tell the world the truth about his age would be enough to have him sprint down to the museum, where I would then murder him, but that was beside the point.

"Oh," Michel said. "It's that bad, then, is it?"

"It is."

"All right, love, I'll get hold of him straightaway."

The second he clicked off the phone I got up and moved to the closet. Yanking open the door, I shrugged out of my sweater and took out a black canvas vest lined with over a dozen magnets, hanging on a hook inside the door.

"Wait," Heath said. "You're going to wear *that*?"

The vest was a spare. It was made for us by Gilley's mom a year earlier, and while it was truly sweet of her, the bedazzled *Ghoul Getters* logo on the back was perhaps a bit much for either Heath or me to be seen in public with.

We had subtler clothing at home. "There's no time to go to the condo right now," I told him, pulling out the one that Mrs. G. had made for him. "We'll wear these. They're fine." When he looked at me skeptically, I snapped, "Do you really want to waste extra minutes before retrieving the dagger because you're embarrassed by a few rhinestones?"

Heath opened his mouth but stopped himself. I had

a feeling he'd been about to say yes. Perhaps it was the no-nonsense glare I offered him that made him (wisely) hold his tongue and put on the damn vest.

"At least I've got my boots here," I said, reaching back into the closet for my black leather riding boots. Shrugging out of the modest heels I'd worn on the plane, I slipped into them, feeling the carefully placed interior pockets—the boots were also lined with magnets—slip past my toes.

We'd discovered on a casual ghostbust about a month before we were able to quit the show that magnets in our shoes prevented any of us from being possessed. It had something to do with grounding our energies to the earth, I think. It didn't really matter what the mechanics were; it worked and I was grateful to have discovered it.

Heath stared down at his running shoes. "Mine are at the condo."

"We'll be fine," I said, bending to zip up the boots. "What's important is that we've got enough between us to protect us, and once we get our hands on the dagger, we can use some spare magnets from the vests to pack the dagger in until we get it back here."

"Worst-case scenario, Oruç and his demon could get blinded by the rhinestones," Heath said as he took the vest and unzipped it to take out the hanger.

I sighed. I was in no mood for jokes. This was a scary and deadly serious situation, but sometimes my husband made jokes to help lighten his own anxiety. And I got it, but at times it was still a little annoying.

Once I was done getting dressed, I nodded to Heath, who had also just finished getting into his own gear.

Within six minutes of hanging up with Michel, we were out the door and headed to the museum, ready to wage war against the nastiest spook and demon you'd never want to meet.

Chapter 2

We arrived at the Museum of Modern Science twenty-eight minutes after walking out the door of my office. And they were twenty-eight anxious minutes, believe me.

The museum itself is a gorgeous structure—lots of glass and sharp angles—a very modern showpiece not far from Boston Harbor and situated right on the water. If I'd been in the mood to tour a museum, this would've been the one I'd have chosen, but I was more in the mood to murder a certain five-foot-six, one-hundred-sixty-two-pound thirty-seven-year-old who was unceremoniously dumped by his previous boyfriend for cutting his toenails while eating a doughnut in bed. (Oh, gee golly whiz! Did I just spill Gilley's most tightly guarded secrets? Oopsies . . .)

Anyway, we had to pay ten bucks for parking, then sprint to the museum itself. Once there (and after paying thirty bucks to get us both inside), I was sort of at a loss for where to go. I'd told Gil to meet us at the museum, but not specifically where.

"The exhibit is upstairs," Heath said, and I turned to look at him and saw that he was pointing to a poster next to the central hallway. On the poster was an ad for the exhibition and a few shots from the movie, including a close-up of the Grim Widow herself. It was enough to make me shudder.

"Maybe he's already here," I said.

Heath arched a skeptical eyebrow.

I frowned. "Yeah, I know, but let's head up and look for the dagger and someone to help us get it back."

We walked toward the elevators, but there was a line, so we took the stairs. I was a little winded by the time we reached the top but ignored the urge to catch my breath in favor of getting to the exhibit as quickly as possible. To my absolute horror, I saw a line of people waiting to enter the exhibit where Oruç's dagger was on display. It hit me that we'd arrived at the exhibit just a few hours after it'd officially opened to the public on its first day, and I'd been unprepared to find it so popular already. I'd figured that if any kind of crowd was going to show up, it'd be in a few hours when Gilley was set to make an appearance and talk about his time on the show and some of the ghostbusts we'd done. To see a long line of people already waiting to get in felt a bit surreal and, to be honest, highly flattering, but then I remembered our mission. I was about to tell Heath that we should look for someone in charge to speak with when a woman in line turned and pointed at me. "Oh . . . my . . . *God*! It's them! It's M.J. and Heath!"

I stiffened in shock as a whole line of heads turned, eyes bugged, and then about forty people rushed right toward us. Heath grabbed hold of my hand and pulled me close to him as we were swarmed. I resisted the urge to run, but barely. Smartphones flashed as people took pictures, and more phones were raised high as others recorded our shocked faces. My hearing was flooded with a barrage of excited chatter: "I can't believe you two are here! Are there cameras?"

"Will you sign my program?"

"Ohmigod, Heath, you're so hot! Will you sign my chest?"

"M.J., are you and Heath really dating?"

"Ohmigod! Is that a *wedding ring*?! Heath! Did you and M.J. get married?"

"Where's Gilley? Are the others coming?"

"My house is haunted and I really want you guys to come do a show about it . . ."

Belatedly, I realized I'd not only lost hold of Heath's hand but my sight of him, and I was now backing away from the crowd. Several months earlier I'd been mobbed by a group of possessed mental patients, and I found this situation to be no less threatening or scary. "Heath!" I yelled as several programs and pens were pushed at me, while hands gripped my arms and pressed on my back. The memory of being overrun by those possessed patients was starting to press in on me, and I found it hard to breathe. *"Heath!"*

My husband suddenly stepped in front of me, and in a loud, booming voice he commanded, "Everyone, *back the hell up!*"

To my immense relief, the shocked crowd fell silent and took several steps away from us. I pressed against his back, shaking and trying to get a grip. Heath then reached back for my hand again and pulled me to his side, where he then wrapped a protective arm around me. "We're not here to sign autographs today, folks," he said. The crowd groaned, but it felt only halfhearted, probably because they were still in shock at Heath's outburst.

"Excuse me," said a voice somewhere beyond the crowd. "What's going on here?"

A gentleman stepped forward wearing a blue blazer and dark gray dress slacks. He wore a lanyard with a badge that looked official, and carried a walkie-talkie in his left hand. I assumed by his surprised and annoyed expression that he represented museum security.

Shaking off the fright I'd had, I said, "Do you work here?"

"Yes," he said brusquely. "What are you two doing to incite this crowd?"

"We're from the show," I said, pointing to a blown-up image over the entrance of the exhibit that pictured Heath and me running across a bridge as if our lives depended on it. (Which, at the time, they definitely did.)

"Nobody told me there'd be any public appearances until later on tonight," the man said. I saw the name Murdock on his employee badge.

"We're not here for a public appearance!" I snapped. (The mobbing of the crowd had seriously rattled me. I think I took it out on poor Murdock.) "Sir, you have a *very* dangerous relic on display in there!" For emphasis I pointed to the entrance of the exhibit. "And we've come to collect it before it can cause anyone harm."

All around us there were gasps, and I realized my mistake immediately. Whispered murmurs of "Which relic is she talking about?" and "I'm totally going in there!" and "Quick, let's go see what she's talking about before she takes it away!" filtered out to my ears as the crowd turned away from us and rushed back toward the exhibit entrance.

I watched them go and palmed my forehead. How could I have been so stupid?

"We need to get in there," Heath said to the guard, who'd thankfully been the only one who'd remained next to us.

"I can't let you take anything from in there!" he said, as if he were offended that Heath would even ask.

"You don't understand," Heath insisted, squaring his shoulders and standing up to his full height. Heath isn't overly tall, or overly brawny, but he can put out the most powerful presence when he wants to.

Murdock took a step back and lifted his walkie-talkie. "Rob, we've got a situation up in the ghost movie exhibit. I need Mr. Sullivan here. Stat."

There was a garbled reply that I couldn't quite make out, and I could feel my impatience and anxiety mount as more and more people crammed into the exhibit room.

For his part, Murdock simply stared into space as he held the walkie-talkie about face level. It appeared he was waiting for orders.

I tapped my foot impatiently, ignored the occasional lifting of a smartphone in our direction followed by the occasional flash, and muttered a few obscenities under my breath.

"Why are we standing here?" Heath finally asked the guard when he continued to stare into space without explanation.

"I gotta wait for the boss to tell me what he wants to do with you two," Murdock growled. It was clear he had no love for us, and vice versa.

"Well, we don't," I said. Squeezing Heath's hand, I turned away from the security guard and marched with authority toward the exhibit entrance.

"Hey!" Murdock yelled. "Get back here!"

I ignored him and ducked into the crowd, weaving between people who, thankfully, made way for us, but not without excited murmuring as we passed. At last we came out into the exhibit room, and as I stepped to the middle and looked around, I was too shocked to speak.

The exhibit was impressive. It lined all four walls and unfolded the story of our show like a timeline. There were photos galore—all the haunted spaces that the show had investigated, the scary still shots of the spooks we'd busted, and profile pictures of each member of the GG crew.

Another wall had small snippets of our show playing on a loop, and on a third wall there was a poster-sized photo of some ectoplasmic fog filling the floor of a room, which was taken from one of our ghostbusts in Europe. Belatedly I realized that a dry ice machine was pumping out a similar fog along the floor of the exhibit. Glancing down, I shuddered when I realized I couldn't see my feet; it brought back dark, nightmarish memories.

Yet another wall held memorabilia from the show. There was a whole section filled with nothing but the weapons we'd used over the past couple of years against the various nasty spooks we'd encountered. Everything from our magnetized railroad spikes to the tennis racket strung with magnetized wire we'd used against the Grim Widow, to the Ghost Enhancer, which was a contraption that looked like a radio but amped up the electromagnetic field around a given area, something that actually made the spooks stronger, and which we'd needed for two particular busts we'd done. It was a fairly dangerous contraption in the wrong hands, and I made a mental note to ask for that back as well.

Nearby I saw that one of our crew jackets had been framed, and there was even a female mannequin wearing nearly the exact same outfit I had worn on many of the *Ghoul Getters* episodes.

Amid all of this, playing eerily in the background was a recording of a compilation of terrifying sounds—disembodied footsteps, a series of faraway screams, muttering whispers, and what could only be described as long nails raking against wood, but I knew better. The sound was actually a set of talons, etching deep grooves slowly and terrifyingly into a wall. The sound bite had been pulled from the hotel in San Francisco where Oruç's demon had been set loose to terrorize and kill.

Another shudder traveled through me and I focused

my attention on a display case toward the back wall. There, with a light trained on it, was the dagger itself. Crowded around it were several people, reading what was likely a description of the dagger and the dangers it held. Luckily, there were enough magnets surrounding it, and the people in the room, to protect us all—at least I hoped so.

"There," I said, pointing to it.

"I see it," Heath replied. "And I think there're enough magnets in here to hold Oruç and the demon inside the dagger, at least."

"Excuse me!" we heard from behind us. We both glanced over our shoulders to see a very fit-looking man with intense eyes, a crooked nose, and thick black eyebrows approach us. "What are you two doing here?" he demanded, slightly out of breath, as if he'd rushed to the exhibit from downstairs. "I wasn't told about any public appearances by the stars of the show until later on. We're not staffed with enough people to accommodate this right now!"

Behind him I realized that the crowd currently attempting to enter the exhibit had grown almost exponentially. People were literally flooding in, and the scene was making me more and more anxious.

I shook my head at both the unfolding scene and what the newcomer had just said. I don't consider myself famous—certainly not a star—and yet, everyone who came through the door seemed to have a hand raised with a phone that was either flashing or recording. It was *super*-disconcerting. "This was a spur-of-the-moment thing," I heard Heath say to the man. And then he stuck out his hand, as calm as could be, and said, "Heath Whitefeather, sir."

"Phil Sullivan," the man replied, shaking Heath's hand, but there was little warmth to his expression. "I'm the museum director. We should've been notified that you two were coming."

"We had no idea this would happen," Heath said, blinking in the flashing lights of several smartphones.

I was starting to lose patience with this whole thing. Pointing to the display case with Oruç's dagger, I said, "We just came to collect that, Mr. Sullivan. As soon as you open the case and let us retrieve it, we'll be on our way."

Sullivan's gaze followed my index finger to the display case across the room. He then looked back at me as if I'd asked him to hand over all his cash. "You're kidding me, right?"

"No," I said to him. "I'm definitely serious. That relic has no business being on display. It's insanely dangerous. We need to remove it. Now."

He stared at me as if he expected me to wink at him, and when I didn't, his face flushed red with irritation and he put his hands on his hips. "Listen, I've got a museum to run, and I don't need any publicity stunts today. Not when two members of my security staff are out sick with the flu!"

Heath stepped a little closer to Sullivan, projecting that glorious presence again. "Mr. Sullivan, I can assure you this isn't a publicity stunt. That dagger houses a ghost and a demon, and both are among the most dangerous we've ever dealt with. That dagger needs to be locked up away from the public, not on display here where there could be exposure to its influences."

Sullivan rolled his eyes and then glared angrily at Heath. "Listen, buddy," he said, "I know you two gotta keep up the pretenses for the sake of the movie, but I'm telling you to drop the act and leave before this situation gets out of hand."

Around us I could hear the excited murmurs ratchet up a notch—the crowd sensing the tension in the air. Others, though, must have overheard me talking about Oruç's dagger, because the group around the display case where it was housed was growing and people were hovering dangerously close.

Taking Heath's cue I drew myself up to my full stature (keep in mind, I'm not very tall) and inched closer to Sullivan. "Sir," I said sternly. "This is not an act. That relic over there was entrusted to us to look after and we can't do that if it's here. I demand that you give it back."

But Sullivan wasn't budging. He folded his arms across his chest and said, "I have a signed contract from the movie studio paying us for this display. I'm not about to put that contract into breach just because the two stars show up and try to throw their weight around. If you want it back so bad, you're going to need to go through the museum's attorney, and good luck with that, Miss . . . Miss . . ."

Heath glared hard at him. "*Mrs.* Whitefeather," he said angrily. "And I'll thank you to speak respectfully to my wife."

My breath caught. I'd had every intention of keeping

our marriage under wraps until after Gilley's wedding, but Heath and I had gotten so used to calling each other Mr. and Mrs. that of course it rolled easily off his tongue. The excited murmuring around us ratcheted up another notch. "Ohmigod! Did you hear that?! They got married! M.J. and Heath got married!"

I wanted to groan. There'd be no keeping the news from Gilley now. But speaking of Gilley, I started to wonder where that little—

"You're married?!" came a shrieking voice.

The crowd fell silent. Then it parted to let through my oldest and dearest friend. Who looked ready to murder *me*. Raising both fists above his head, Gilley fell to his knees and shouted, *"Why, God, why?"*

"Great," I muttered. "Could this day get any worse?"

And then the lights went out and the place was plunged into darkness.

Screams erupted all around us—the loudest of which I recognized as Gilley's. I waited for someone to turn the light on from his or her cell phone, but among all the frightened screams, there were other shouts from people claiming that their phones were dead.

As I fumbled for my own phone, Heath grabbed my hand and pulled me to him, and together we carefully wove through the crush of rushing bodies toward Oruç's dagger, which had to be responsible, because it was the only thing powerful enough in the room to douse the lights and drain every single phone. Well, save mine.

I slid my finger across the surface of the phone, and it lit up—the only light in the dark room. A wave of relief washed over me, until I realized that I held *the only light in the room*.

A mass of footsteps from all around us rushed straight for me, like moths to a flame. I shut off the phone fast, and Heath pulled me sharply to the right and off the track we'd been on, which was wise, because a lady I'd just been standing next to appeared to be suddenly swarmed by people. "Get off me! Get off me!" she cried.

"Turn on your phone again!" someone else shouted. "Dammit! Turn it on!"

Heath maneuvered through the crowd, which was working itself up into a frenzy of fear. The energy was insane, and I could feel the vibrations of intense alarm and mounting panic bouncing around us as people tried to figure out where they were in relation to the exit. "We have to get out!" many shouted. "Where's the door? How do we get out of here?"

The fog from the dry ice machine wasn't helping matters, because what feeble light did trickle in from the hallway was obscured by the fog that was getting kicked up by people rushing around the room.

I also found it a little odd that at least some people weren't finding the situation humorous—the way some individuals can move through a staged Halloween haunted house and find it funny. There didn't seem to be anyone within hearing distance of me who thought the whole thing was a publicity stunt—*everyone* was scared, and I do mean petrified.

"Are we close?" I called to Heath, who was still pulling on my arm.

"I think so!" he called back to me, using his shoulder to push aside someone who, in his panic, was trying to get between us. Abruptly, Heath stopped and I nearly bumped into the back of him. "It's here," he said, and I felt around a little with my free hand and found a velvet rope near my waist. I then heard a clicking sound and the rope fell to the floor. Heath guided me forward and then my hands were on the glass case that housed the dagger. I could feel a wave of the foulest energy waft over me, and then, all of a sudden, it was gone and all the lights came back on.

I blinked in the sudden brightness and the nearly immediate shocked silence that rippled through the crowd. People had frozen in place when the lights came on—many were clinging to each other in fear. One poor soul had soiled his pants, and he was the first to bolt out of the exit. Many of what remained of the crowd followed. Hastily.

Turning my attention back to the dagger, I tried to lift the glass housing it, but it wouldn't budge. I then scanned the crowd for any sign of Gilley, as I was hoping he'd know how to get into the display, but he was nowhere in sight. Frustrated, I dug into my vest and pulled out a few extra magnets, placing them directly on the metal podium that held the glass case and the dagger. They stuck there nicely, and while I could tell that there were a whole lot of other magnets already placed there, my four extra certainly couldn't hurt.

"Do you see Gilley?" I asked Heath, who was also scanning the crowd.

"No," he said. "I think he might've made it to the door and out."

I stepped away from the display and looked at the dispersing crowd anxiously. I wasn't leaving without the dagger, and Gil was the key to getting the glass case unlocked. More scanning of the crowd failed to reveal my best friend, but Phil Sullivan and Murdock were still in attendance. They both appeared quite shaken by the ordeal. But then Phil's petulant expression returned and he stalked over to us. "I'm going to call the studio and complain," he told me with a snarl. "Maybe they can't fire you for pulling a stunt like this, but I hope they fine you or withhold some of your royalty checks. And then I'm gonna call the police and see if they can issue you a citation!"

"Wait," I said. "You think *we* did this?"

Phil pulled up his own smartphone and eyed it with irritation. "I don't know how you managed to drain everybody's phones, but I'm not in the mood for stupid stunts like this. There're laws against inciting a panicked riot like this, you know!"

"Mr. Sullivan," I said firmly, my voice rising, "we didn't have anything to do with this. Not us and not the studio."

"Then who did?" he demanded, his face flushing yet another time.

Next to me, Heath pointed to the glass case holding Oruç's dagger. "I'm guessing the ghost and his demon, housed inside that dagger, are flexing their collective muscle."

I glanced around the room. There were magnetic spikes everywhere. *"How* did they get through the field created by all the spikes?"

Heath shook his head, his expression grave. "Don't know. But it's something to worry about, Em."

I turned back to Sullivan. "We need that dagger back," I said. "And we need it now."

If Oruç was simply giving us a demonstration of how easily he could get through the magnetic field in the room, then I was worried indeed.

Sullivan glared at me, then turned to Murdock. "Charlie, throw these two outta here, and if they come back, call the police."

Murdock stepped forward and squared his shoulders, and my husband did the same. For a moment it looked like things were about to get physical, but then two other security guards rushed into the room and even Heath knew he stood no chance. Still, when they surrounded us and made it clear they weren't averse to getting rough with us should we resist, Heath managed to stare one of them down enough that the guy took a step back.

"We'll call Gopher," I whispered to Heath. "He's got to be able to use his clout to help us get the dagger back."

"Yeah, but how long will that take?" Heath said, looking over his shoulder at Oruç's dagger.

"Hopefully, not long," I said, and crossed my fingers. "He knows full well how dangerous that dagger is. He'll help us get it back."

We made it out of the building behind a stream of shaken pedestrians. All anybody was talking about was the ghostbuster exhibit and how freaky and frightening it had been. It was also surprising to see how many people were really upset about their phones being dead—of course this was a regular occurrence in our ghostbusting world, but to those folks so used to having a charge on their phones to accompany them throughout their day, it was shocking and upsetting to them on a level I barely understood.

We found Gilley in his new car, crying big wet tears. I rapped on the window and he shrieked. *"Don't* do that!" he shouted at me before he rolled down the window.

"We need to talk," I said sternly. I was in no mood for Gilley's bullshit. "My condo. Thirty minutes. Be there, or I'm going to hunt you down, Gillespie."

Gil bit his lip. I almost never called him by his last name, so he knew I meant business. He nodded meekly and I grabbed Heath's hand to head toward the parking garage, more furious with Gilley than I could ever remember. And given how difficult my best friend could be, that was saying something.

Gil actually beat us to the condo. I figured he might've headed to his own unit ahead of us, which was only down one flight of stairs from mine, but he stood in front of my door dutifully and didn't mutter a peep as Heath unlocked the door to let us all in.

Doc—my African grey parrot—welcomed us with "Hi, birdie!" I walked over to him and kissed him on the head. He was such a sweet birdie. I'd had him since I was a little girl, and I treasured and adored him like my own child. I figured that standing close to him would keep me from erupting, which I was damned near close to.

"What the hell were you thinking?" my husband roared the moment Gilley took a seat on the sofa. I should add here that he wasn't standing anywhere close to the birdie. "That dagger is the most dangerous relic in New England and *you* think it's okay to put it on display?! Seriously, Gil . . . *what the hell*?!"

"I only loaned it to them for two weeks!" Gil replied. "Heath, it's still completely surrounded by magnets, and I personally inspected the exhibit to make sure no one could steal it or get too close to it, and I ensured that it'd be in the center of a magnetic field so powerful that there was no *way* Oruç or his demon could get out. I swear to you I followed every protocol, took every precaution, made every attempt to keep that thing in check before I even considered bringing the dagger to the museum! Oruç and his demon should *not* have been able to do that!"

Heath stared at Gilley like he didn't even know him. Shaking his head as if he still couldn't fathom Gilley's insanely stupid decision, he said, "But that doesn't tell me why, Gil. *Why* did you loan it out? Of all the things to hand over to the public, why the dagger?"

Gil's eyes misted and he began to cry again. I knew he hated being yelled at like that, but I had little sympathy for him. "It was the studio's idea," he said. "One of the producers called me, and he said that he'd seen photos of the exhibit before it opened up to the public, and the studio heads thought it was a little boring. He said that we needed something big to draw in the crowds, and that he'd heard about the dagger from Gopher and had gotten the okay from him to ask M.J. about it."

My brow furrowed. "No producer ever called me about the dagger," I snapped.

"Yeah, I know," Gil said. "And that's because, before you left on your trip, you told me not to give out your location or phone numbers to *anyone*. And you told me not to call you unless somebody was on fire or dead. So, I made the executive decision to handle it myself."

I shook my head. "Oh, cut the crap, Gil! You didn't call us because you knew I'd say no!"

Gilley picked at a thread on the seam of his jeans. "Well that may have had something to do with it," he admitted.

I shook my head, so angry I could have actually punched him. "Why?!" I demanded.

Gilley sighed and he seemed full of regret. "The studio threw a lot of money at me and I caved," he admitted. Looking up at me, he added, "Seriously, M.J., the money was too good to turn down."

"You don't need any more money!" I yelled. "Gil, you were already paid handsomely for the movie, and there are more box office royalties to come!"

Gil's expression shifted to something a little closer to petulance. "First of all, Michel and I received a *lot* less than you and Heath. You guys got the biggest piece of the pie by far. And before you start yelling at me again, yes, that still meant that we got a really nice check, *but* weddings are expensive, M.J.! Between the caterer, the venue, the photographer, and the DJ, it's a

ridiculous amount of money! And that's before the down payment on the new apartment in Manhat—"
Gilley suddenly covered his mouth with his hand and shook his head as if he'd just let out a huge secret. Which, of course he had.

"New apartment?" I said, jumping on the admission. "New *Manhattan* apartment, Gil?"

Gil dropped his hand and went back to staring at his lap. "We were going to tell you when Michel got back from the shoot in New York," he said.

A lump formed in my throat. Even though Heath and I were heading to Santa Fe sometime in the next few months, somehow, having Gilley announce his move first both stunned and deeply hurt me. "Ah," I said, blinking hard to fight back tears. "I see."

Gilley shook his head sadly, and when he spoke his voice hitched with emotion. "It's Michel's job," he said. "All the best-paying photography gigs are in New York, and he's starting to be requested by some of the top magazines. We just feel he'll get a real shot at having his career take off if he's closer to their offices."

To hear Gilley tell me that he was leaving me—it went right to my heart. I'd never lived farther than ten minutes from him since I was eleven years old. And as frustrating, aggravating, annoying, and infuriating as Gil could be, he was still family to me. It hit me all of a sudden that I could never simply just walk down the stairs to have breakfast with him again. Or watch old movies with him on Sunday. Or be wined and dined at one of his fabulous dinner parties. I'd have to fly clear across the country to see him, and we'd probably do that quite a bit for a few years, fly back and forth to see each other, but then our lives would go in different directions and we'd see less and less of each other.

I realized that the first step in having Gilley mostly out of my life had already been taken, and it upset me more than I could say.

"Em?" Heath said, moving to my side. "Are you crying?"

I buried my face in my hands and tried to choke back the emotion, but it came out in small sobs anyway. And then I heard Gilley begin to cry in earnest and a moment later both Heath and Gilley were hugging me.

After a little while, Gil and I settled down and he squished into the chair with me and wrapped his arms around my shoulders. "I don't know how I'm going do it, sugar," he said. "How do I leave my best friend?"

I caught Heath's eye and he smiled sadly. "We love our husbands," I said, laying my head on Gil's shoulder. "And to have the best life with them that we can, we need to let go of each other a little."

He nodded and made a little squeaking noise like he was trying not to cry again. "I'll always love you, M.J."

"I know," I told him. "Me too."

For a while no one spoke. Heath got up after a bit and moved to the kitchen, and Gilley and I just sat cuddled together. I heard the sounds of a meal being prepared, and still Gilley and I sat together. I was still furious with him over the dagger, but there wasn't much I could do about it at the moment.

"I'm sorry," Gil said at last.

"For . . . ?"

"For the dagger. For wanting to move to New York. For leaving you here in Boston to fend for yourself when Heath hogs the remote on Sundays to watch football."

I smiled. Little did Gilley know that I wouldn't be staying in Boston. "It's okay," I said. "Well, it's okay about everything except the dagger."

Gil pulled back from me a little. "I have a call in to Gopher," he said. "I think he'll support us if we tell him we need to get the dagger back."

"Can you reach him?" I asked. "I mean, he's still in Nepal, right?"

"He is, but I put a call in to his assistant. She says that he might call in from there in the next couple of days."

"The next couple of days?! Gilley, we can't wait that long! We've got to get that dagger back immediately."

Gil winced, likely because my voice had risen. "I'm trying," he said.

"Call that producer who talked you into giving up the dagger," I said. Gilley winced again. "What?" I asked.

"I haven't gotten the check yet," he muttered.

"Why does *that* matter?"

"Because I was hoping to keep at least some of the money," he admitted. "I mean, I did loan out the dagger for the exhibit and it was there on the day the *Ghoul Getters* exhibit opened to the public."

"Gil," I said sternly. "Call him and have him talk to the museum. That dagger comes out of there tomorrow morning. First thing."

"Okay, okay," Gil said. "I'll call him."

"Good." And then I had a moment to reflect on what'd happened at the exhibit, and I said, "You know, I saw all the precautions you took to keep the dagger neutralized. What I can't figure out is how that damned spook, or his demon, or both of them, managed to douse the lights and drain every cell phone in that room. I mean, how was that even possible?"

Gilley scratched his chin. "I don't know, M.J. It shouldn't have been. The only thing I can think of is that there were so many people there tonight who were nervous and afraid—especially around the dagger—that maybe they supplied a little fuel for Oruç or his demon to zap the lights and drain all the batteries."

I had to concede that Gil had a point. Spooks *love* inciting fear. For the meaner ones, there's the added bonus that all that outpouring of terror can actually fuel them; like a vampire sucking blood, it can make them incredibly strong and powerful, able to do things like appear fully formed, or move stuff, or throw things, or launch a vicious attack.

The more fear emitted by unwitting innocents, the more powerful a spook or a demon could become, so I could understand Gilley's theory, but it still shouldn't have been possible given all the magnets in the exhibit room. What I also wondered was, why was every phone in the place drained of battery life—except for mine? Shrugging out of my vest, I set it on a chair with Heath's. I'd take them back to the office in the morning. "Gil," I said as I moved to the sofa. "Assuming it takes us longer than the next sixteen hours or so to get the dagger back, can you do a little checking with one of the EMF meters at the museum tomorrow? I want to know if Oruç or his demon is gaining enough strength to overpower all the magnets and escape the dagger."

Gil frowned. "Aren't you and Heath better equipped to do that?" he asked.

I had a feeling he was scared of going back to the museum by himself. "We can't," I told him. "We've been banned from showing up there again."

"Great," he muttered.

"Gil . . ."

"Okay, okay," he said. "I'll go."

"Good man," I said, softening toward him again.

Heath called to us from the kitchen. "Hey, guys, dinner's on."

Gilley clapped his hands and said, "Hey, over our meal, maybe you two fools can explain why you went off and got hitched without either telling me or including me."

A new note of pain lit up in Gilley's eyes, and a sharp pang of guilt settled into my chest. "We didn't want to steal your spotlight," I said gently, reaching for his hand as we headed to the bar off the kitchen. "Heath proposed to me the second day we were there, and, what can I say, Gil? It wasn't something we gave a lot of thought to. We just didn't feel like waiting a year or so to be married. In fact, once we were engaged, we both agreed that what we really wanted wasn't an engagement, but a marriage, right away. And that left us with the choice to either elope, or come back here and risk upsetting you by having our own wedding so close to yours. The last thing in the world I wanted to do was to upset you or your wedding plans. So, we decided to elope and not tell anyone—not even Daddy or Heath's mom, Gil. You were the very first person I planned on telling, because, next to Heath, you're the person I love most in the world."

The hurt faded from Gil's eyes and he lifted my hand to kiss my knuckles. "You mean all that?" he asked.

I nodded. "Yes, honey. And, like I said, we had planned to keep it a secret until after you got hitched, but in all the hurry to get to the museum and reclaim the dagger, Heath forgot to take off his wedding band."

Gil looked down at my bare left ring finger. "Where's yours?"

"It's in the safe, where Oruç's dagger used to be."

Gil narrowed his eyes and pursed his lips. "I'll take that as a hint to get moving on making those calls to Gopher, et cetera."

"Nothing gets by you," I said to him with a wink and a nudge of my shoulder.

Gil sighed and went to his phone on the counter, where he'd left it to charge from the plug there. I took a seat on one of the barstools as Heath set a plate of steaming vegetables and noodles mixed in a heavenly smelling white wine sauce. "Bon appétit, Mrs. White-feather," he said with a wink.

"Merci, Monsieur Whitefeather," I replied before tucking in. The dish was sublime. It was so good, in fact, that I nearly forgot to listen as Gilley spoke to Gopher's assistant. "Rachel, it's super important that I get ahold of him," he was saying. "Isn't there any way you can contact him and tell him it's an emergency?" There was a pause, then, "His sat phone was malfunctioning and you haven't heard from him in three days? Are you kidding me?"

My shoulders slumped and I looked at Heath, who was also listening. He pressed his lips together and shook his head.

"When will he get a new sat phone?" Gil said next. There was a pause, then, *"What do you mean probably not for a week or two?"*

I reached over and laid a hand on Gil's shoulder. It wouldn't do us any good to upset poor Rachel, who was a young girl in her twenties and had no control over the situation.

Gil looked up at me and took a deep breath. "Sorry," he said to Rachel. "Just . . . if he gets ahold of you at all in the next twenty-four hours, I need to talk to him. It's an emergency."

Gilley clicked off and turned to us. "You guys heard?"

"We did," Heath said, sliding Gilley's meal over to him. "I guess Gopher can't help us, so, Gil, you've got no choice. You've got to call that producer back and tell him the deal with the dagger is off, and he can keep his money."

Gilley bit his lip, and for a moment I thought he might protest, which made me wonder exactly how much money the studio had put up for the dagger, but then Gil said, "Yeah. Okay. I'll call him right now."

I gave Gil an encouraging pat on the back and went back to my dinner. I hadn't realized how ravenous I'd been, and Heath chuckled at the way I was eating with gusto.

Meanwhile, Gilley apparently got voice mail and left a message for someone named Bradley. It wasn't a name I recognized, but I didn't think much about it. The movie had so many names attached to it, there was no way I could keep them all straight.

"He'll probably get back to me," Gil said, putting his phone back on the charger.

"He'd better," I heard Heath mutter.

Gilley appeared pained, but I thought we needed to talk the issue through. "What do we do if we can't get anyone to make the call and get the dagger out of that museum?" I asked them.

Heath and Gilley were quiet for a moment, and then Gil said, "We could sabotage the exhibit. Shut it down so that no one can enter and get close to the dagger. That should keep it isolated long enough to have the loaner period expire, and then the museum has to give it back to us."

I frowned. "How? I mean, Heath and I have both been banned from the premises. What kind of damage could we do that wouldn't get us sued or arrested and would ride out the next two weeks?"

"I could mess with their computer network," Gil said. He's an incredibly skilled hacker, and he flexed his fingers and grinned slyly to show me that he welcomed the opportunity to work a hack on the museum.

"What if it comes back to you?" I asked.

He shrugged. "It's not like I'm tinkering with a

government agency, M.J. I'll just mess with the sprinkler system."

"The sprinkler system?" Heath said.

Gilley chuckled slyly. "The museum has an extensive fire-prevention sprinkler system. I could make it rain, rain, rain."

"But what about the other exhibits in the museum?" I said. "Gil, we can't destroy or damage anything but the movie exhibit. If you mess with the sprinkler system, it has to be in that room only."

"I'll look into it," he promised.

"Good. And remember—it can't get back to us."

Just then Gil's phone rang and we all jumped a little. He looked at the display, gasped, then ran off to my home office in the spare bedroom. Heath and I shared a look and a sigh. "Want some popcorn?" he said, getting up to take my plate and his to the sink.

He and I were eating very healthy these days. We'd turned vegetarian a couple of years earlier, and now we were on a no-sugar kick. He'd been so good about it that I didn't have the heart to tell him how very, very, *very* much I missed ice cream. And brownies. And especially ice cream over warm brownies.

"Sure," I said, trying to muster up some enthusiasm.

He grinned at me and there was a knowing look in his eye. "Why does the image of ice cream and brownies keep popping into my head?"

I sucked in a breath. "Whoa," I said. "Who ratted me out?"

Heath, like me, was a medium—able to communicate

with the dead as easily as the living. The dead are funny—and I mean that literally. They're big on pulling pranks and teasing, and I had no doubt that one of the spirits connected to me had told my husband what I'd been too chicken to say. That I hated the "absolutely no sugar ever, ever again" diet and really wanted to switch to a "sugar every once in a while when I'm really craving it" diet.

"It was your mom," Heath said with a laugh. My chest filled with warmth, but my eyes misted just a bit.

My mom passed away when I was eleven. Her loss was the most devastating thing that'd ever happened to me. It was like a terrible earthquake that'd caused me to fall from a high shelf and shatter into a thousand tiny shards. All these years later I was still picking up the pieces and trying to reassemble them into something whole and unbroken. But no matter how hard I tried, I could never get the pieces of myself to come together in a way that made me feel sound. Her loss was always there, pronounced and ready to level me. I'd come to realize that I could glue back all nine hundred and ninety-nine pieces, but the most important piece, the piece I needed more than all the others and the one piece that could actually make me feel fully myself again—well, that piece was her. And she was gone. So I'd never be whole. I'd never be sound. I'd never be quite healed. I'd be okay, I'd be happy, I'd be loved and love in return, but a part of me would forever remain broken, like a china doll with a chip in it. I knew that about myself, and it was something I accepted, but there were times when I couldn't hide how very much I missed Mama. Sometimes, that chip in my armor was the only thing I saw or felt.

Blinking furiously and turning my face away from Heath, I forced a laugh and said, "Mama shouldn't rat me out like that!"

I felt his arms around me a moment later. He knew. "Why don't we go out for ice cream?" he said. "We can sneak out while Gilley's on the phone and come back with a scoop for him."

I leaned back against him. "We'd have to go, like, right now," I said.

"I'm game," he replied.

"Ohmigod!" Gil shouted, coming out of the study. "You two will *not* believe who just called me!"

Heath sighed and whispered in my ear, "We were so close to a clean getaway."

I stifled a laugh and said to Gil, "Please tell me that was Gopher or the producer and one of them is going to help us get the dagger back."

Gil's excited smile faded. "No. But I'll figure out something. Don't worry."

"Who was it, then, Gil?" Heath asked.

"None other than *the* Catherine Cooper-Masters!"

My brow furrowed. "You mean Cat Masters? Abby's sister?" Abby Cooper was a very dear friend of mine. She was also a psychic, but the kind who predicts the future, not the kind who talks to dead people. She lives in Texas, and her sister, Cat, was a tiny woman with an enormous, and often overpowering, presence. Oh, and an insane amount of personal wealth.

Gilley bounced on the balls of his feet. "Yes! That's her!"

"She called you?" Heath said.

"Yes!"

Heath and I exchanged a look. "Why?" we said together.

Gilley fanned himself and went over to sit in one of the living room chairs. "I sent her a note two days ago just to say hello and let her know that I was getting married, and to tell her that I'd so admired all the hard work she'd put into her sister's wedding—"

"You mean the disaster you and I nearly didn't live through?" I interrupted. Was he kidding? That wedding had been one of my worst nightmares.

Gilley waved his hand dismissively. "It was a gorgeous ceremony with unfortunate and unrelated extenuating circumstances."

"Unrelated," I said flatly. "Are you talking about when swans attack, or when little people dressed as cupids start shooting wedding guests in the butt with their bows and arrows? Or maybe when a team of stallions runs away with the wedding carriage?"

"Wasn't there also a swarm of moths or something too?"

I held up my hand and splayed my fingers. "They were butterflies *this* big!" I said. "Which I think were also carnivorous."

Gilley glared at us. "Will you two stop? Seriously, that kind of extravaganza is a tough thing to pull off— and all that stuff wasn't Catherine-Cooper-Masters' fault." He said Cat's name like he said Sarah Jessica

Parker's name. As one word. "And you *know* what extenuating circumstances I'm talking about, M.J."

I sighed. I did know. "So what'd Cat have to say?" I asked, reading Gilley like a book. He had more to tell.

"Well!" he said, excited again. "In my note I'd told her how much I'd admired her ideas, and asked that if it wasn't too much trouble could she recommend a good caterer—I'm having the *worst* trouble with ours—and when she called me just now she said that she had a whole binder full of great ideas and contacts, and would I like any of her input?! I mean, can you *believe* it? Catherine-Cooper-Masters wants to help *me* plan our wedding!"

I stared at Gil. After the horror show that'd been Abby Cooper's wedding ceremony, she and I had talked at length about what a nightmare her sister had been when she'd taken on the task of planning Abby's wedding. Cat had big ideas. *Big.*

Of course, she also had the money to execute most of those plans, but in Abby's case, it had all gone terribly wrong. To be fair, it'd gone terribly wrong for reasons other than just Cat's crazy weddingpalooza, but that'd been a freak show unto itself.

"Did you accept the offer?" I asked, already knowing Gil would've jumped at the chance.

"Of course!" he said. "We're meeting for brunch tomorrow. Isn't that amazing?"

Here's the part where I really should've stepped in and cautioned Gil about the wisdom of joining forces with another impossibly impulsive and headstrong person. Here's also the part where I remembered my earlier vow that no matter what drama unfolded from Gilley's wedding plans, I was not going to have an opinion or give my input. That was the quickest way to get sucked into trying to fix it when things started to go south, and no way did I want to get caught up in that whirlpool. So instead I pushed a huge smile onto my face and said, "I think that's amazing, Gil!"

He beamed at me and clapped his hands together. "I've got to call Michel!"

He left us again to hurry into the office, and I grabbed Heath by the arm and said, "I now need ice cream more than ever."

"Let's roll," he said, and we rushed out the door.

Chapter 3

"*Where* have you been?" Gil yelled the second we came back from the ice-cream shop. I've read that when a dog is barking like crazy, it's best to distract it by offering it a treat.

FYI, this works with Gilley too.

I shoved the only slightly melted triple scoop at Gilley, and his yap stopped flapping almost instantly. "Peanut butter fudge brownie atop rocky road atop death by chocolate," I announced. "You're welcome."

To my surprise, Gilley shook his head and stepped away. "No! No, no, no! My diet! I have to stick to my diet!" And then he licked his lips hungrily, his eyes never leaving the cone.

I moved it back and forth in front of me. "It's deeeeelicious . . ."

Beads of sweat broke out over Gilley's brow. "You're hateful," he said. "I hate you, M.J. You're mean. So mean!"

I sighed dramatically and brought the scoop closer to me. "You're right. I shouldn't tempt you. I suppose Heath and I will just have to eat this ourselves . . ."

Gilley darted forward and grabbed the cone right out of my hand. His mouth then descended on the ice cream, much like a viper dislocating its jaw to consume dinner, and he moaned with pleasure. "Hate. You," he said between bites.

I waved a hand at him. "You can work that off tomorrow on a run with me."

"Hate. Hate. Hate," he repeated.

I was about to tease him some more when there was an unexpected knock at the door. I glanced at the kitchen's wall clock. It was nearly ten. "Are we expecting someone?" Heath whispered.

I shook my head and gazed at the door. I had a bad feeling. Nobody moved to answer the knock. Maybe I wasn't the only one with a bad feeling.

Three firm raps came again. They had the ring of authority to them. "Miss Holliday?" said a woman's voice. "This is Detective Olivera. Please open up. I need to speak with you and Mr. Whitefeather."

A bolt of alarm traveled from the top of my head all the way down to my toes. "Shit," Heath whispered. I was certain he felt it too.

Taking a deep breath, I crossed through the kitchen to the front door and opened it, finding a tall, lanky woman with enough presence to make me take a step back. She radiated authority. And confidence. And badassery. (It's a word. Coined by badasses. Trust me.)

As looks went, she was. Gorgeous, I mean. Wavy

brown hair, olive skin, big brown eyes, and a figure that probably belonged on the cover of *Sports Illustrated* at the peak of bikini season.

I could just imagine my husband working hard to rein in the barooga eyes. A quick glance behind me suggested he wasn't working so hard after all. It was all I could do not to slam the door in her face. Consequences be damned.

As if sensing I might try something like that, Detective Olivera pushed one boot subtly forward into the doorframe. Great. She was gorgeous *and* smart. My lucky day. "M. J. Holliday?" she said, flipping open the leather billfold that contained her picture ID and shield.

"Detective," I said. "What's this about?" (As if I couldn't guess . . .)

Instead of answering me, she looked over my shoulder. "Heath Whitefeather?"

I felt a hand on my back as Heath said, "Yes, ma'am. What's happened?"

Tucking away the badge, Olivera pulled out a small leather-bound notebook and flipped it open expertly. "I was hoping you could confirm a few facts for me."

My brow furrowed. Facts? "Of course," I said. "Has something happened, Detective?"

Again she ignored me and read from her notes. "Were the two of you at one zero six Mount Vernon, earlier this evening? The Museum of Modern Science, say, around six p.m.?"

"We were," Heath and I said together.

"What was the nature of your visit there?" she asked.

I mentally groaned and my heart rate ticked up. She

knew damn well what the nature of our business was. Something had obviously happened at the museum. Something very likely involving Oruç's dagger. "We were there on a matter of personal business," Heath said. "A relic belonging to us had been loaned to the museum without our knowledge while we were on our honeymoon. We went to the museum to try to get it back."

Something flickered in the detective's eyes. I didn't like it. "What relic?" she asked.

"A dagger," I said. No point lying. She knew what damned relic. "It belonged to a Turkish warlord."

"How did you come to own this relic?" she asked.

Crap. We were getting into dicey territory here. "It was put into our care by a police inspector in San Francisco," I said. "And I'd prefer to keep his name out of it."

Olivera's granite-hard expression showed a tiny crack. "You're kidding, right?"

"Why do you need to know?" I demanded. She was making me feel defensive, and I knew it wasn't the tone to set with her, but I couldn't help it.

Olivera considered me with a steely gaze. "Miss Holliday—"

"Whitefeather," I corrected, just to be a pain. "And that's Mrs., Detective."

She gave a tiny nod of acknowledgment for the error. It felt a little condescending. "Mrs. Whitefeather, the dagger has been stolen from the museum. And I'd like to know what you might think or know about *that*."

I felt the blood drain from my face, unable to take even a breath for a long, long moment. The dagger had been stolen? It was the worst possible news. "Detective,"

I said quietly after I'd taken that in. "You've *got* to get that dagger back. Seriously, you've got to."

She cocked her head, and her eyes never stopped assessing me. "Again, Mrs. Whitefeather, that's what I'm doing here. I'm looking for the dagger."

Heath's hand on my back moved to my shoulder and he stepped forward to stand next to me while my brain raced with all the awful implications of a relic such as Oruç's dagger free of its magnetic bonds, able to inflict all kinds of terror upon the city of Boston. "Detective," he said, and a sideways glance at him told me he was every bit as alarmed as I was by the news. "What's really going on? You wouldn't be here at ten o'clock at night for just a stolen relic from a museum with little to no market value. So why don't you come out and tell us what else happened?"

Olivera lifted her chin slightly. It was clear she was surprised Heath was cutting to the chase. Maybe she'd underestimated him. "How would you two feel about coming down to the precinct to talk about what else happened?" she said.

I reached for Heath's waist to steady myself. Oh, God. Someone had died. It had to be that. Oruç's dagger had struck again. "We'd be happy to," Heath told her. "As soon as I can arrange for an attorney to meet us down there, of course."

"Why would you need an attorney?" she asked him.

"Why would we need to go down to the precinct to discuss what else happened?" he replied.

"Ohmigod!" Gilley gasped behind us. I jumped a

little, as I'd all but forgotten he was there. "Someone was assaulted at the museum in a robbery gone bad!"

I turned to see him scrolling his finger along his iPad. Why hadn't I thought of that? Turning back to Olivera, I said, "Will they be okay?"

"Who?" she said, looking like she wanted to punch Gilley. He'd clearly stolen her control of the conversation. And then she turned those steely eyes back to me.

"Whoever was assaulted," I said impatiently. "Will they be okay?"

"No," she said evenly.

I sucked in another breath and Heath wrapped his arm around me, which was good because I thought my knees might give out. "Oh, God," I whispered. "Who was it? A patron? Or someone who worked there?"

But Olivera was done giving up information. Handing us her card, she said, "Mr. and Mrs. Whitefeather, I'd appreciate it if you'd come down willingly to the precinct for a conversation. If you feel you need to be represented by counsel, fine. But one way or another I'm going to get to the bottom of this, and you can either cooperate now, or I'll build my case around the two of you."

"I'll call someone," Gilley said, heading off toward the spare bedroom, and I knew he meant he'd be calling an attorney.

I began to tremble. This had all gotten way out of hand so fast. I mean, I'd been worried about Oruç's dagger being on display, but even I'd figured we'd have at least twenty-four hours to get it back before the worst happened. And the exhibit had been blocked off as we were being led from it by museum security—probably to prevent any further scenes like the one we were involved in. I'd figured that they'd keep the exhibit closed at least until morning and we'd have a chance to work the back channels to get the dagger out of there.

What I still couldn't understand was how the dagger had overcome all those magnets. Even with the amount of fear that'd been generated after the lights went out to fuel either Oruç or his demon, the lights had still been turned off and all the batteries drained *before* anyone had gone crazy with fear. So how had that anomaly happened, and why hadn't anything like it happened when we had the dagger hidden in my office safe with just a few magnets to surround it? At the museum, none of the spikes had been touching the dagger, but it'd been surrounded by half a dozen of them only inches away. The whole room was decorated with magnets, in fact, and that kind of electromagnetic field should've kept even a demon as powerful as Oruç's quiet.

And then I thought of something even scarier. What if Oruç's dagger had been stolen by a fan of the show? No one but myself, Gilley, Heath, Gopher, and a dear friend in San Francisco really understood the magnitude of danger the dagger represented. If some brazen fan had decided that the dagger was a collector's item worth stealing, then we had a gigantic problem on our hands. "Detective," I said as Heath took her card, "I'm sure by now you've heard that the dagger is a very dangerous relic—"

She smirked at me. "Obviously," she said. "It played a major part in a murder tonight, Mrs. Whitefeather."

She had no idea how right she was, but I didn't want to fill her in any more than I had to about how we came into possession of Oruç's dagger. It'd probably come out anyway, but for now, I figured Detective Olivera was on a need-to-know basis. "It goes beyond that," I told her. "The dagger isn't just some antique knife. There is a very powerful—very dangerous—set of forces that're associated with it, and in the wrong hands, they could become a *serious* problem."

She cocked her head again. "You don't think murder is a serious problem?"

"Of course I do!" I snapped. "And please don't think I'm not every bit as concerned as you are. But, ma'am, that dagger *is* evil. It needs to be locked away in a safe, lined with enough magnets to choke a whale." I was beginning to regret very much the fact that we hadn't at some point thought to take the dagger, wrap it in magnets, throw it down a deep hole, and cover it in concrete. In hindsight, simply leaving it in my safe seemed like the stupidest thing I'd ever done. There was no help for it now, but I silently vowed that once I got the dagger back, I was gonna bury that thing in a dry well and pour enough concrete over the top to seal it up for all time.

"You keep talking about this dagger like it's got a life of its own," the detective said. "Come down to the station and explain that to me."

I sighed. Why were cops always so skeptical of the supernatural? I'd had my fair share of encounters with law enforcement, and it was always the same deal: suspicion and skepticism until they saw the demon du jour up close and personal, and then they were all, "Oh, please help us, M.J.!"

"Fine," I told Olivera. "We'll follow you to the station."

Heath was quick to protest. "Em, we'll need to wait for the attorney to meet us there."

"No, we won't," I told him. When he opened his mouth to argue with me, I laid a hand on his shoulder and said, "Heath . . . the dagger. Someone has it."

He pressed his lips together and nodded. "You're right. Okay, let's go."

I called to Gil, who came out from the spare bedroom looking frustrated. "I'm waiting on a callback," he said.

"It's okay. We're headed down anyway," I said, as Heath handed me my jacket.

"Without a lawyer?" Gilley said. "M.J., don't be stupid!"

"Don't be stupid?" I repeated angrily. "Gilley, somewhere in this city someone has Oruç's dagger—which *you* offered up to the museum on a silver platter, and in so doing, *you* placed it within the public domain, where it obviously tempted someone into stealing it. And now someone appears to be dead, so I gotta ask you, who's really the stupid one in this scenario?"

Gilley's face flushed with shame and he dropped his gaze. "Me," he said softly. "You're right, and I'm so, so sorry, guys. I really thought I could keep it safe."

"Come to the precinct with us," Heath said gently

while I continued to fume a little. "I think we're gonna need you to confirm our whereabouts for tonight anyway." For emphasis he glanced at Olivera, who nodded subtly. So it was true. We were under suspicion for the crime. Great. Just great.

We met Olivera outside the precinct and then followed her inside, up a flight of stairs, and down a long hallway to the back of the building. Once through a set of double doors, we came out into a large room with desks arranged in a kind of haphazard fashion, some facing each other and others simply by themselves like little islands floating in a sea of paperwork.

I wasn't used to seeing actual desks at a police precinct—all of the previous investigative offices I'd visited had always been arranged in cubicles, which I personally hated. I never knew how people could spend hours at a time in a tiny three-walled area with barely enough room to turn around and which gave only the pretense of privacy. Looking at the area Olivera had led us to was like stepping back in time before corporations became so uniform. I liked it.

"Over here." The detective gestured, waving us to the far corner of the room, where a door stood open. We filed in one after the other and sat down in one of the four chairs assembled in the room. I thought maybe Olivera had called ahead and told someone to put enough chairs in the room.

Behind us, a gentleman, probably in his late fifties or early sixties, entered, and he brought his own desk chair with him. Taking a seat in the corner, he crossed his beefy arms over his portly belly and studied us one by one. He also gave off a vibe of authority, perhaps one notch above what Olivera was putting out.

"This is Lieutenant Wilgus," Olivera said, with a subtle wave of her hand in his direction. "He'll be joining us for the duration of our talk."

I shifted a little in my chair. If the precinct lieutenant was sitting in, then something really bad had to have gone down at the museum.

Olivera took her seat and opened up her notebook. "Talk to me about earlier this evening," she began. "Why did you go to the museum, and what happened there?"

Heath took the lead and talked slowly, carefully, and in great detail about our trip to the exhibit. He had more presence of mind than I did, it appeared, and certainly more patience. I tried not to fidget or look guilty—a tough thing when two cops are staring at you like they've got you dead to rights.

At last Heath was finished and Olivera asked him a few follow-up questions, mostly focused on the timeline he'd offered. She even tried to trip him up once or twice, just to see if she could, but he had the timing down solid. We'd been at the museum from about five thirty to about a quarter past six, when we'd been tossed out by Phil Sullivan. We'd then headed straight home, arriving at close to seven p.m., where the three of us had discussed the dilemma of getting the dagger back; then we'd eaten dinner; and, right around nine p.m., Heath and I had gone out for ice cream, arriving back home shortly before ten, when Olivera had shown up. Heath told her that there were plenty of people at the ice-cream parlor who could vouch for us—the place had been fairly crowded. She took down the name and location of the place and then said, "Okay, so talk to me about this dagger. Why is it so special?"

Heath glanced at me and I nodded, then leaned my elbows on the table and folded my hands together. I'd do the talking now. "Several years ago, me, my husband, and my business partner were asked to participate in a cable TV show featuring haunted possessions. The dagger was one of the items that Heath and I had to focus our intuition on, and within seconds it became quite clear to us that the dagger had a particularly violent history."

Gilley cleared his throat, and when I turned to look at him I saw that he was swiveling his iPad around to show Olivera and Wilgus something. "I have the video," he said and pressed the play button.

I turned my face from the monitor and shuddered. I'd lived through that first encounter with the dagger— no way did I want to see it again. But I did watch the detective's and lieutenant's reactions. They both leaned forward to peer at Gil's tablet, and I noticed that Olivera jumped when the talon marks started etching themselves directly into the table where Heath and I were sitting.

But Wilgus wasn't at all convinced. "Special effects," he said before the video had even stopped rolling.

"No," I said firmly, and stared right into his eyes to let him know I wasn't fibbing.

"It's real," Heath said.

Olivera must've been bolstered by her boss's skepticism. "We're supposed to believe a couple of professional filmmakers?"

"We're not professional filmmakers," I said testily. "We're the talent. That film was shot on Gil's phone. It's real." For emphasis I stood up, turned around, and lifted up my jacket and shirt to expose my back and the long white scars that still marred my body from where the demon had dug its talons into me. Looking at Gil, I said, "Play the part of the video again where I got raked," I told him, and then waited for Gilley to rewind and play that part again slowly. Over my shoulder I said, "You'll notice those marks appear exactly where my scars still are."

I watched over my shoulder as Olivera's gaze darted between my back and the screen. I could see she was at least a little rattled. I let go of my clothing and sat back down. "The dagger houses an evil spook named Oruç, who was a sadistic, murderous Turkish warlord several centuries ago. He was killed by a woman he'd been trying to murder with the dagger, and he became a ghost who has attached himself to the dagger. He's a powerful spook who likes to possess anyone either near or holding the dagger, and if that weren't bad enough, he's somehow also attached himself to an evil demon that's capable of doing what you saw on that tape . . . and a lot more."

"It's because of the 'lot more' that we need that dagger back," Heath said. "We have to find it."

Olivera considered all three of us for a bit before she

pulled up her own iPad and flipped it around to us. Turning it on, she tapped on the photos icon and said, "I'd say it's definitely imperative that we find your dagger."

Her finger stroked the iPad to one particular photo that caused me to suck in a shocked breath. The victim was someone I recognized. It was Phil Sullivan, the museum director, and in the photos of his body, he appeared to be lying faceup on the museum floor staring sightlessly upward with his mouth hanging open as if in midscream. The scene was quite gruesome; the top of Phil's head sported a terrible wound, and the area behind him was covered in a pool of blood.

There are things in life that you don't really need to see. A man murdered like that is one of them. Turning my face away from the screen, I whispered, "My God . . . that poor man."

"When did this happen?" Heath asked.

"We believe it happened between eight fifty and nine p.m.," she said.

"That's pretty specific," Gilley said, and I knew the three of us each felt a tiny hint of relief that we all had alibis for the time Sullivan was murdered. Heath and I had been at the ice-cream parlor, and Gilley had been at our place, on the phone with his fiancé for almost that entire time.

"The museum closed at seven and the last employees left at eight," Olivera explained. "An alarm in the exhibit was triggered at eight fifty p.m., and we think Sullivan was in his office working late when the alarm sounded upstairs and he went to investigate. Officers responded to the alarm, and they got there at two minutes past nine, finding Sullivan already dead at the scene, the dagger gone from the display case, and no sign of the killer."

"Security footage?" Heath asked hopefully.

Olivera said, "All fed to a computer that was housed on-site at the museum. A laptop kept in a security closet on the same floor as your exhibit. The closet was broken into and the laptop was also stolen."

Gilley's jaw dropped and he became visibly upset. "Why would the museum have such a stupid setup for their security footage?" he demanded. "Everyone knows that, these days, you send the feed off-site to make sure law enforcement always has access to the footage!"

Olivera shrugged. "Sullivan was the one who set up the system. So we can't really ask him why he had it set up that way."

"Fingerprints?" I asked. "DNA? Other witnesses?"

"We're still processing the scene and canvassing the area," she said. "It'll be a while before we know if we have anything to go on."

"Was anyone else hurt?" Gilley asked, and I could hear the guilt in his voice. A sideways glance at him told me he was on the verge of tears.

"No," Olivera said, but I knew it was just a matter of time, and truthfully we had no way of knowing if there weren't already more victims. Maybe there were other casualties that simply hadn't been reported yet. Still, I wasn't going to mention that to Gilley. He felt bad enough.

"How can we help?" Heath asked the detective. But it was her lieutenant who answered.

"You can't," he said, crossing his arms over his chest. "And frankly, even with your alibis I'm not convinced you three aren't behind this as some kind of publicity stunt."

I felt myself getting really angry. It was one thing to accuse us of faking the footage from that hotel in San Francisco when Oruç's demon had first reared its ugly head, but it was another thing entirely to suggest we'd conspired to commit murder just to make ourselves famous.

"Would it help if we offered you the name of someone who could vouch for us and the veracity of the story behind the dagger?" Heath said.

I stiffened and put a hand on his arm. The person I was protecting was an inspector on the San Francisco police force. He'd risked his job—hell, he'd risked getting charged with obstruction—to get us the dagger, because he knew that we were the *only* people it'd be safe with. "Honey," I whispered. "Don't."

Heath looked meaningfully at me. "I talked to *our friend* a couple of months ago, Em. He saw our show and called. He left his job last December—took early retirement. He told me that ever since the thing in San Francisco—ever since Oruç got inside his head—he's been suffering from panic attacks. He says he has nightmares all the time and he can't shake 'em. He swears that there's still a little bit of Oruç left in his mind, toying with him. I told him that was unlikely, but now I'm not so sure. Maybe there's something to it."

I put a hand to my mouth. "I had no idea."

"I know," Heath said. "I didn't want to tell you because I knew you'd feel bad, but I think it's important to loop him in on this. For a number of reasons."

I bit my lip. Could it be true? Could the last person Oruç had tried to possess really have a bit of that vile spook still roaming around inside his mind? Turning to Olivera, I said, "What I'm about to tell you is off the record."

Olivera frowned and tapped her finger on the table like I had to be kidding.

"I'm serious," I said.

"I'm not a reporter," she said flatly.

"No, but the information I'd be giving to you could be used to prosecute."

"Prosecute?" she said. "For what?"

"Tampering with evidence," I said. "And probably obstruction."

Olivera's left eyebrow arched. "If you two tampered with any evidence at my crime scene, I'll have the DA prosecute the hell out of you," she warned.

"It wasn't your crime scene, and we weren't the ones who tampered with the evidence. Well, at least not directly. And the crime scene was from several years ago and well outside your jurisdiction."

"Then why would you be worried I'd have the DA prosecute you for obstruction?"

"I'm not," I told her. "I'm worried that you'll make a few calls and have someone important to us prosecuted when all he was trying to do was protect the public."

"Explain," she said.

"First, your word, Detective. And you too, Lieutenant."

Olivera and Wilgus exchanged a look. They seemed to consider my offer a trap, but Wilgus finally shrugged and Olivera said, "Okay, Mrs. Whitefeather. We won't pursue an obstruction or evidence-tampering charge with you, your husband, Mr. Gillespie, or whomever else you're protecting, as long as what you're telling me about this crime scene being outside of our jurisdiction is true."

I let out a breath of relief and said, "The footage we showed you on Gilley's iPad was taken at a historic hotel in California. While we were there filming for a show called *Haunted Possessions*, there were a series of murders and this dagger was at the center of them. In the end, Heath, Gilley, and I helped solve the case and we were entrusted with the dagger for safekeeping.

"Anyway, the evil spook housed inside that dagger likes to take over the minds of anyone within range of the weapon. You don't necessarily even need to be holding it to be taken over."

"How exactly is this ghost 'housed' inside the dagger?" Olivera asked, using air quotes.

"Well . . . ," I said, pausing for a moment to think about it. "The dagger is basically a hole in the electromagnetic energy that surrounds all of us, and it allows entities like Oruç and his demon to go from one plane of existence to another."

"Come again?" Wilgus said. I could tell he thought I was full of shit.

With a sigh I tried explaining it another way. "For the sake of argument, I'm going to explain this as if we all agree that ghosts are real. Now, to the average ghost-believing layperson, ghosts are sort of that disembodied spirit that wakes up at night, floats down the staircase, and might freak you out on the way to the bathroom at two a.m. The truth, like most things, is a lot more complicated than that.

"See, most ghosts are the result of people who don't quite grasp that they're dead. They exist in a sort of murky reality, an almost dreamlike state where they try to pretend that nothing has changed. They still wake up and find themselves in their own homes; it's just that the furniture has been moved around. They sometimes spend decades in denial, but usually there will be a moment when they'll sort of wake up to the reality that they're no longer alive and can't affect their surroundings anymore. At that point, they typically allow themselves to cross over . . . into heaven, if you will.

"Now, having said all that, there is a sort of subset of spooks that come from far more sinister backgrounds. These were very bad people in life—murderers, rapists, serial killers, and the like. In death they have no interest in crossing over and facing any form of judgment, so they too become disembodied spirits without a lot of purpose. Unlike the other spooks, who live in a bit of a fog, these guys know full well that they're dead. The problem for them, though, is that being a normal spook is pretty boring.

"So, typically within a matter of a few decades, they begin to figure out that they can use some of their energy to create a sort of doorway that leads them to one of the lower realms."

"Lower realms," Wilgus repeated. "You mean like hell?"

"Not quite hell per se," I said. "But close. We call it a lower realm because for us mediums, heaven, if you will, always appears to us as a light feeling upward—an ascension, if you will—and the lower realms feel, for lack of a better word, downward, or lower than where we are. Now, lots of bad stuff floats around in the lower realms. Within them, these evil spooks figure out pretty quick that they'll be able to spend the day in a place that doesn't drain them of energy, and come out at night when the higher humidity will allow them to affect their environment and the people in it. Within the lower realms these spooks will also have access to knowledge and even a little bit of extra power, and a few of them, like Oruç, will even bring back through that doorway a demon they've somehow managed to partner with.

"But, to answer your question specifically about the dagger," I said with a nod back to Wilgus, "think of our realm—where we live, work, eat, sleep, et cetera—and the lower realm as two separate nations with a really well-sealed border between them. If a spook like Oruç can find a place along that border where the barrier is weak, he can create a portal. Essentially, a portal is a rip or a tear in the fabric of what we see as reality, and it allows for these spooks to float between our reality and the lower realms. Most portals are fixed within something immovable and permanent. Over the years we've seen them in walls, floors, trees, tombstones, caves, roads, monuments, and even the side of a cliff. The dagger was one of the very first portals we ever came across that was small and portable—I mean, up until we encountered it, we'd never thought that a portal could be located anywhere that wasn't large, solid, and fixed. I'd never even heard of an object like a relic containing a portal, but Oruç's dagger is a very real portal, and its size has not limited the amount of evil that's able to escape from it."

"So how did you come into possession of this evil portal?" Wilgus pressed me in a voice dripping with skepticism.

I reined in the urge to snap at him and, without giving him the specifics that I knew would get our friend in San Francisco into hot water, I said, "The dagger came into our possession because it was too much of a threat to the general public in any hands but ours. It was linked to a series of murders in San Francisco. They occurred at the location where we were filming our very first TV show together, and after we suspended filming, Gilley, Heath, and I assisted the police with the apprehension of those people responsible, and we also made sure that Oruç and his demon were shut back behind the portal in the lower realms."

"How'd you do that?" Wilgus wanted to know.

"It's a long story," Heath said, cutting in. "But basically, we got the dagger away from the murderer and covered it in magnets."

"Why magnets?" the lieutenant asked next.

"There's some science involved," Gilley said, also jumping in. "Spooks are very sensitive to changes in electromagnetic frequencies. When you introduce a magnet to a spook's environment, it's like setting off the fire alarm. To a spook, it's extremely uncomfortable to be around, and enough magnetic energy can actually burn a spook. When you shove a magnet into the center of a portal, you shut it down permanently. As we couldn't really do that with Oruç's dagger, we settled for wrapping it in magnets."

"But how did *you* three come into possession of the dagger?" Olivera pressed.

Gil looked to me to answer. This was the third time we'd been asked that specific question, and I understood then that there was no dancing around the answer anymore. With a sigh I said, "While assisting the police with the murder investigation, it became apparent to all of us that Oruç had developed the ability to possess the minds of anyone near his dagger. Once the police apprehended those responsible for the murders and we neutralized the dagger, the inspector on the case thought it best if the dagger didn't end up in his evidence room to be handled by various police and DA personnel. He felt that would simply be too risky, so he asked us to look after it, and we agreed."

Olivera swiped a lock of her hair behind her ear and looked to Wilgus as if to say, "You believe this bullshit?"

He ducked his chin and covered his mouth, as if he were stifling a laugh; then he shook his head to let her know that, no, he definitely didn't believe it.

I wanted to shout at them, "We're right in front of you, you know!" but instead I settled for fuming in my seat.

"Let me get this straight," Olivera said after a lengthy pause. "A couple of years ago, you three managed to convince some idiot inspector from SFPD that there was an evil ghost and his demon responsible for a series of murders, and he then helped you tamper with evidence in a murder case?"

I glared at her. She wasn't listening. Turning to Heath, I said, "They don't get it, and I'm not putting our friend in jeopardy. Let's go."

"Whoa, whoa, whoa!" Olivera said, holding her hands in a T for "time out." "I gave you my word that I wasn't going to pursue a criminal charge for anything having to do with a crime scene that isn't ours, but, guys . . . I mean, come on! This is all a little too crazy to believe."

A thought came to my mind and I glanced at her iPad, and my memory flashed to the shock in her eyes that'd appeared when she'd looked at my scars and the footage from Gil's tablet. Pointing to her iPad, I said, "There were talon marks at the museum, weren't there, Detective?"

Her chin tilted up slightly and she crossed her arms over her chest, mirroring Wilgus's posture. "What makes you think that?" she asked me, but I could tell I'd just struck gold.

I smirked. "Because it's the demon's signature. He likes to mark up the walls and tear up the furniture and, occasionally, a person. I'm guessing some part of the exhibit was torn to shreds or at least shows three talon marks. Just like the ones on my back."

Again Olivera and Wilgus exchanged a look. They looked perhaps a bit less confident in the belief that we were big fat fibbers. "Let us talk to your inspector in San Francisco," she said at last. "I want to hear what he has to say about all this."

It was my turn to hesitate. I didn't really want Ayden to get sucked into this mess, but I was also very worried about him after what Heath had told me. "Let me call him and explain what's going on, first," I said. "I'll leave it up to him as to whether or not he wants to talk to you."

Olivera shrugged. "Okay," she said. "In the meantime, we'll check your alibis." She got up, effectively dismissing us, and both she and Wilgus turned to the door, but Olivera paused to turn back to us to say, "Don't leave town."

I bit back the retort that was on the tip of my tongue. No way did she have the authority to dictate where we went, but her warning was still pretty intimidating, regardless of the fact that I'd had no plans to go anywhere as long as the dagger was missing. I just prayed that we'd find it before the body count rose. Something told me we weren't going to be so lucky, though. And that had far less to do with my keen intuition and much more to do with a wealth of past experience in such matters.

Ain't my life grand?

Chapter 4

An hour later we were back home and in the midst of a deep discussion. "We've got to make sure that we stick together as much as possible and account for our whereabouts at all times," Heath said, heading to the window to peek out at the street, as if he expected there to be an unmarked cop car below with a detective on stakeout duty. "If BPD thinks we're involved in Sullivan's murder, then they'll be looking to us if any other bodies turn up."

"You mean *when* other bodies turn up," Gilley said miserably. "I keep going over it and over it in my mind, and it just doesn't add up. I checked the museum's security before I loaned them the dagger. How is it that the central alarm wasn't triggered when the thief broke in?"

"He could've been there the whole time," I said. "I mean, there was a lot of chaos earlier tonight when the lights went out and everybody's cell died. The thief could've been hiding in a restroom or something until after closing."

Gilley shook his head. "No way. The security guards check all the restroom stalls before closing, and they're supposed to do a sweep of the building too. And there are motion sensors throughout the whole place. I'm telling you, it would've been impossible for the killer to have moved around freely without triggering at least one alarm. I know because I went over the security for the whole building to make sure it was sound."

"And yet you missed the part where the security cameras all fed to an on-site computer," Heath said with a hint of anger. I couldn't fault him, because Gil had been reckless in his decision to loan out the dagger, especially the part about not bringing us in on the discussion, but Gil was still my best friend and I felt a pang of sympathy—especially after he winced at the rebuke.

"I did miss that," he said, dropping his gaze to the floor. "I don't know how I did, but you're right. That got right by me. And now Sullivan is dead and the dagger is missing."

"I think we need to stay on topic here, guys," I said softly. There was no point in making Gilley feel any worse than he already did. "If we figure out how the killer got past all the security except for the alarm in the exhibit hall itself, maybe we'll be able to give Olivera a lead she can follow instead of looking at us as suspects."

Gil tapped his lips, thinking, and then he snapped

his fingers as if he'd figured it out. "I know how it was done!" he said.

"How?" Heath asked before I could.

"Well, if Sullivan was still there, he might not have turned on the motion detectors inside the building until he was ready to leave. Maybe the killer was walking around freely until Sullivan was ready to go. Before leaving, Sullivan would have flipped the central switch for the motion detectors, which then activated the one upstairs in the exhibit room where the killer already was. The man's movements would have set off the alarm up there. Sullivan probably then raced upstairs to investigate, and bam! He gets murdered."

"Yeah, but it still doesn't explain how the killer got inside the building in the first place," I said. "How'd he bypass the initial alarm into the building?"

"The same way our spook and his demon drained everyone's cell and turned out the lights. Oruç must've drained the power to the central alarm for the building."

"Wait, what?" I said. "Gil, how could Oruç target something so specific, and for that matter, how did he coordinate with the living, breathing thief? I mean, until tonight, we have no evidence that the thief had any prior contact with Oruç, who couldn't have known that his portal would be stolen from the exhibit."

Gil scratched his head in a frustrated gesture. "Okay, so I have no idea how the thief bypassed the exterior alarm, but you're raising an even bigger question, M.J.," he said. "Even without any prior contact with the dagger, someone had to know what kind of power was locked away in it, and they targeted that possessed relic specifically."

"What'd the sign on the dagger display read?" I asked him, wondering if he hadn't imparted the dagger's history to anyone willing to walk by the display.

He shook his head. "Only that the dagger was an ancient relic said to be a haunted possession of a Turkish warlord. I wrote it up myself, making sure to leave out any specifics."

"Did you identify the warlord?" I pressed. Maybe someone had looked into Oruç's history.

"No way," Gil said. "I mean, I'm not stupid, M.J."

I sat down with a tired sigh. "*Someone* had to know how powerful that dagger was," I said.

Heath came to sit down next to me. "Maybe not," he said. "Maybe some obsessed fan saw it and wanted to steal a little piece of our history."

I eyed him skeptically. "No way," I said. "There's no way, Heath. If you're an obsessed fan and you want to steal something from our show, then you're gonna go after something like my leather jacket that was hanging on the wall. Or a couple of the spikes, or even some of Gopher's notes from the shows. You're not going to risk a long prison sentence by breaking into a museum after hours for a relic that may or may not be haunted, and then you're definitely not going to murder someone over it."

"Once he got his hands on it, would he have even known he was killing Sullivan, though?" Gilley said.

I motioned to Gilley with my hand. "I don't know that the dagger would've worked *that* fast, Gil. Still, I seriously doubt that a fan, even an obsessed one, would be willing to risk his freedom for what he thinks is probably just some dusty dagger—especially one that was never even featured on *Ghoul Getters*."

"That's another good point," Heath said. "The dagger and its history were a secret, right? I mean, none of us has ever talked publicly about Oruç or his dagger. But someone knew. They *had* to know; otherwise, why risk so much for a stupid knife?"

I looked at Gil. "You never put anything online about it?"

"No!" he said, as if I'd insulted him.

"Okay, okay," I said, holding up my hands in surrender. "Just making sure." There was a pause before I spoke again. "So who could've known about the history of the dagger?"

We all looked at one another. The people who had knowledge about Oruç and the dagger were almost all accounted for in my living room. "There's Gopher," Gil said.

"You think he told someone?" I asked.

"Well, he did tell that producer who called me from the production company," he reasoned.

I palmed my forehead. "Shit," I said. "I'd forgotten about him. So if Gopher told *that* guy, who knows who else he told?"

"Great," Heath said. "That means it could've been anybody. And what the hell is Gopher doing shooting his mouth off about the dagger anyway?"

I shook my head. "I don't know. I've never heard him talk about it to anyone. Maybe he got together with this producer for a few drinks one night and that loosened his lips."

"Maybe it had nothing to do with the production side," Gil said. "Maybe Gopher telling someone from the studio was just a coincidence, and other people we haven't even thought of heard about it."

"From whom?" I said.

"Well," Gil said, blinking while he thought his theory through. "Anyone from that original shoot could've blabbed about the dagger and the demon inside it. I mean, guys, think back to that shoot. There was a camera guy who walked off the set after the demon showed up—remember?"

"I've never seen anybody turn so pale," I said with a smirk.

"Yeah," Gil continued, "and that actor . . . What was his name? That former child star?"

"Matt Duval," I said with a roll of my eyes. "He was a piece of work. Just wanted a ticket back to the fame and fortune of his yesteryear."

"Fat chance," Gil said with a giggle. Heath and I chuckled too, because Matt Duval had gained a considerable amount of weight since he'd been a teen heartthrob. "I heard he's now living in a trailer park."

"Ouch," I said. "Oh, how far those stars fall when they come back to earth."

"Well, the point is that he was there that day, and he saw what came out of the dagger."

"I can't see fat, broke Matt Duval coming after the dagger, Gil," I reasoned.

Gilley shrugged. "We've got to consider everybody

who was there on the day the demon first made his appearance," he said. "And Matt doesn't have to be the one who stole the dagger, just the guy who blabbed about it. Anyone there could've talked about it, in fact."

Heath snickered. "You mean like that washed-up hack they partnered me with? Em, what'd you call him again?"

I grinned. "Captain Comb-Over." We all laughed. "I also called him Count Chocula. I mean, the dude wore a cape!"

"Can you imagine going to a medium who looked like him and had a name like Bernard Higgins?" Gilley said. He'd remembered the man's real name at least.

"He sucked," Heath said bluntly. My eyes widened. "What?" he said to me. "You thought he was good?"

"No," I said. "But no worse than who they paired me with. What was her name?"

"Elvira, mistress of the dark," Gilley said in a spooky voice. We all laughed again. That hadn't been her name, but nobody seemed to recall it. "Do you remember when she threw that lady's bowl on the floor?" Gil asked me.

I put a hand over my mouth, remembering the scene. It'd been an awful afternoon, suffering through the filming of a show I never wanted to be on, and all of the resulting disasters thereafter. And the smashing of the family heirloom had been well before Oruç's dagger had even shown up. "I can't believe that woman didn't bitch-slap Elvira for that," I said. "She destroyed a family heirloom."

"See? You should've been paired with Captain Comb-Over," Heath said.

"No way!" I told him. "That guy was a letch!"

"I thought I caught him staring hard at the girls," Gil smirked, waving a hand in the direction of my chest. "Which I might add are looking marvelous in that sweater tonight, honey."

I wagged my finger at him. "Eyes off the ladies, Gillespie."

"Oh, please, I'm a great admirer of décolletage, which you've never been in short supply of, thank your lucky stars."

I felt heat hit my cheeks, and I wanted to get us back on track. "Okay, so to Gilley's point, there were quite a few people in the room when the dagger showed up and who knew what it held. Any one of them could've blabbed over the years. But the thing that doesn't hold water with that theory is, other than Gopher, who knew that we even had it?"

"Ayden," Gil said after a pause.

"No *way* did he say a word about the dagger or that we had it," I insisted. "Not when it could've gotten him in serious hot water."

"Which means it had to be Gopher who said something to someone," Heath said. "We'll need him to give us a list of the people he's told about the dagger being in our possession."

"He's unreachable for the next two weeks, remember?" I said.

"I do," he said with a sigh. "But other than trying to

get ahold of him, I'm not sure what we can do to figure out who stole the dagger and murdered Sullivan."

"Maybe we start at the scene and work our way backward," I suggested. "I mean, starting from a list of suspects only Gopher could name isn't an option, so let's work this like the police do. From the scene and work our way back."

"Do you have access to the crime scene photos?" Gil asked me. "Because I don't."

"Oh, please. We all know you could hack your way into the BPD system to take a look if you wanted to."

Gil eyed his fingernails modestly. "Yes. Yes I could."

"But that's not the scene I'm talking about," I told him. "I'm talking about the scene from the exhibit when the three of us were in attendance. Somehow, some way, Oruç and his demon overcame all those magnets enough to douse the lights and drain the batteries on . . . what? Seventy-five? A hundred cell phones?"

"Yours wasn't affected," Heath reminded me.

"That's right!" I said. Turning to Gil, I asked, "How was it that my cell wasn't affected?"

"Where were you carrying it?" he asked me.

I patted my chest. "Right pocket of the . . . hey, where're the vests?" I looked around and didn't see the vests we'd taken from the office.

"I put them in the car," Heath said. "There's no room in the front hall closet and they're better off at the office."

I hid a smirk. I knew that Heath really just didn't want to look at them. It'd been so nice of Mrs. Gillespie to make them for us, but they were definitely a crime of fashion. "Thanks," I told him. "I'll put them back tomorrow."

"*Any*way," Gil said, "if you had your cell in your vest pocket right next to a magnet, then it probably protected it."

"But all of the other magnets in the room didn't protect the other cell phones?" Heath asked.

Gil got up and started to pace. "I know, I know!" he said. "It doesn't make sense. The magnetic energy in that place was insanely high. There's *no way* Oruç or his demon or even both of them should've been able to pull a stunt like that!"

"And yet they did," I said.

"Unless there was something else at play," Heath said. "Could the lights have been taken out and the batteries drained by some other means, Gil? Something man-made?"

Gil frowned, tapped his lip, thought for a long moment, and said, "Nothing I've heard of could've done that," he said. "There's no electronic device I know of that could drain several dozen cell phones in a room all at once. I mean, that's just *insane*!"

"So it had to be Oruç and his demon," I reasoned.

"Afraid so," Gil said. "But how, I still can't figure out." He went back to pacing again, and after a moment he added, "I need to get into that building! Something's super fishy about this whole thing."

"The police will have the crime scene sealed until they're through investigating," Heath said. "I doubt they're going to let us walk in and take a look around."

"We still have to talk about Ayden," I said next.

Heath sighed heavily. "I hate to get him mixed up in this, but I don't know how else to convince the Boston PD that we're not making any of this up."

"It bothers me that he had to leave the force because of the panic attacks," I said. "How is he surviving?"

"I asked him that too," Heath said, "and he told me that his dad passed away a year ago and left him a nice inheritance. He's also got his pension, which probably isn't a whole lot, but he insisted that he's doing okay. Plus, he said that he'd just gotten his PI license, so I don't think he's given up the investigative life."

"Do you think there's any truth to his theory that the demon left something behind in his mind?"

"I don't know, Em. I mean, it's possible, but have we ever encountered something like that?"

"Maybe with Lester," I said, referring to an old case we'd worked. The memory of all that made me shudder again.

"Why did Ayden think Oruç's demon is still in his head?" Gil asked.

"He's been having really bad nightmares for the past couple of years," Heath said. "Ayden didn't go into detail, but he said they were graphic and always involved murder. He said the nightmares were what brought on the panic attacks, and he's seen every shrink in town and hasn't been able to get them to go away."

I frowned. "Lester had nightmares too," I reminded them. I didn't like the coincidences.

"We should call him," Gilley said. "Ayden, I mean."

I nodded and glanced at the clock on the wall. It

was nearly midnight. "It'll be close to nine on the West Coast," I said. "Ayden should still be up, right?"

We made the call and our friend the former inspector picked up on the third ring. "MacDonald," he said formally.

"Ayden?" I said. "It's M. J. Holliday. How are you?"

"I don't know any M. J. Holliday," he said gruffly. The tone of his voice threw me a little, and as I had him on speaker, I looked around at Gilley and Heath, who also appeared taken aback.

"Don't know me?" I said. "Are you kidding?"

"Nope," he said curtly. "Like I said, I don't know any M. J. Holliday." There was a pause as I tried to figure out what to say to that, when Ayden suddenly said, "Now, I *do* know an M. J. Whitefeather. Would you be any relation to her?"

I couldn't help it; I busted out laughing, as did Heath and Gilley. "Funny, man," I said to him. "You had us all going."

"Who's us all?"

"Gilley is here, along with my husband. Heath Holliday." I winked at Heath and he grinned at me, enjoying my little joke.

"Oh, yeah, I know those guys. Heath owes me a beer the next time he's in town. I'm gonna hit him up for a double-malt scotch, though, 'cause he didn't invite me to his wedding."

"Nobody was invited," I was quick to say. "Not even Gilley."

Gil narrowed his eyes at me. I could tell he was still miffed about it. "I think the thing to do is to hold a reception and invite all our family and friends," Heath said. That was news to me, but I liked the idea. "After Gilley's wedding, of course."

"Am I at least invited to that?" Ayden asked.

"You're invited to both," I said, ignoring Gilley's pointed head shaking. I knew he already had a bajillion people he planned to invite, so what was one more?

"Awesome," Ayden said. "Count me in. Anyway, I figure you're not calling me about the weddings so much as you're calling me to talk about what happened at that museum tonight, right?"

"Ayden, *how* do you know anything about what went down at the museum?" I asked.

"Hey, I Facebook," he said coolly. "And I'm a fan of your show's page. It's all over social media, how you two got married and there was some sort of crazy publicity stunt that nearly caused a riot. I was about to send you guys an angry e-mail when I recognized Oruç's dagger in one of the photos posted before the lights went out. What the hell is that thing doing on display anyway?"

Heath and I looked pointedly at Gilley. He gulped and said, "Hey, Ayden. So, in a moment of serious weakness, I agreed to loan out the dagger to the museum for the exhibit. It was stupid, but in my defense I personally loaded the room with enough magnetic spikes to build a railroad. There's no way the dagger should've been active, and we're still trying to figure out what happened and what to do."

"Well, for starters, how about taking the dagger out of that exhibit, like, right now?"

Again we all looked uncomfortably at one another. "About that," I said. "Ayden, the real reason we're calling is because the dagger has been stolen from the museum."

There was a very long pause, and into the silence I even called out to Ayden to make sure he was still on the line. "I'm here," he said. "Just taking that news in. And now I need details."

Heath filled him in and ignored the parts where Ayden cut loose a swearword or six. "So, one man dead, one missing dagger, and one loose spook and his demon, is that about right?"

"Yes," I said. "Only, the Boston PD suspects that we must've had something to do with it, which is actually why we're calling. We explained to them that we're legit and that the dagger is super dangerous and we need to get it back, but they're not buying it. We were hoping to have you—a former inspector with the San Francisco PD, vouch for us."

As I finished speaking I heard some distinctive clicking sounds in the background. "How about I do you one better, M.J. There's a direct flight to Logan from SFO, no tickets available online, but I might be able to squeeze on going standby. It leaves in an hour and forty-five minutes and gets in at seven thirty a.m. It'll be tight getting to the airport in time, but if I don't make it onto that flight, there's the first flight out at six that I'll nab, and that'll get into Logan at three p.m."

"We'll pick you up," I said immediately, and pointed at Gilley. Let the fool who put the dagger on display get up early and pick up Ayden.

Gilley scowled at me.

"Great," Ayden said, and in the background I could hear what sounded like dresser drawers opening. "I pack light, so I won't be checking a bag. Where am I staying?"

Gilley shook his head furiously again and I waved my hand dismissively at him. "With us, of course." I had a full-sized bed in the basement storage room for just such an occasion. We'd have to haul it up four flights of stairs, but I could have the spare bedroom ready by the time Ayden got here.

"Excellent. Hopefully, I'll see you at seven thirty a.m. Barring that, I'll see you at three." With that, he hung up and we all looked around at one another, a little stunned.

"What the hell just happened?" Gil said.

"We got ourselves some true investigative help," I told him. "And we'll be thankful for it."

Gilley stood up and stretched. "Yeah, okay. So, I guess I'm gonna turn in since I have to be up at the butt crack of dawn. Good night, you—"

"Don't even think about it, mister," I told him, stepping in front of him. "You're going to help Heath bring up the spare bed from the basement."

Gilley groaned. "Ugh, but it's so *heavy*, M.J.!"

"Get over it," I said. "If Ayden makes the flight out tonight, he'll be exhausted by the time he gets here, and he'll probably need a power nap before we head to the station. I'm not going to make him sleep on the couch, and no way are Heath and I getting up at six a.m. to haul that bed upstairs. So that leaves the two of you to do it tonight."

"But, M.J.—!"

"Oh, shut it, Gil," I snapped. "The sooner you guys head downstairs to the storage room, the sooner you can drop off the bed and go get some sleep. It'll probably take you all of fifteen minutes, unless you continue to whine about it."

Gilley pouted his way over to the door, and Heath followed with a slight chuckle. In the meantime I headed to the linen closet to root around for clean sheets and pillows. Once I found them, I brought them to the spare bedroom. As I set them down on the side of my desk, however, I heard Doc in the other room let out a horrible screech that had me racing out of the study to the living room.

Doc's cage had been covered for the night when we got back from the precinct. I use a big green blanket to cover his cage. It's there to prevent any drafts from chilling him during the night, and to make him feel safe.

When I came around the corner into the living room I saw the blanket . . . bulging and moving as if an unseen force was beneath it. Doc continued to screech at the top of his lungs, and as I took in the scene I screamed in both terror and rage. Lunging for the covering, I tore it off the birdcage and threw it aside. My beloved bird was clinging to the far corner of his cage, staring at the blanket behind me and panting in fear while continuing to scream in small frightened bursts.

I turned and pressed my back to the cage, spreading my arms wide as I eyed the blanket. It continued to undulate and roil, moving this way and that as it swished across my bare wood floors, sometimes flattening out, sometimes bubbling; it never stopped moving, and it moved like a predator playing with a cornered prey. Here's the part where I also admit that the scene was absolutely terrifying.

As I tried to fight through my own fear, my right hand went instinctively to my waistline, but I wasn't wearing my belt with the spikes. That belt and the rest of my usual ghost-hunting gear were in the front hall closet, clear across the condo. The blanket suddenly stopped undulating and began to slither on the floor, snaking its way toward me, which meant that I had two choices. I could sprint across the condo, heave open the closet door, grab some spikes, and run back to stab it, which would leave my bird totally vulnerable, or I could face whatever was under the blanket head-on, which would leave me totally vulnerable.

In the end, the choice was easy. "Come on, you son of a bitch!" I yelled, shielding Doc the best I could. "You wanna dance? I'm right here. So, let's dance!"

The blanket rose a little, like a viper, and a trail of ectoplasmic fog rolled out from underneath. I ignored the fog and focused on what appeared to be the head. It swayed back and forth and then shot up and at me, spreading out the edges of the blanket as if it were going to smother me.

I didn't duck or turn away; instead, I lifted my right leg as high as I could, kicked the head of the blanket away from my face, then brought the other leg up to land with both feet right on the fabric. There was a hissing sound and some resistance to the weight of my body, but then the blanket flattened out and lay still.

For a few seconds I just stood there panting, but then I began to stomp on the fabric as hard and as quickly as I could. "Ha!" I yelled at it. "I might not have any spikes on me, but these boots are packed with magnets, you motherfu—!"

The front door suddenly burst open and Heath and Gilley rushed in. "We heard screaming!" Heath said, while I stomped around on the blanket several more times for good measure. "What happened?"

"Something tried to attack Doc!" I yelled, still stomping and kicking the blanket across the floor.

"I think you got it, M.J.," Gilley said drolly.

I paused long enough to glare at him. "Not funny." I then pointed to the small puffs of ectoplasmic fog around the room that were quickly dissipating.

"Holy shit," Heath swore, marching across the room to inspect the fog. "That's ectoplasm!"

"I know." Working up the courage to bend down and pull up on the blanket, I lifted it with two fingers and flung it away from me to see if something might shake out.

Nothing did.

Meanwhile Gilley crossed the room and went straight for Doc's cage. Opening the door he cooed to my parrot and got him to step onto his fingers. Snuggling him close he said, "He's not hurt, M.J. Just scared."

I glanced over my shoulder at the trembling bird

before I kicked the blanket several feet away from me. I was so furious that Doc had been terrorized. Lifting my chin, I shouted, *"Whatever showed up here tonight, I swear on my mother's grave that I will not rest until I kick your spook ass straight back to hell!"*

Heath considered me with widened eyes, but I didn't apologize for the outburst. Fuck that. Doc was my baby, and *nobody* and *nothing* threatens my baby!

After a little bit of an awkward silence, Gilley said, "Do you think it was Oruç's demon?"

My hands were still clenching into fists and I had to take a couple of deep breaths before I was able to reply. "I don't know. Maybe. Maybe not. It wasn't here long and I wasn't focused on its origin so much as I was focused on keeping it away from Doc."

Gilley shuffled over and handed the birdie to me. "Here," he said. "He needs you."

I folded Doc into a protective cuddle, tucking him under my chin and cupping his back with my free hand. He made a few clucking noises, then put his beak to my throat and made a loud kissing noise. I could've cried with relief.

Gilley moved to his backpack on the floor and pulled out four spikes. I figured he kept those for emergencies. Bringing them back over to Doc's cage, he slid two of them into the bottom tray and put the other two on the top of the cage. "I'll grab my sleeping bag and a pillow," he said, looking pointedly at the couch.

If I hadn't been holding Doc, I would've hugged him. "Thank you," I whispered hoarsely.

He nodded once, eyed Doc's cage, and took one of

the spikes back, tucking it into his waistband for the trip down to his place. "I'll be back in a sec," he said, hurrying out the door.

Heath went to a chair and sat down. "There's a trace of something heavy and dark still here," he said. "It feels a little familiar, but I can't place it."

I went over to sit next to him in the other chair and extended my own senses. There was something still lingering in the ether, and I understood what Heath said about it feeling familiar. I swore we'd encountered it somewhere before, but where? And why was it showing up in my condo of all places?

"It doesn't feel like Oruç," I said after a bit.

"No," he agreed. "Which means something else came in here tonight. Something we've dealt with before."

"Heath," I said softly, "we've locked down tight every bad spook we've ever encountered. How could whatever this thing was come here tonight?"

"You know what it feels like?" Heath said with a hint of recognition in his eyes. "It feels a little like the Slayer."

My breath caught. Sy the Slayer was a horror show all unto himself. I wanted to shake my head at Heath because I couldn't quite face it if he was back to his old haunting ways, but I also couldn't deny that my husband was right. The energy did feel a little like the Slayer. "If it is him . . . ," I said, "how?"

He shook his head and took my free hand. "I want to say that it's not possible, but we didn't think Oruç and his demon could overcome the magnets either."

"But the Slayer was shut down!" I insisted. "Heath, his portal was destroyed. *Beyond repair. How* could he come back?"

"Again, Em, I don't know. But he has been here before, so if it was him, it was easy enough to find you."

I shuddered. And then I thought of something else and shot to my feet. Covering Doc, I raced for the door. "Gilley!" I cried. Sy the Slayer had once gotten inside Gilley's head, and if Sy was back to visiting old haunts, he could be downstairs with Gil at that very moment.

As I reached for the door handle, however, it turned unexpectedly and the door shot open. Doc squawked and flew out of my hands while I jumped back and narrowly avoided getting hit in the face by the door. "What's happening now?" Gilley said, standing in the doorway with his sleeping bag, his laptop, and every article of magnet-stuffed clothing he owned.

Heath bent down to retrieve Doc and moved quickly back toward the birdcage to tuck him inside. My poor bird had certainly been frightened enough for one night. I grabbed Gil by the collar of his fishing vest— which his mother had also bedazzled for him and lined with magnets—and pulled him inside, slamming the door shut behind him. "Are you okay?" I asked him.

His eyes pinched with worry. "Yes. Why? What's going on? Did something happen? Did it come back? Is it here? Is it after us? *Is it behind me?!*" Gilley then shrieked, threw aside his sleeping bag and pillow, and launched himself into my arms, where he proceeded to cling to me and shake like a leaf.

No *way* was I gonna tell him that Heath and I thought

Sy the Slayer had somehow managed to invade my home tonight. "Nothing's happened, Gil," I said, patting him awkwardly on the back. "You were just gone a long time for someone only retrieving his pillow and a sleeping bag."

Gil shuddered against me. "I had to put on my gear," he whimpered.

"I know, honey. I see that now. You're totally protected, so not to worry." Gilley finally let go of me, but he was still a little pale. "Would some hot cocoa help?" I asked him.

He shrugged and said, "It wouldn't hurt."

I smiled. "Okay, then, let me warm up some milk while you make up the couch for yourself."

"What about the bed in the basement?" Heath asked.

I sighed, feeling weary down to my toes. "We'll get it tomorrow," I said, reaching under the counter for a soup pan. "If Ayden needs a power nap, he probably won't mind taking the couch. I would rather have had his room already made up for him, but it's not like he'll mind if the place isn't perfect the second he arrives. We can move the bed up from the basement tomorrow afternoon."

"What do we do about covering Doc?" Heath said next. He eyed the blanket, still on the floor, a little nervously.

I set the pan on the stove and headed right for the blanket. Picking it up, I carried it to the door and dropped it on the mat outside. "I'll take that to the Dumpster in the morning. It might still have spook residue on it and I'm not getting it anywhere near Doc."

"Okay, do we have another blanket to cover him with?" Heath asked.

"We have something better," I said. Getting the milk out of the fridge, I handed that to Heath and then headed to the linen closet again. Pushing aside all the extra blankets and sheets, I reached for one of my most prized possessions and lifted it out carefully.

For a moment I simply stared at it, until my eyes watered so much that I couldn't really see it. "What'cha got there?" Heath said from the hallway's entry.

I held it up so he could see it. "It's a quilt," I said, clearing my throat, which was choked with emotion. "It was the last quilt Mama ever made. The last thing she ever gave me too. She made it for my eleventh birthday."

"Aw, Em," Heath said, coming to me for a hug.

I let him embrace me, holding the quilt to my chest to let it feel my heartbeat. Maybe the essence of my mother was still in the fabric of all those panels, sewn by hand with so much love and care. Maybe through the quilt she could feel my heartbeat.

"Your mom is showing me a heart," Heath said, and my breath caught. "She's making me feel like it's beating with love for you."

I swallowed hard, pushing down the sob that wanted to bubble up. For a long time I just hugged Heath and let the beat of my heart drum out the love I felt for Mama. At last I pulled away and wiped my cheeks. I'd been very teary lately, no doubt a result of so much travel and so much drama in one day. Wiping my eyes,

I whispered, "Thanks, sweetie. I'm so happy you're my husband."

Heath offered me a warm smile and tilted my chin, about to plant a kiss on my lips.

"My cocoa is burning!" Gilley yelled.

I rolled my eyes and laughed a little. Leave it to Gil to ruin a tender moment. With a sigh Heath let go of our embrace and we moved back to the living room. "I've got the cocoa," Heath said. "Why don't you cover Doc's cage."

I moved over to my birdie, who was cleaning himself and settling all his feathers back into place. Even so, one look at him told me he was very tired. It was going on one o'clock by now and well past his bedtime. I made an effort to unfold the quilt and show it to him before attempting to place it over his cage, lest he be frightened by any covering after the earlier incident.

He wiggled his tail and fluttered his wings a little, but then he picked up one foot and tucked it underneath him, so I knew he was ready for bed and not bothered by the quilt. Still, I very gently placed it over his cage, tucking it in a bit to make sure no cold drafts could sneak in and chill him.

"That's a gorgeous quilt, sugar," Gilley remarked from the couch. "Didn't you used to have that on your bed when you were little?"

"I did."

"Is that the one your mama made you?"

"It is."

"Aw, well, that's perfect," Gil said. "No spook is

gonna mess with something Madelyn Holliday put so much love into."

I turned and smiled at Gilley. He'd called it exactly. "That's what I was thinking."

"We should've brought that quilt with us on a few ghostbusts," he remarked with a yawn. "It probably works better than a pound of magnets."

"I just want it to keep Doc safe," I said.

"Here," Heath said, and we both looked up to see my hubby holding two mugs. One he handed to Gilley and the other he handed to me. I took a whiff of it before indulging in a sip. "Peppermint?" I asked. "I didn't know we had peppermint-flavored cocoa."

"We don't," he said, grinning. "But we do have some leftover peppermint schnapps from last Christmas."

"Did you make mine a double?" Gilley asked.

"Oh, yeah," Heath said with a bounce to his eyebrows.

Gil took a sip and sighed. "Ahhh," he said. "Perfect."

I took my hot cocoa into the bedroom, and Heath came with me with just a shot of schnapps. We fell into bed and I blew on my cocoa while he rubbed my shoulders and assured me that everything would be okay. "We'll figure this out. Don't worry."

"Yeah, well, until we do, Doc can't stay here," I said sadly. "He's too vulnerable."

"Mama Dell?"

Mama Dell was a dear friend of ours who'd looked after Doc almost the entire time we'd been in Europe shooting our cable show. "I've imposed on her so much, though."

"How about Teeko?"

Teeko is my other best friend. Her name is actually Karen, but she's such a knockout that Gilley had nicknamed her TKO, which had morphed into Teeko.

With a sigh I said, "Yeah. I'll call her tomorrow. Until then, I can't leave Doc here alone."

"We could take him to the office," Heath suggested.

I brightened at the idea. My office had plenty of magnetic spikes driven into the walls and covered in plaster. It was a precaution Gilley and I had taken when we'd first started out in the ghostbusting business. Back then we'd thought that, if anything followed us back to the office, it wasn't gonna hang out for long. "The office is perfect. I'll keep him there until Teeks can pick him up. Thanks, honey."

"Anytime," he said with a yawn. I felt my eyelids begin to droop and I set the cocoa aside. I was so tired that I'd taken only one or two sips. "I should brush my teeth," I said, sliding farther under the covers.

"I think you can go one night without a squeaky-clean mouth." Heath chuckled.

I believe I mumbled something in reply, but I don't have any memory of it. That night, I slept like the dead.

The next morning I woke up while Heath was still sleeping and found Gil rolling up his sleeping bag. "I didn't get a text from Ayden," he whispered with a yawn. "I think he made the plane, so I'll head over and pick him up."

I glanced at the clock on the DVR. It was a minute or two before seven.

"Do you want coffee?" I asked him as he shuffled toward the door.

"I'll pick some up on the way," he said. He paused at the door and said, "I checked on Doc when I first woke up. He's still sleeping like a baby."

I let out a sigh of relief. "Thanks, honey."

Gil left and I put on the coffee, hoping that Heath would wake up and join me, but that man can sleep through anything.

Around eight I got a text from Gilley who let me know that, apparently, Ayden hadn't made the flight. Gil said he was heading to his favorite coffeehouse and he'd call me later.

With a sigh I got up, uncovered Doc, fed him some breakfast, and then put him in his travel carrier. After leaving a note for my husband, I headed to the office with Doc.

It's a very short drive to my office—hell, I could easily walk there, but I didn't want Doc exposed to the cold, so we drove.

Once there he settled into his cage beautifully, and I retrieved my wedding and engagement bands from the safe. "No sense pretending it's a secret," I muttered.

Just as I was about to leave again, my cell rang and with an excited squeak I answered the call. "Abby!" I sang. "How the hell are *you*?"

She laughed. "I'm great, M.J.! I've just had you on my mind for a couple of days, and then I heard that my sister was going to be helping Gilley out with his wedding and I wanted to call and lend my support, because, as the best person, you're gonna need it if Cat is getting involved in Gil's wedding."

I sat down at my desk and shook my head. "Oh, I remember the cray-cray that was your wedding, Abs. No *way* am I getting involved in that hot mess again. Gil's on his own. Although I have a feeling I'll be talking Michel down from the ledge between now and September."

"Might I recommend alcohol?" Abby said. "In a pinch, some heavy doses of chocolate also help to take the edge off."

I chuckled. "Noted. So what's new and exciting?"

"Oh, nothing much, actually. At least not much since we last talked right before you went on vacation with that hot man of yours. And I'd ask you how *that* went, but I can already tell that congratulations are in order!"

My eyes widened. Abby's a damned good psychic, and sometimes she blows even *me* away. Of course, she also could've read it on the Internet, but Abby's the type to confess if she's cheated or not. I took it as her turning on her radar and picking our wedding up out of the ether. "Yes, they are," I told her. "Heath was so sweet. He proposed on the beach and we got married a week later."

There was a pause, then, "Hold on, you got *married*?!"

I blinked. "Yes. Isn't that why you were congratulating me?"

Abby paused again, but I'd heard her suck in a

breath. "Uh, no. Actually, I was congratulating you on the baby. Please tell me you know you're pregnant, M.J." Blood drained from my face and I slid out of the chair and right onto the floor with a thump. I think she heard me because she said, "Oh, crap. You didn't know."

I put a hand on my belly and looked down. Gilley was right; my décolletage was impressive as of late. My boobs were definitely swollen and tender to the touch, and come to think of it, they'd been that way for a couple of weeks. I was also a bit thicker around the middle, but I'd attributed that to being on vacation and indulging in all the great restaurant food. And I'd been eating a *lot* lately. It seemed I was hungry all the time.

Pulling myself back up into the chair, I skimmed my desk calendar and realized I was well over a month late. Which normally wasn't a huge deal for me. My cycle had never, ever been normal, and it wasn't unusual for me to skip a month. I'd had a burst appendix when I was in my teens, and the doctor had once told me that I might have difficulty getting pregnant. I wasn't on the pill, because the added hormones just made me crazy, and as Heath and I had been together for a couple of years now, it wasn't like we practiced safe sex a hundred percent of the time. "Oh . . . my . . . God," I whispered. I hadn't really paid my cycle or the tenderness in my boobs much attention because I'd been having too much fun with Heath on the beach. I'd figured it was just a blessing that my period hadn't happened while we were on our vacation/honeymoon.

Now I realized, it really was.

"M.J.?" Abby said. "Honey, are you there?"

"I . . . we . . . it . . ." I was still so stunned that I couldn't really think. Holy shit . . . I was pregnant. *Pregnant!*

"M.J.," Abby said again, "I'm not a medical intuitive. You might not actually *be* pregnant yet. It may be that you're just really fertile and that's what I'm picking up in the ether."

"No," I said quickly. Even I knew that Abby didn't believe that. She'd picked up baby, not fertility. "No, Abs, I think you're right. I think I really *am* pregnant."

"Is there a drugstore nearby?" she asked calmly.

"Uh, yeah. Why?"

"You can go get a home pregnancy test and make sure," she said. I could hear the worry in her voice. I think she thought that maybe I wasn't happy about the situation. But I was. At least, I thought I was. Wasn't I?

Children had always been a part of my plan, and Heath had mentioned them once or twice in the "Someday when we have kids" kind of way, but I knew that neither of us had planned on it happening so soon.

"Yeah," I said, shaking my head to clear it. "Yeah, that's exactly what I'll do." And then I thought about that whole process: peeing on a stick, sitting there waiting for the results. I didn't want to do it alone, but I didn't really want to bring Heath into it until I was sure I was pregnant.

"Do you want to call me back when you get the test? We can wait for the results together if you want a friend to talk to," Abby said, as if she'd actually read my mind.

"Call you in ten minutes?" I said.

"I'll be here," she said.

I hung up and raced for the door. There was a Walgreens at the corner.

Chapter 5

Fifteen minutes later I was sitting back in my desk chair, on the phone with Abby, and I was staring at the little pink positive sign on one of the five sticks I'd peed on. They'd *all* come up positive. "Congratulations!" Abby sang. "Are you okay, honey?"

I nodded, too choked up to reply at first, but finally I managed to squeak out a "Yeah. Yeah I am."

"Oh, M.J., you're gonna make the *best* mom!"

I'd had the best mom. In the back of my mind I kept repeating to myself that all I had to do was do what she did, and my kid would be okay. "Thanks, Abs. Thanks for telling me and for being here. I wish you were here in person so I could hug you!"

"Aw, me too!" She paused again before she said, "Do you want to know if it's a boy or a girl?"

My heart hammered hard in my chest. "You can tell that already?"

"In this case, I can," she said. "It's very clear to me, but if you'd rather wait, then I won't say another word ab—"

"I want to know!" I cut in. And then I crossed my fingers and said a prayer.

"It's a girl, M.J. A little girl. I keep seeing little pink bows all around you. And she'll have your gift too."

I burst into tears. It was exactly what I was hoping for. Whenever I'd envisioned children for myself, I'd always seen a little girl with long chestnut-colored hair and big brown eyes, and I'd picked out her name long ago too. "I'm going to call her Madelyn," I said when I could speak again.

"Aww!" Abby replied. "After your mom, right?"

"Yes."

"I'll bet she'll love that."

Just then my phone buzzed. Pulling it away from my ear for a second, I quickly returned to Abby and said, "That's Heath. I gotta go."

"Okay, honey, no worries. And congratulations again!"

When I picked up Heath's call he said, "Hey! Where are you? I got your note, but I've been waiting for you to come back. Is everything okay?"

I bit my lip. Should I tell him now? Or wait? Making a quick decision, I said, "No, everything's cool. I was just on the phone with Abby Cooper."

"Ah," he said. "Well, that explains it."

My brow furrowed. "Explains what?"

"Your mom," he said. "She's the one who woke me up. She mentioned you and Abby, and then she kept giving me the feeling that there was a little baby girl on the way. Did Abby mention to you that she's pregnant?"

I glanced at all the pregnancy sticks lined up on my desk and started to laugh, and then I couldn't stop. At last I composed myself and said, "Heath, I think you need to come to the office. There's something I want to show you."

Later, around eleven thirty, Heath and I were tangled up together in the soft sheets of our bed, and Heath lifted my left hand to stare at my wedding ring. "Should we tell people we got engaged, married, or pregnant first?"

I giggled into his chest. I'd never been so happy. Even thoughts of Oruç's missing dagger felt far away and not nearly as important as they had only twelve hours before. "Maybe we can hire Gilley's flash mob to dance it out and put it on YouTube," I said.

"That's one way," Heath said. "God, my mom is gonna freak with happiness! She loves kids, and her first grandkid is gonna get spoiled rotten."

I squeezed his hand until he looked at me. "Are you sure you're ready for this?" I said. "I mean, this all happened pretty quick."

"It did," he agreed, "but isn't it awesome, Em? I mean, we get to really start our lives now. No more ghostbusting. No more cable show. No more worrying over bills and mortgages and money. And no more bullshit. Just us. A family. You, me, and our little girl. How perfect is that?"

"It's pretty damn perfect," I said.

"Yeah," he agreed and cupped my face to kiss me. Then he said, "And you gotta make an appointment with the doctor. Get some vitamins and stuff."

I couldn't stop smiling. "I will. I'll make it for this week."

"And we gotta meet with the Realtor and put this place up for sale. And I'll call the builder in Santa Fe and tell him that we're moving up the deadline. I'll want us in and settled there before you get too far along."

I closed my eyes and thought about the home that Heath and I would share. We'd found the perfect series of lots, high in the hills. One lot for us, one lot for his mom, and one lot for a guesthouse. It would cost a fortune, but Heath and I now had two fortunes between us, so we were covered.

I would've stayed content with him like that right up until Gil and Ayden arrived if it hadn't been for the fact that my stomach was not having any of the skipping-meals bit. "Babe," I said when my stomach growled.

"We need to feed the two of you, don't we?"

"We do."

Heath sat up with me still in his arms. "Let's go out," he said. "I feel like celebrating."

"It's not even noon."

"We can celebrate with brunch."

"My baby girl is gonna have the smartest dad," I said. "Let me take a quick shower and then we can go."

"Want company?"

I smiled slyly. "Isn't that how the two of us became the three of us?"

"More than likely."

My stomach grumbled in protest.

Heath put a hand on my belly. "Okay," he said. "You win. No company. Just brunch. I'll get dressed. You go take a shower."

"We'll need to talk about a game plan to find Oruç's dagger again," I called over my shoulder as I headed to the bathroom.

"Yeah, yeah," Heath said. But I knew he hadn't forgotten about it. Just like I hadn't. "We'll call that Detective Olivera after brunch and see if there've been any new leads."

I closed the bathroom door and turned on the shower, letting the room get nice and steamy. I love hot showers. The only problem is, once I step in, it's hard to find the motivation to leave.

Still, I was hungry, and I knew that Heath was waiting, so, much as I wanted to, I didn't linger.

Stepping out of the shower, wrapped in two towels, I went to the sink and flipped on the fan. The mirror had fogged over, so I took the towel that was wrapped around my head turban-style and wiped the mirror down. The fan helped as well, and I almost had the mirror clean when a face from my nightmares appeared right behind me.

A grotesque woman with ratty, dripping-wet hair, sagging eyes, gaunt features, and skeletal limbs smiled wickedly before her bony arm wrapped itself around my neck.

I got out one tiny squeak before her grip tightened and my air supply was cut off. Clawing at the cold, bony arm, I realized how overpowered I was. She was skeletal, but stronger than hell. "Hello, Mary Jane," the Grim Widow said, her voice gritty and sinister, just like I remembered. "I've missed you."

I tried again to scream, but the pressure on my voice box was too intense to let any sound come out. All I could think about was my unborn child, and the instinctual urge to protect her at all costs kicked in. I thrashed and pushed and did my best to double over, all in an attempt to break free of her grip. But nothing was working and I needed air. Finally I rocked backward and kicked out with my left leg. My heel struck the door, and as fast as I could I kicked at the door again. I got in a third good kick before I was dragged backward away from the door.

By now my vision was starting to darken around the edges and pinpoints of light were sparking behind my eyes. I was blacking out. She was killing me. With cold, deadly precision, this cursed spook from the moors of Scotland was killing me.

Just when I was losing hope I heard Heath say, "Em? Hey, you okay in there?"

I couldn't answer, of course, so I kicked out again and my foot struck the wall. I arched, and in the close confines of the bathroom, my other heel struck the bathroom cabinet. I flailed out with both fists, and each struck something solid. "*Em?!*" Heath called, his voice rising in alarm. I heard the rattle of the door handle. It sounded locked, but I hadn't locked it. I thrashed out one last time, most of my vision now dark and filled with sparks. My fist connected with the door to the shower. The tempered glass held firm against the blow, but it made a nice, loud racket.

A moment later the door to the bathroom exploded inward. My vision cleared a fraction and I saw Heath standing there, his form lit with a glow that seemed surreal, and behind him stood a warrior every bit as brave, strong, and fierce as my husband. A streak of white that matched Heath's trailed down from his long black mane, and tied to a braid at the back of his head was a lone white feather.

The hag behind me hissed and immediately let go. I dropped to the floor like a rag doll and blacked out for a few seconds. The next thing I was aware of was Heath, holding me in his arms; then I was lifted and carried to the bed. A moment later I was wrapped in the comforter and felt him stroking my wet hair. "Babe," he whispered. "Em, I'm calling an ambulance. Just try to breathe for—"

A jolt of alarm helped bring me to my senses. "No . . . ambulance!" I whispered hoarsely. With relief I saw that Heath was holding his phone and had only managed to dial a nine and a one.

My husband studied me for a moment. "Love, I'm shaking too hard to drive you to the hospital myself, and Gilley's not here. I'm calling an am—"

I knocked the phone out of his hand and it clattered to the floor. He stared at me as if he couldn't imagine what the hell I might be thinking. Taking a ragged breath, I said, "Can't go to the hospital. They'll ask questions."

"So?"

"Heath," I said, lifting my chin to show him my throat. I knew the area would be red and might have already begun to bruise. "You really want to tell the doctors a spook did this?" I panted a few more times before I added, "They'll have you in custody and me at a women's shelter before sundown."

Heath paled. He knew I was right. "Shit!" he swore. He looked ready to murder someone. *That* wouldn't help us if I ended up at the ER.

"Can you get me some ice?" I asked.

He looked again at me, and his expression was so torn, so angry, so guilt-ridden, that I reached up to stroke his cheek. "I'm okay," I insisted, even though I hardly felt it. "I just need some ice. And maybe some water."

Without a word he eased me from his arms and moved quickly from the room. I heard him rattle around in the kitchen, and that gave me time to stare toward the bathroom. Heath had shut the door, which had a hole about the size of his heel next to the handle. I tore my gaze away from it and took note of the magnetic spike on the nightstand next to me, but I still shuddered.

"Here, honey," my husband said when he returned with a baggie of ice and some water. I took both and felt only a small sense of relief the moment I took a sip of the water. That's the worst part about the aftermath of being choked—assuming you survive, it's hard to find anything that brings relief from the heat of the violence to your throat, your voice, your larynx. It hurts to swallow, talk, and breathe. It's terrible.

Heath sat down next to me and laid a few more

spikes on the nightstand. "If that bitch weren't already dead, I'd kill her. Slowly."

After a bit I said, "The bigger question is, what the hell is the Grim Widow doing, showing up in our bathroom?"

Heath was so stiff against me. I could feel his rage wafting out from every part of him. "Hell if I know," he said. I leaned away from him so that he could get up and pace, something I knew he was itching to do, simply to work off a little steam. "How can *any* of this be happening?"

I shook my head, but stopped when the muscles in my neck protested. "I can't think of a single explanation that makes sense," I said. "In the past day and a half we've encountered three spooks we *shut down*. None of them should be rearing their ugly heads. Well, except maybe Oruç. But how could his dagger have anything to do with the Slayer or the Grim Widow?"

Heath paced angrily back and forth. He stopped suddenly and looked at me to say, "I want you to get checked out by a doctor, Em. That hag could've hurt you and the baby and maybe you're not even aware of it."

I took that in and checked it against my own intuition. "I'm okay," I said, knowing it was true. Well, at least physically. "And the baby's okay too."

I then expanded my intuition to get a feel for the room. I wanted to know if there were any other spooks hiding out. To my surprise, there were.

Chapter 6

"Whitefeather's here," I told Heath.

He glanced over his shoulder at the corner where I was staring. "He is?"

"Yeah," I said, pointing. "He's right there."

The room was dimly lit, as all the blinds were closed, but enough light was seeping in to form shadows against the walls, and one shadow in particular was a little darker, or should I say thicker, than the background it stood out against. The shadow had the vaguest outline of a person. Someone tall and broad shouldered. Just like my husband.

Centuries ago, when Heath's tribe was still fairly young, a great warrior named Whitefeather had saved his tribe from an unimaginably evil demon. Whitefeather had entombed it in a sacred clay vessel, but hundreds of years later, grave robbers had broken the vessel and unwittingly released the demon inside.

That demon had very nearly killed us all, but White-feather and Heath had worked together to bind it back up. Afterward, Whitefeather had gone back to the land of spirits with his spirit tribe and we'd not heard from him since.

Until now.

"Is he talking to you?" Heath asked.

"No," I said. "He's just standing there. I think he's standing guard."

Heath looked from the wall back to me, then back to the wall. "It's you," he said. "You're carrying my baby. He's protecting the newest member of his tribe."

I felt a warmth settle over my shoulders and I knew that Whitefeather was confirming what Heath had just said. It gave me great comfort that Heath's ancestor was protecting a baby girl as fiercely as he would've pro-tected a baby boy. In the land of spirits, they get it. *All* lives have equal value.

"How long do you think he can stay with us?" I asked. The longer a spirit had been away from the mortal plane, the harder it was to show up here and hang out. It had to be costing Whitefeather a tremendous amount of energy to linger in the corner of the bedroom. But then, Whitefeather was a tremendously powerful spirit.

"Probably as long as it'll take to get you packed," Heath said, and moved to the closet.

"Packed? Heath, we can't leave. What about Oruç's dagger?"

"We're not leaving Boston," Heath said. "We're just going to a hotel with lots of people and their noisy energy where the spooks won't like to follow us."

He had a point. Spooks find it hard to connect with people in a crowd. You'll never see a ghost at a concert, and even the ones that haunt theaters almost always wait for the patrons to leave before they start following the actors and set crews around.

While Heath got out our suitcases and began to shove clothes into them, I sat numbly with the bag of ice pressed to my throat, shivering a little. It was probably a reaction to the attack. "She picked the exact right moment to come after me," I said, looking toward the bathroom door again. "I was naked, without any magnets, and the room was filled with steam. The perfect environment for a spook." (Humidity and ghosts go hand in hand. The electrostatic energy gets amped up when there's water in the air. Again, why you'll never find a spook haunting a desert at high noon.)

Heath paused in the packing of my things. "We'll have to carry spikes with us at all times," he said. "Or wear our vests. From now on, we're never away from some heavy-duty magnets."

I sighed and put a hand across my stomach. "Is it ever going to be over?"

He paused again to look at me, and his eyes were pinched with worry. "We'll figure out a way to protect ourselves, Em. We will."

The shadow in the corner of the room moved closer to Heath, and Whitefeather seemed to be taking a stand behind his descendant, the same way he had when Heath kicked open the bathroom door. The move suggested that Whitefeather had our backs.

"I'm kind of surprised your grandfather hasn't chimed

in. I thought we'd hear from Sam by now." Even as I said that I felt a presence enter my mind. *Hello, Mary Jane,* he said. *I see Whitefeather beat me here.*

I pointed at Heath, then upward. "Speaking of Sam . . ."

"He's here?"

I nodded.

"What's he saying?"

"Nothing other than he's acknowledging White-feather. Hang on while I get the skinny." Focusing on Sam, I mentally said, *Can you tell us what's going on, Sam? I was attacked by the Grim Widow a few minutes ago, we think Sy the Slayer showed up in my living room last night, and Oruç's dagger has gone missing and we suspect the demon is free of its bonds.*

Sam's spirit came closer to me, surrounding me and making me feel truly connected to him. That in and of itself was a very paternally protective thing; not quite a hug, but as close to it as a spirit could physically manage, and when the essence of him surrounded me, there was a note of something . . . something that felt like fear and worry all mixed up—a disquiet that was as intense as his love. And just to let you know how extraordinary that is, I've never felt a soul who'd crossed over to the other side emote anything even remotely close to fear. The other side is a blissful, happy place where nothing bad happens; there's only love and joy and freedom from worry—fear, worry, anxiety, have no place there, but Sam's energy was giving it off in spades. And that shook me to the core.

Mary Jane, he said in my mind. *I and the other members*

of your spirit counsel believe a portal has been opened to the lower realms and only those dark spirits whom you and my grandson have sent there have been called through. Oruç's dagger is at the center of this, but we can't tell who's behind the theft. Or where the portal is. It seems to be in motion. And it seems that the darkest demons you've entombed in the lower realms are coming for you.

Sam's words both stunned and chilled me to the bone. For a long moment I couldn't even breathe I was so scared.

"Em," Heath said softly. "Talk to me."

I opened my eyes and they immediately misted. I was terrified for myself, for my unborn child, and for Heath. "They're all coming back," I said to him.

"Who's coming back?"

"All the demons. All the spooks we've locked up. They're coming back for me all at once."

"Is that what Sam said?" Heath asked. He too looked extremely shaken.

I nodded. "Oruç's dagger has opened up a portal which is allowing the spooks to come find me."

Heath walked over to the bed and sat down next to me. "But that shouldn't be possible, right? I mean, spooks create their own portals so that only they can go through them. They don't share."

"It doesn't mean they can't," I said. "A portal is just a portal, Heath. If one spook creates the hole and gives his permission to the others to use it, there isn't anything that should stop them from doing that. And if a spook like Oruç, who not only hates women, but hates me in particular, decides the best way to get his revenge is by forming alliances with other spooks who'd also like to see me dead, then there's not a lot stopping him from opening up that portal and letting all our worst nightmares run free."

Heath stared at me with widened eyes. "Oh, *shit*!"

"Yeah."

And then Heath said, "If the dagger is opening up the portal, then that means that son of a bitch who stole it and just let the Grim Widow attack you has to be close by, right?"

Another jolt of alarm went through me as Heath raced to the window and looked outside. I watched him as he lifted the blinds and peered this way and that. "I don't see anybody suspicious," he said.

"He could be in the building," I told him.

My husband's back stiffened and he stepped away from the window, paused, then flew out of the bedroom. I heard the front door open and close, and I wasn't sure what to do. I was still reeling from the attack, and didn't think I could chase after him until I'd caught my breath. Finally, Heath came back into the condo and the bedroom. "I couldn't find anybody who didn't belong here in the hallways or outside," he said. "He might've already gone."

"And if we don't know who this guy is, then we won't be able to recognize him when he does show up with the dagger again."

Heath looked shaken by my words. "We've got to get you out of Boston," he said. "We'll go into hiding. Maybe we can head to Santa Fe and find a hotel or an apartment there for you to stay."

"Where will *you* be?" I asked.

Heath got up and began to edge toward the suitcase on the floor again. "I'm gonna shut Oruç's portal down."

I thought about that for a minute. Heath was a damn good ghostbuster. He'd fought by my side on dozens of ghostly encounters, and he'd always had my back, but he'd never faced anything like what was coming at me right now.

One on one, Oruç's demon, the Grim Widow, and Sy the Slayer had been almost more than Heath, Gilley, and I could handle. How the hell did Heath think he'd be able to take them all on alone?

And then another thought occurred to me—and that was, if these spooks and demons were coming after me, wouldn't they also be coming after all of us? Gilley had been on more ghostbusts than Heath, and one of those had involved one of the most vile, disturbing ghosts I'd ever had the great displeasure of meeting. A ghost named Hatchet Jack, who'd enjoyed torturing and murdering young boys.

A chill traveled down my spine when I thought of Hatchet Jack and Sy the Slayer getting together to conspire about taking us down. "I can't go anywhere," I said to Heath.

He paused the frantic motions of pulling open dresser drawers long enough to say, "You're going, M.J. I'll call my mom and my cousins and my granduncle. We'll get you on sacred ground and protect you and the baby."

I stood up and bent to retrieve my jeans and a clean hoodie that'd missed the suitcase when Heath had heaved it over his shoulder. "Heath, we both know that even on sacred ground I could still be vulnerable. If Oruç's demon has opened this portal and he's encouraging every spook and demon we've ever encountered to come back through it, then there's a certain demon out in Santa Fe who's gonna love to come visit me again, sacred ground or not."

"Whitefeather won't let that happen," Heath said defensively.

Pulling on my jeans, I sighed. "Honey, there isn't going to be an inch on this earth that's safe for me as long as that dagger's portal is open." I just knew that to be true, and looking at him, I had the feeling that my husband did too.

Heath was holding an armload of my clothes tight to his chest. I saw him waver as his gaze traveled to the suitcase on the floor, then back to me. "I'd die if anything happened to you, Em," he said. "Please let me take you to my family. The tribe will protect you."

I moved over to him and pulled the clothes out of his arms. Setting them aside, I cupped his face and said, "Don't you think I'd also die if something happened to you? I can't be in this world without you, Heath. I know what it does to you to lose the person you love most in the world. You never get over it. You never heal. And if I leave, they'll all come after you. And Gilley. And the rest of the crew. You can't face them alone. You need me, and I need you."

Heath's face was a mask of pained indecision. He knew I was right, but his protective spirit and fatherly instincts were at war with the truth.

I turned away from him to let him think it through, and quietly put my clothes back in the dresser. Then I went out to the front hall closet and got dressed in all my ghostbusting gear. When I looked up after pulling on my boots, Heath was standing in the kitchen, staring at me. "Okay," he said when I caught his eye. "You win. It's you and me in this thing to the end." I knew it cost him something to admit he wouldn't be able to deal with all the spooks on his own.

I nodded to show him that I understood and we never needed to talk about it again.

"Where d'you want to start?" he asked, after I'd handed him his own magnetically lined clothing.

"The museum," I said, grabbing an infinity scarf to hide the bruises around my neck. It was a loose scarf, but I figured I could fiddle with it in the car using the vanity mirror. I didn't really want to be in the condo one minute longer, so, to hurry Heath along, I reached for the handle of the front door. "If we can't reach Gopher and we don't know who might've blabbed something to the wrong person about the knife, then we've got to work backward starting with the crime scene and figure out how the thief broke in without triggering the outside alarm, and also figure out how Oruç's demon overcame all the magnets. There has to be a clue to the killer's identity in all of that. And, in order to get a look at the crime scene, we're gonna have to play nicey-nice with the police. Which means we'll start by paying a visit to Olivera at the precinct."

With that I turned and pulled open the door, ready to march down to the car, but stopped short and even jumped back a little when I saw the very person I'd just mentioned, standing on my doorstep with raised fist, ready to knock.

The police, it seemed, had saved us a trip, and the look on Olivera's face, as her gaze settled on my neck and then shifted to Heath standing behind me, made me quickly understand that nicey-nice had up and gone out the window.

Chapter 7

"Detective Olivera!" I said a little too loudly.

"Mrs. Whitefeather," she replied. "What happened to your neck?"

I wrapped the infinity scarf around my throat twice and pulled it up a little to cover all of the exposed skin between my chin and my collarbone. "It's a rash," I said. "I'm gluten intolerant and I must've been served something with gluten in it this morning at the restaurant we ate at for breakfast."

She cocked her head and squinted at me. "Oh, yeah? I'm gluten intolerant too. I'd hate to go to that same restaurant. Where'd you eat?"

My mind went blank. I couldn't think of a single restaurant. Not one. "Um . . . ," I said, fumbling for the name of literally *any* restaurant. "I . . . it was . . . McDonald's."

She cocked one eyebrow. "You're gluten intolerant and you ate at McDonald's?"

"I figured the egg and hash brown special would be safe," I said, fiddling nervously with the scarf.

Her eyebrow remained cocked. "I've never seen anybody break out in a rash quite like that," she said. "Mind if I take a look?"

"Yes, actually," I said, tucking the scarf more snuggly into the top of my jacket. "Anyway, my rash isn't important. What is important is that we need to talk to you about the break-in at the museum."

Olivera studied me suspiciously. "I'm listening."

"We want your permission to take a look at the crime scene," Heath said from over my shoulder.

"Why?" she asked, her eyes narrowing even more at him.

"Because what happened shouldn't have happened," he said simply. "There's no way that demon could've overcome the electromagnetic field created by all the magnets in that room. Something else was at play there, and if M.J. and I can just take a look at the scene, maybe there'll be something there that will offer up a clue about the killer's identity."

"My CSI team has been all over that room, Mr. Whitefeather. If there was a physical clue there, we would've found it."

"So what's the harm in having us take a look?" I asked.

She crossed her arms. "I'm not sure yet. But your names keep getting connected to trouble, which is why I'm here."

A note of alarm went off in my mind. And I knew some other terrible thing had happened, even as Detective Olivera continued. "You mentioned a former detective in San Francisco who could vouch for you. It took me almost two hours, but I finally found a murder case connected to an Inspector MacDonald where the victims were stabbed and the murder weapon—an antique dagger—mysteriously went missing from the evidence room."

Olivera pulled out a file from the inside of her coat. From that she extracted a photo of the dagger. Of course it was Oruç's. "The murder weapon was photographed before it came up missing," she said. "Look familiar, Mr. and Mrs. Whitefeather?"

"Okay," I said, with a shrug. "So what? Inspector MacDonald entrusted us with the dagger. Yes, that was wrong, but people still went to jail. Justice was still served."

"I'll say," she said. "I talked to an inspector this morning about your old pal. He came up in a police report from last night, as a matter of fact."

A cold shiver vibrated along my shoulder blades. "What happened?" Heath asked urgently.

"Ayden MacDonald was found in the airport parking garage beaten to a pulp. He's sustained severe injuries."

I gasped and put a hand over my mouth. My knees buckled slightly and Heath caught me, steadying me as I absorbed the news. "No!" I whispered. "No, no, no, no, no!"

"In his pocket," Olivera continued as if I hadn't

reacted at all, "was a one-way ticket to Logan. I'm assuming he was coming here to meet with you about the missing dagger?"

"He was," Heath said. "We were expecting him around three this afternoon."

I took an unsteady breath and tried to hold back the tears that were flowing down my cheeks. Even though I hadn't had a lot of contact with Ayden since our time in San Francisco, I still considered him a dear friend.

"Yeah," she said. "I figured."

My mind was spinning. I couldn't imagine Ayden dropping his guard enough to let somebody sneak up on him and pummel him nearly to death. He was too much of a seasoned investigator for that. "Do the police have any leads?" I asked.

"Nope," she said. "His wallet and watch were stolen, so the police initially thought he was mugged. That is, until I told the inspector all about the two of you and the murder at the museum. Said you two could be involved in MacDonald's attack, and I'm here to inform you that he's pretty anxious to talk to you."

I wanted to yell at Olivera. She was being mean on purpose. "Of course we didn't have anything to do with Ayden's attack!" I snapped. "We were with you until close to midnight last night, remember? There wouldn't have been time to catch a plane, fly to California, beat up Ayden, then get back here in time for *this* stimulating discussion!"

"How much money did you make last year, Mrs. Whitefeather?" she asked nonchalantly.

I shook my head. "What the hell does that have to do with anything?"

"Humor me," she said. "What'd you pull down last year?"

It was my turn to cross my arms. "Well, let's see, I made a sum total of none of your damn business, Detective. What'd *you* make last year?"

She smirked. "Funny. I made a whole lot less than that last year, which is my point. You two had to pull down some serious cash for this movie, and that cash can be spent in a lot of ways. If you two did steal back the dagger, and this former inspector got wind of it and wanted to come investigate, you've certainly got the means to hire someone out in San Francisco and shut MacDonald down before he even gets on the plane."

I turned to look at Heath. "Can you believe this bullshit?"

"Em," he said softly, and laid a hand on my shoulder.

I took a deep breath. He was right. She was pushing my buttons on purpose, trying to see how I'd react. Reining in my temper, I turned back to her. "Detective, we didn't hire anyone to hurt Ayden. He's our friend. A close friend actually. Which means one of two things is at play here: One, he was actually mugged, or two, whoever stole the dagger has an accomplice and they're the ones who made sure that Ayden didn't get on the plane. Which means this thing is a whole lot more complicated than we originally thought."

"What does that mean?" she asked me.

"It means that stealing the dagger and unleashing

the spooks and demons was only part of the plan. The other part seems to be causing those of us trying to keep it under wraps harm."

Olivera tapped her finger on the side of her arm. I knew she believed me, but I also knew she didn't want to. "Okay, Mrs. Whitefeather, who do you think took the dagger and murdered Phil Sullivan?"

I sighed. "I don't have any suspects in mind, but if you'll just let us look at the crime scene, maybe there'll be something there that will stand out to us. And it'll help us help you."

"All right," she said easily, and I breathed a sigh of relief.

It was short-lived.

"I'll take you to the crime scene, but only after you tell me why it looks like *someone*"—she paused long enough to look meaningfully at Heath—"choked you hard enough to cover your neck in bruises."

My hand reflexively went to my throat to make sure the scarf was still in place. With a sigh, I realized she was waiting for exactly that reaction. "It's not what you think," I said.

"It never is," she said drily.

"The problem with the truth, Detective, is that you won't like or believe it. But the truth is that I was attacked here just half an hour ago. My husband was the one who saved my life."

Her arms fell away from their crossed position. "Did you call nine-one-one?"

"No."

"Why not?"

"Because, as far as I know, your station doesn't have a demon investigation unit."

She rolled her eyes and shook her head. "Are you really going to make jokes with me right now, Mrs. Whitefeather? Do you *get* that I could haul your husband down to the station on suspicion of domestic abuse? The bruises *alone* are enough to send him to a holding cell."

I took a step toward her. "Have you *watched* our movie, Detective Olivera? Seen any of the footage we took in Scotland?"

"Nope."

"Then you're right. Of course you don't know that I'm not joking. I'm not joking about any of this. The demon spook we encountered in Scotland is back. She attacked me in my bathroom as I stepped out of the shower. She did this," I said, pulling down the scarf, "and a couple of years ago, she nearly drowned Heath and put him in the hospital. She's a killer, and she's loose, and this dagger is at the center of everything."

Olivera squinted at me. I held her gaze. "You guys ever see a shrink or spend time in a mental institution?"

I sighed heavily. "We're not crazy. You need to watch the movie."

"What's that going to prove?" she said. "Other than Hollywood is very good at special effects?"

I turned back to Heath and threw my hands up in the air. How do you reason with someone so skeptical?

"We could take her to Mrs. Ashworth's place," he said, and I brightened.

Lucy Ashworth was an elderly woman who owned

several old apartment buildings all around Boston. Heath and I had been working to clear a couple of spooks from her properties in the weeks leading up to our newfound wealth and success. We'd easily taken care of all of the spooks that'd been causing disturbances in her apartment buildings, save one, and that spook had *refused* to leave. No amount of cajoling or coaxing could get Mrs. Grady—who'd died in 1999— out of the Ashworth Commons Apartments.

As spooks went, Mrs. Grady wasn't especially dangerous—just mean. Or, better yet, she was temperamental . . . emphasis on *mental*. She liked to shove people and throw things. She also liked to shriek in your ear at two a.m., and I can tell you from personal experience that spook was *loud*.

She began haunting the Commons shortly after she tripped down the stairs of the apartment building and snapped her neck. Initially, she stuck to her former apartment, sending the new tenant screaming in terror on his first night there. Five other tenants had come and gone since then, and Mrs. Ashworth had given up trying to rent out Apartment 4B in 2000. But then, about a decade later, Mrs. Grady figured out that she could travel easily through walls. She started checking out other apartments in the building, found the extra room appealing, and began to terrorize all the other tenants until they left too. One by one every renter moved out until the place was abandoned. Enough one-star reviews on the Internet—all with the notation that the place was haunted—had halted any prospective tenants from even applying.

In desperation, Mrs. Ashworth had called us to tell us about the Commons, but she was also wary of our actual abilities. She tasked us with helping to rid two other apartments she owned of their spectral tenants (far tamer than Mrs. Grady), and based on that test she'd let us have a crack at the Commons.

We'd passed her test with flying colors, of course, and she'd given us a key to the building. We entered that place on the first day, all confidence and bravado. Within a few hours, however, we'd realized this spook was playing for keeps.

Mrs. Grady refused to cross over, and we'd no sooner chased her off the first floor than she'd moved up to the second. Then the third, and finally the fourth. We thought we had her cornered then, but she outsmarted us by heading back down to the first. The Commons had twenty-four apartments. They were large and spacious, with plenty of closet space. *Lots* of places for a spook to hide. The task quickly proved to be way bigger than we'd ever anticipated.

So, we'd offered Mrs. Ashworth the only solution we could, which was a proposal to haul in several hundred pounds of magnetic spikes and drill them into the walls and floors of every single apartment and each of the central hallways. Our estimate had been nearly ten thousand dollars, and it was no surprise to us when Mrs. Ashworth balked. She'd told us that she'd have to think on it, but it'd been over a month, and she hadn't gotten back to us, and no new tenants had moved in, so it was a pretty good assumption that Mrs. Grady still had free run of the Commons.

So I considered Heath's idea. And I liked it. The worst Mrs. Grady had ever physically done to one of us was to shove Heath into a wall, and me to the floor. She was a pushy bitch, that Mrs. Grady.

Meanly, I thought Olivera could do with a little shoving. I'd probably enjoy watching it. "Yeah," I said with a wide smile. "Seeing is believing, Detective. You don't believe we're actually dealing with the supernatural? Well, how'd you like to meet a spook up close and personal?"

Her brow furrowed and I saw her move her hand subtly to the gun in her shoulder harness. "What's the deal here?" she asked.

"We know of an apartment building where there's a very active ghost," Heath said. "She's basically harmless, but she doesn't like visitors. We're thinking that within a few minutes of making her acquaintance, you'll be convinced we're not making this stuff up."

"That sounds a lot like a setup," she said.

"Not at all," I said sweetly, turning away for a moment to scribble Mrs. Ashworth's name and number and the apartment building's name and address onto a piece of paper. Handing it to Olivera, I said, "Make a few calls, Detective. This is the name of the owner of the apartment building, and that's her phone number. Check her out. See that she's legit and then meet us at the Commons in an hour."

With that, I motioned to Heath and we stepped out into the hallway, shut the door, and left Olivera to stand on the front mat, probably confused and frustrated.

* * *

Once we were in the car, Heath said, "What now?"

"I have to get ahold of Gilley," I said, tapping my iPhone. "I've got to tell him about Ayden and warn him about the portal."

"He'll freak out about the portal," Heath said.

"I know, and I was against telling him about it last night, but now, after the Grim Widow's attack on me and Ayden's attack at the airport, we can't *not* tell him, sweetie. It'll leave him too vulnerable."

"He already knows about Oruç's dagger," Heath persisted. "Telling him more of the freak show is coming after him is only going to make him go all squirrelly on us, babe. He'll pack a bag and get out of town faster than either of us can say 'cupcake.' And away from us he'll *really* be vulnerable. Especially if Sy the Slayer was one of the spooks who came through the portal with Oruç."

I sat with that for a second before placing the call to Gilley. Heath was actually right. Keeping Gilley in the dark to a degree wasn't a bad idea, for him or for those of us who had to deal with him when he got freaked-out and tried to flee. "Okay," I relented with a sigh. "I'll make that part subtle. But I'm still telling him about Ayden."

Heath made a motion for me to go for it and I placed the call. "Go for Gilley," he said by way of answering his phone. He typically answered like that only when he was with someone he wanted to impress. I wondered where he was.

"It's me," I said.

"Hi, me," he sang playfully. "Listen, I can't talk right now, I'm with my *dear* friend Catherine-Cooper-Masters, and we're just sitting down to some brunch, so, unless it's an emergency . . ."

"It's an emergency."

There was a pause; then I heard Gilley's muffled voice say, "Catherine, would you excuse me one teensy minute? M.J.'s having some sort of wardrobe crisis." I didn't hear her reply, but I did hear Gil say, "Girl, I know *you* know what I'm dealing with!"

I could guess that Cat had made a mention of her sister's wardrobe choices too. Abby and I weren't fashionistas, but we sure as hell weren't slobs either. I could've gotten all snotty with Gil about it, but I decided to pick my battles.

"Okay, what's up?" he said after a moment during which I assumed he'd removed himself from Cat's presence. Wise, as I didn't really want her brought into the drama we were currently dealing with.

"Olivera was just at our condo."

"That hot detective lady?" Gil said. "What'd she want?"

"Well, honey, I'm going to need you to brace yourself. It turns out that Ayden didn't make the red-eye last night because he'd been attacked in the parking garage at the airport. He's hurt pretty bad, from what I understand."

"Wait, *what*?" Gil gasped. "Start from the beginning."

I did, and told him everything that Olivera had said to us about Ayden's attack. "Ohmigod," Gil said breathlessly. "Poor Ayden! Has anyone called the hospital?"

"Not yet," I confessed. "I was hoping you could do that and maybe see if his next of kin has been notified?"

"I'm on it," he said.

Fearing he was about to hang up on me, I called out to him. "Gil, wait!"

"What?"

"I . . . I just wanted to check and make sure you're wearing your gear."

"My gear?"

"Yeah, you know, your vest and boots and stuff."

"I'm wearing khakis a white shirt and a blue blazer, M.J. What one wears in the springtime for brunch with Catherine-Cooper-Masters."

With effort, I kept my voice light. "I'll bet you look gorgeous." (When in doubt, go with flattery.)

There was a pause during which I imagined Gil looking down at himself. "Well, duh," he said.

"And I hate to ruin what must be a fantastic look for you, but maybe you could humor me and put a couple of magnets in your pockets."

"Why?"

"Because Oruç's dagger is still out there somewhere, and we did have that attack last night."

"The blanket?"

"Yes."

There was another pause. "You think Oruç's demon could come after me?"

"Well," I said quickly, "it's not likely. I'm pretty sure he's still focused on me and Heath, but it wouldn't hurt anything to be extra, *extra* cautious, you know?"

Gilley sighed. "Fine. I'll stop by the office after brunch and pick up some magnets. Is Doc there?"

I did a face palm and said, "Yes. And I forgot to call Teeko. Dammit!"

"Well, reach out to her after you hang up with me, and tell her I'm bringing the bird to her around two o'clock. I'll call the hospital and get the deets on Ayden right now and text you what I find out."

"Thanks, honey," I said with relief. Sometimes Gilley really came through for me, and I had another little pang of sadness thinking that we wouldn't get to see each other every day.

After clicking off with Gilley, I took a look around and saw that Heath had driven us to one of my favorite Thai restaurants. Realizing again how famished I was, I beamed a smile at him. "You're the best husband slash father-to-be ever!"

He put a hand on my cheek and leaned in for a kiss. "I'll always take care of you, babe."

We grabbed our lunch to go and headed over to Mrs. Ashworth's apartment building to see if Olivera would make an appearance. "How're we getting in if she does show up?" I asked in between bites of my red curry dish with tofu. "Do we call Mrs. Ashworth?"

Heath smiled slyly. "I never gave her back the keys," he said. Reaching over my legs, he opened up the glove box and pulled out a set of keys I recognized. One was to the side entrance; the other was a master to all the apartments.

"Thief."

"She can have her keys back anytime she remembers to ask for them," Heath said.

"Why'd you keep them, anyway?"

Heath leaned forward to look up at the four-story apartment building. "I guess it's always bothered me that we couldn't convince old Gertrude to move across to the other side. I think I was trying to figure out a way to get through to her."

"Honey," I said, "there's no getting through to full-on crazy. Gertrude Grady was mentally ill in life, and she carries that in death too."

"Only for as long as she remains stuck here, Em."

"True," I agreed. There's no crazy in heaven, thank God. "But we'd still have to be able to get through to her enough to convince her to go to the light, and we tried and tried that and she wasn't having any of it."

"I kinda feel sad for her," Heath said, his gaze trained on the fourth floor of the apartment building.

"Yeah, I know, you big softie. But if she won't listen, then I don't know what we can do to get her to leave."

"Me neither," Heath said. "Which is why I kept the keys. If I ever find a new technique or something that might work, I want to come back here and try again."

"Okay," I said. "But let's not tell Olivera, if she makes it over here, that technically, we'll be trespassing."

"I won't if you won't," Heath said with a wink. "She probably won't show anyway. She's too suspicious of us."

"And yet, this address is in the middle of a nice part of town, with plenty of foot traffic. She's got to know that if we wanted to cause her trouble, we sure wouldn't do it here."

"Let's hope she knows that," Heath said.

We ate silently for a bit and then my cell rang. "Gil," I said, picking up the call. "What'd you find out?"

"Ayden just went into surgery," he said, getting straight to the point. "He had a punctured lung and they had to wait to inflate it again before proceeding with the surgery to close the wound from his rib."

I made a face. That sounded terrible. "So he's hurt really bad, huh?"

"No, actually. Other than the punctured lung, a concussion, a busted ankle, and several cracked ribs, he's not doing too bad."

I made another face. "Yeah, other than a broken *body*, he's in great shape."

"M.J.," Gil said. "He's not dying. He's expected to make a full recovery. It'll just take time."

"How'd you find all this out?" I asked.

"I pretended to be his brother. They ask you a few security questions to make sure you're family, but lucky me, with my mad typing skills, I have access to all of Ayden's personal information, like his birthday and his address and stuff. The nurse totally bought it. Anyway, the bummer is that, according to her, Ayden didn't see his attacker. She said the cops were in with him for almost an hour, and he couldn't give them a description of the guy because the first blow was a crack to the head. He says he blacked out and doesn't remember getting all the other injuries."

"That's a small blessing, I guess," I said.

"Yeah, in a way, but without a description, the cops have nothing to go on."

"When will we be able to talk to him?" I asked next.

"Hopefully tomorrow. I know you're worried about him, but his nurse assured me that his surgery was pretty routine and that he should be able to take visitors and phone calls starting tomorrow."

I relaxed a little. I'd been very worried about Ayden. "Okay, Gil. Keep me posted if you hear anything else."

"Will do. Now call Teeko and let her know I'm bringing Doc over."

After hanging up with Gil, I called Teeks, who was on her way out the door for an appointment, but luckily she was more than happy to take my bird for a few days and told me that she'd inform the doorman to let Gilley in with the bird when he came over.

After that, I relayed all the details to Heath, who said, "When are you gonna tell Gil and Teeks that we're pregnant?"

I offered Heath an odd look. It always sounded weird to me when expectant fathers offered up the "We're pregnant" thing. Heath wasn't going to get fat, have swollen ankles and raging hormones, and pop a watermelon out of his vajajay.

"What?" he said as I continued to furrow my brow at him.

"Are *we* really pregnant, honey?"

Color tinged his cheeks. "I thought that's what you were supposed to say."

"I think it's okay to say that your wife is pregnant,

and you're the supportive, understanding, ice-cream-with-a-side-of-pickles-fetching father-to-be."

Heath saluted. "Got it." Then he added, "For the record, it sounded weird coming out of my mouth."

That made me laugh. "Well, now that we've cleared that up . . ." And then I sat up in the seat. "Well, would you look at that?"

"What?"

I pointed across the street and down a row of cars. "Olivera just showed up."

"Huh," Heath said. "I didn't think she'd come."

I reached for the door handle. "She has enough curiosity and skepticism to be a pain in the ass," I muttered. Like I said, I've had to convince a lot of detectives that paranormal doesn't mean fake—it simply means "other than" or "beyond" normal.

We reached Olivera just as she stopped in front of the apartment building, hands on hips, assessing it from the sidewalk. "Good to see you, Detective," Heath said cordially.

It could've been my imagination, but I swear she jumped a little at the sound of his voice. "I spoke to the owner," she said. "She said it'd be okay if we checked out the place as long as you two accompany me, which I think is a little weird."

I snuck a meaningful look at Heath and said, "This way, Detective."

Leading the way inside, I headed straight for the stairs. The elevator was always iffy, and I'd long wondered if Gertrude had anything to do with that—I suspected she did.

We hoofed it up to the fourth floor, and I paused on the landing, waiting to feel anything out of the ordinary with my intuitive feelers. A moment later Heath placed a hand on my shoulder and said, "I doubt we're gonna pick up anything with all this armor."

Looking down at myself, I realized how right he was. There was no way anything was coming out of the woodwork while we were wearing so much protection. "What do we do?" I asked him. "I mean, the point of all this is to show the detective that we're for real, right? But if we take off our protective gear, then we'll be vulnerable."

"Only to Gertrude," he said with a shrug. "And she's a crazy bitch, but she's not gong to kill anyone."

He began to shrug out of his jacket and peel off his boots, and I started to follow suit when he said, "Why don't you keep your stuff on. I can escort the detective around the apartments. You can stay here where I know the two of you are safe from harm."

I chuckled. "Are you going to be this protective my entire pregnancy?"

Heath looked me in the eyes and said, "Count on it."

"Did I hear you right?" Olivera suddenly asked. "You're pregnant, Mrs. Whitefeather?"

I turned to her and noticed she was studying me again with those same calculating eyes that hadn't let up their suspicion for even a minute since we'd met. "I am," I said. "We just found out this morning."

She focused her next comment on Heath. "I used to work a beat, and the worst domestic abuse cases were always when the wife or girlfriend was pregnant. There's something about a pregnancy that seems to put men on edge."

She'd said that so casually, you might've thought she was merely making small talk, but given the bruises on my neck and where she clearly suspected they'd come from, it was very hard not to spit something mean at her in reply. I did my best to keep my voice level when I said, "I understand your concern, and I know your heart is in the right place, but Heath didn't hurt me, Detective. He'd never hurt me, but you're right about the bruising on my neck. I was attacked by something that would blow your mind if you knew how very real it was. We'll save those details for later. Right now, I'd like you to meet Gertrude. She seems most unhappy to meet you."

With a little smile, I pointed down the hall, and there, silhouetted against the light filtering in from a dirty window at the end of the hall, was an angry-looking woman in a long silk robe, her arms crossed over her chest and a deep scowl on her features.

Oh, and she was also floating two feet above the floor.

"What . . . the . . . *fuck*?" Olivera gasped when she spotted Gerty. Then she took several steps forward and Heath and I both reached out to grab her before she could get too close to the spook. Gerty's temper was nothing to trifle with.

"Easy there, Detective," Heath said. "Whenever we see her, we give her plenty of breathing room."

Olivera blinked several times and squinted toward the ghost. "It's a trick," she said at last, folding her arms over her own chest in a perfect imitation of Mrs. Grady and making a point to look at Heath's cautionary hold on her shoulder.

I sighed. *Why* were some people so stubborn? Glancing at Heath, I saw a flash of anger sweep across his features. He'd had enough of the skepticism too. Removing his hand and making a sweeping motion toward the corridor ahead, he said, "After you, then."

I felt a jolt of alarm but saw that Heath began to walk right behind Olivera, just in case things got tricky, and I relaxed a fraction. Still, I was pretty tense.

And I will give Olivera some credit; she didn't falter on the way to Gertrude's ghost. I think she must've been pretty convinced we were big fat fibbers. Even when the temperature dropped by a good twenty degrees in the span of about three seconds, Olivera kept on striding down that hallway. I wrapped my arms around myself; there's nothing that cuts through you like a ghost chill.

When Olivera was about ten feet from Gertrude, things got interesting, and by "interesting" I mean things went the freak-show way they normally do around me and my crew. It began with a wicked smile from Gertrude, and then she disappeared. "Here it comes," I whispered, but I never could've predicted what happened next.

Olivera paused for half a second, then darted forward and looked from side to side. She stood smack-dab between Apartment 4B on one side and 4E on the other. Both doors suddenly opened and a scream so earsplittingly loud that even I covered my ears erupted from both doorways.

Olivera ducked and drew her gun. Heath closed the distance between them and was just about to reach out to the detective when she was jerked in a half circle and then pulled right into 4E by an unseen force.

She screamed—which I couldn't blame her one bit for—and as Heath reacted by changing direction toward her, the door to 4E abruptly slammed shut.

"Oh, *shit!*" I swore, launching myself down the hall-way. I didn't really think Gerty would hurt Olivera beyond pushing her around a little, but I wasn't certain about that. She'd looked pretty mad when Olivera had approached. From beyond the door where Olivera had disappeared, there was another sharp cry, followed by gunshots.

What I did next was instinctual; I dived for the floor. A moment later I felt Heath's weight hovering over mine protectively. More shots erupted, followed by shouts from Olivera that sounded an awful lot like "Boston PD! Drop your weapon!"

I think Heath and I had the same thought at the same moment. He ducked his chin to look at me, and we both mouthed, *Weapon?*

Something slammed against the interior wall right next to us and Olivera's gun measured out several more shots. I wondered when she would run out of bullets.

Heath continued to cover me as the *pop-pop-pop* from Olivera's gun went on a few more times. Then all was deathly still.

No gunfire, no screaming, no slamming around of heavy objects . . . nothing at all. It was freaking creepy.

Heath slowly got off me, but as I tried to get up, he pushed me back to the floor. "Stay down!" he whispered. I glared at him but heeded the command. He moved to the door of 4E and put his ear to it. We locked eyes and he shook his head slightly. He couldn't hear anything. I watched as he tried the handle. It didn't move. Stepping back from the door, Heath raised a leg to kick it in when all of a sudden it opened on its own, and what stood there . . .

"Heeeeeath!" I screamed, popping up to my feet in an instant. My husband was already backing away from a spook I knew he'd never seen before, the one I'd prayed we wouldn't encounter. Hatchet Jack stood in the doorway with the evilest, most sadistic grin on his face you'd ever not want to see. He was a bony figure, all sharp lines and angles, with wisps of black greasy hair on a somewhat bald head. His nose was too large for his ugly face, and his eyes were recessed and sinister, but his worst feature by far was his black, rotting teeth, exposed by thin lips pulled back in that menacing smile. Clutched high in one skeletal hand was a hatchet, it's edge razor-sharp and dripping with blood.

I was light-headed even looking at it. Had he killed Olivera?

Heath took a step back from the nightmare spook. I couldn't seem to get my legs to move fast enough. My husband wasn't wearing any kind of protection. No magnets, no spikes, nothing. He was totally exposed. And as I looked at Hatchet Jack, I realized that in the many years since we'd encountered each other, he'd gained some power. It was in his stance, the way he gleefully approached Heath holding his weapon. I had little doubt the spook had gained the ability to kill, and there was that matter of the dripping blood from the blade he wielded.

"Heath!" I cried again. The distance between us was too far; Hatchet Jack was much closer to him than I was.

I prayed for a miracle, but what I got was something on the opposite end of the spectrum. Detective Olivera appeared in the doorway behind Jack, her gun raised and a determined yet frightened look on her face. "Drop your weapon!" she shouted at the spook.

Hatchet Jack paused long enough to turn his head around and stare at her, but the way he twisted his head—one hundred and eighty degrees—was like something right out of *The Exorcist*.

Olivera's already pale face whitened even more, and a second before her finger pulled the trigger I shouted, *"No! Don't shoot!"*

Jack was, of course, unfazed by the bullet fired from her gun, but Heath's head snapped back and he dropped like a stone. The scream that came out of my lungs was unlike anything I'd ever uttered—just a raw, agonized, primal cry as the man I loved was gunned down right in front of my eyes.

Chapter 8

I was mindless of Jack. Mindless of Olivera. Mindless of the hallway, the apartments, the freezing cold. My entire focus was on Heath, who lay facedown, unmoving. I ran to him.

The floor at the edge of his scalp was tinged with red, and even in those last two steps I knew that Olivera's aim had been higher than I'd first realized—she'd shot for Jack's head, and in turn had hit Heath's.

I was still screaming when I reached him, shaking so hard, denying the scene and begging for it all to be a mistake. A dream. A trick of the light. As I fell to the floor beside Heath, more blood pooled away from his scalp and I sucked in a ragged breath, only to expel it in another primal scream. Rage, terror, and hopelessness poured out in that cry in an eruption of noise that bounced and echoed off the narrow corridor. *"Whyyyyy?!"* I wailed. I shouted it to every spirit I'd ever helped. To every ancestor I'd ever prayed to. To Heath's ancestors and to God. In that moment—I hated Him with such intensity that I could've easily walked myself into the lower realms and lived for eternity with the very souls I'd banished there—all because I'd never forgive the God that took my beloved from me.

"Aw, shit!" I heard somewhere in the background. "Jesus! *Jesus!*"

I covered Heath's body with my own, gently laying myself across him, sobbing. I couldn't turn him over. I couldn't see the hole that Olivera had put into the center of his head. I couldn't look upon his dead eyes and ever hope to stay sane. *"No, no, no, no, no, no, no!"* I wailed, curling around him protectively.

"Mrs. Whitefeather," I heard Olivera whisper a second before I felt her cold hand on my shoulder. "Let me see him."

"Get off me!"

She backed away, and I was racked with sobs, clutching at Heath's shirt, begging him to stay with me. A moment later her hand was on my shoulder again. "Please," she said. "Let me check for a pulse."

That rage came back with a vengeance, and I lifted myself away from Heath's body long enough to lunge at her. Catching her by the wrist, I shot to my feet and shoved her back to the wall so forcefully that when her back hit, it shook the whole hallway. "You goddam *idiot!*" I shouted at her. "Why? *Why?!*"

Her eyes were wide and she shook her head. Sweat coated her brow even though it was still freezing in the hallway. "I aimed at the assailant!" she said. "I shot *him!*"

"You shot a fucking ghost!" I screamed back, shaking her by the lapels of her jacket and banging her against the wall again. I wanted to kill her. My rage was that strong. "We told you! *We told you!*"

"Em," I heard a feeble voice call from behind me.

Everything stopped. I held perfectly still except for the tears streaming down my face. For a moment I wondered if Heath's ghost had whispered to me . . . it was a very real possibility.

But Olivera's expression told me the truth. She was looking over my shoulder with such relief that I knew I'd been wrong. Heath hadn't been taken from me.

He lived.

Slowly I pivoted and saw him propped up on one arm, the other hand covering a wound at the side of his scalp. Blood seeped through his fingers and I immediately let go of Olivera and dashed back to him. Gently I took hold of his hand and said, "Let me see it."

His face was twisted in a mask of pain, but he allowed me to peel his fingers away and I saw a long, mean streak of exposed flesh beginning at his temple and continuing for several inches along his scalp. The bullet had skimmed along his skull and missed entering it by millimeters.

"How bad is it?" he asked while I shrugged out of my jacket, removed my sweater, and pulled off my tank top.

Wadding up the shirt, I put it over the wound and replaced his hand. "Hold some pressure on that," I said, my voice quaking slightly. Putting my sweater back on,

I looked back at Olivera. "Shouldn't you be calling someone by now?"

My tone was harsh, the rage barely quelled even though I knew Heath would be okay.

"I tried," she said, holding up her cell. "My phone's dead. It had nearly a full charge when I got out of the car."

I glared hard at her. All that emotion from a minute earlier was simply funneled into anger at her stupid, ignorant, bullheaded actions. It was only then that I realized that Hatchet Jack had disappeared almost immediately after Heath had been shot. "A spook can drain a phone at thirty paces," I snapped. "If you'd listened to us, maybe you would've known that."

It was her turn to get a little testy. "*You're* the ones who invited me here!" she snapped. "How the fuck was I supposed to know this stuff is real?"

"Where's Jack?" Heath said, calling my attention back to him.

I put my coat over his shoulders. His face was pale and he was starting to shiver. I didn't know exactly what'd happened to Jack, so I turned to stare at Olivera expectantly.

"He was standing right here," she said, pointing to the ground in front of her, "and then, the second Mrs. Whitefeather came close, he disappeared."

I looked around the hallway. There was no sign of either Gerty or Jack. Which was odd, because I expected at least one of them to taunt us from the end of the hallway—out of range of my magnets. "Hey," I said to

Olivera before pointing to the landing at the stairwell. "Go down there and bring back Heath's stuff."

I probably had enough magnets on me to cover all three of us, but I didn't want to take any chances. As she took a step in that direction, though, I called her back and held out a spike to her. "Take this," I said. "And I'd sprint down that hall if I were you."

She took the spike gently from my outstretched palm. Her fingertips were ice-cold and I saw that her hand was trembling. She was more shaken than she appeared.

As I began to feel a little pang of guilt over that, I turned back to Heath. "We need to get you to the hospital, honey. That head wound is bleeding bad."

Heath pulled my shirt away from his head. It was soaked in dark red. My stomach turned and I had to quickly look away or I'd lose my cookies. "That's gonna leave a mark," he said.

Leave it to my husband to crack a joke while bleeding profusely. Taking a deep breath, I firmly pushed the shirt back over his wound, then got my arm underneath him and helped him to his feet. He wobbled a little and said, "Whoa, that made me dizzy."

"Lean on me."

"Okay, but go easy."

I moved slowly and carefully with Heath, one step at a time, my entire focus on him. Which is why I didn't immediately notice that anything was off. But Heath did. He stopped in his tracks and whispered, "Em. Look."

I glanced at him first, then to where his gaze was focused, down the hall at Olivera, who was looking all around the stairwell, as if she'd dropped some-thing. Between us and her was Hatchet Jack. He stood facing us, that axe in his hand gripped tightly while he smacked it soundlessly against his other palm. The same sinister smile crept onto his face and, with eyes intent on me, he licked his lips seductively.

I stiffened, because I knew exactly what he intended. "Olivera," I called, trying to keep my tone as neutral as possible. "I want you to put on Heath's jacket, and I want you to do it right now."

She held up a finger, still turned away from me. "I'm looking for it," she said. "But it's not here. I could've sworn he tossed it on the floor of the landing, right?"

Heath and I traded looks of concern. "You still have that spike, though, right?" I asked, staring at Jack, reminding him that if he wanted to attack her, it'd at least be painful for him. His grin widened. Asshole.

I put a hand to my waist. I had a spike there, but Heath's arm was still across my shoulder, and Jack took in the subtle move of my hand and shook his head, grinning at me as if daring me to try it.

Gauging the distance, I knew I couldn't get to Jack before he got to Olivera, and he wanted me to know that he knew it too. Double asshole.

"I think they fell down a flight," Olivera said, now descending the stairs and leaning over the railing.

Jack took a few steps backward, his gaze still locked with mine.

Heath's arm lifted from my shoulder ever so slightly. "You'll have to be fast," he whispered as the figure of Olivera began to disappear down the stairs.

"Keep my jacket," I said in reply.

Jack snickered and stopped palming his hatchet. Behind him I could still hear the faint click of Olivera's footfalls on the stairs.

Jack then lowered his chin slightly in challenge. I snarled at him, and just like that we were off, me freeing the spike from my waist as I raced toward him, him spinning on his heels to raise the hatchet and spring toward the stairs. "Olivera!" I shouted, knowing the spook could move faster than me. "Behind you!"

From the stairwell there was a sort of shocked silence as the detective's footfalls stopped, and then what I can only describe as a surprised gasp. In my mind I imagined her reaching out of reflex for her gun, so I was quick to shout, *"No guns! Use the spike!"*

By then Jack had already reached the landing and leaped high into the air before descending several stairs. As he went down he emitted a victorious shriek, and right afterward a gunshot sent out a deafening boom.

"Em!" Heath shouted.

I ducked and darted to the wall, but I didn't stop. "Dammit, Detective!" I yelled at Olivera. *"Use your spike!"*

Jack's head floated away from my line of vision. Olivera screamed, but it wasn't a panicked cry of terror; it was the scream of a warrior. I willed my legs to move faster and faster, pumping my arms harder and harder to reach the landing and lend her some help. When I did gain the landing, I leaped into the air too. I'd just have to pray I didn't break a leg when I came down.

As it happens, I'm more agile than I thought (must be the pregnancy hormones), and I dropped onto the midfloor landing like something right out of an action movie: hard, but upright. With bared teeth I went straight for Jack, who was taunting Olivera with his hatchet, swinging it in an arc right at her head. She ducked and maneuvered as if she were a trained martial artist, but you could see that she was scared she was gonna lose the dance. I didn't waste any time advancing on Jack. I raised the spike high and drove it into the center of his ectoplasmic visage, and my arm met nothing. No resistance at all.

I was expecting Jack to spin away from my spike, reeling in pain. But he barely noticed. Instead he whirled around, lifting his hatchet to come at me.

I swerved to the side and flattened myself against the wall. His weapon sank into the wood with a loud *thunk*. I raised my spike again and struck, but the thing had absolutely no effect. His evil grin widened yet again, and he yanked out the hatchet where it'd been stuck in the wall and prepared to bring it down on my head.

I reacted more out of reflex than thought. I kicked my leg up hard, and it did meet with something. Not quite a body per se, but resistance for sure. Jack howled in pain and grabbed his nethers just like someone who'd been kicked in the gonads should. He staggered away from me, and, surprised, I pushed myself from the wall and ran at him, kicking outward the whole way. I got in a few good whacks and he snarled and spat and growled at my feet, while feebly trying to lift his hatchet to strike me. In response, I channeled my inner Rockette and kicked it right out of his hand. It fell to the floor and disappeared. I didn't let up. Twisting slightly, I kicked at Jack like I was trying to break down a locked door. "You. Son. Of. A. *Bitch!*" I roared as I struck at him. In the back of my mind, I couldn't figure out why the magnets in my boots worked on him, but the spikes hadn't. That was something to figure out later. At that moment, all I wanted to do was hurt him, and hurt him I did.

He shrieked and tried to block the blows, but almost all of them landed, and I was so amped up on adrenaline, I wasn't even winded. I was like Jackie Chan after a serious bad guy. Relentless.

At last he darted away from me and turned to run straight into a wall, disappearing for a good five seconds before he came shrieking back out again. "Ha-ha-ha!" I shouted, knowing he'd likely run right into the spike that Heath and I had driven into that very spot back when we were trying to encourage Gertrude to leave. "That must've smarted, eh, Jackie-boy?"

Jack didn't even pause to spit at me as he flew up the stairs then, and I gave chase, hot on his heels. He gained some distance between us, but I wasn't about to let him near Heath again. As I crested the landing, I saw him dart through the door of 4E. I stopped in front of it, panting with fury. Trying the handle, I found it locked, so I settled for banging on the door. "You coward!" I shouted. "I put you away in the lower realms once, Jack. I'll lock you away again if it's the last thing I do!"

"Before then, could you maybe get me to a hospital, babe?"

I stiffened and turned to see Heath leaning heavily against the wall. His complexion was gray, and he was still bleeding very badly. Head wounds are like that. They'll bleed for days if unattended.

I ran to him and tucked myself under his arm again, easing him away from the wall and toward the stairs. Olivera had come up to the fourth floor again, and she had Heath's jacket, boots, and spike-lined belt clutched in her arms. I gave her credit for coming back to us. Anybody else would've fled the building.

Still, her complexion was pretty ashen too. I hoped she wasn't about to hurl. I could only assist one helpless person at a time. Figuring that giving her a job might actually steady her, I said, "Can you help support him on the other side to get him down the stairs?"

Her frightened eyes darted around the hallway, then locked onto mine, and she gave a small nod. Coming forward, she tucked Heath's belongings under one arm and wrapped the other around his waist.

We got him down the stairwell and outside of the building with more speed than I would've thought. I suppose we were motivated to get the hell out of there.

Once outside, Olivera and I lowered Heath to the sidewalk, because he told us he needed to sit down for a moment and catch his breath, and I pulled out my cell to call for an ambulance, but the damn thing was completely dead. I pressed my lips together in frustration. "That's not supposed to happen when I'm wearing so much gear," I muttered. And then I looked at the only remaining spike at my belt, and I just had a feeling something was off. Taking the spike out of the belt loop, I glanced around and saw a bottle cap on the ground. I lowered the spike, waiting for the sudden *clink* of the cap rising to stick to the spike, but nothing happened; even when I touched the spike to the bottle cap, the cap never stuck to it.

"What the . . . ?" I said, stooping to pick up the cap.

Turning back to Heath because I wanted to get him to a hospital as soon as we could, I found Olivera standing in the middle of the street, looking around as if she was expecting someone. "Where the hell are my guys?"

"What guys?" I asked, moving back to Heath and getting into position to help him up again.

Olivera swiveled right, then left, looking up and down the street. "I fired thirteen shots inside that building and no one called the police?" she said.

"They didn't hear it," I told her.

"What do you mean they didn't hear it?"

I motioned to our SUV parked across the street, and she came back to help me get Heath there. "Spooks can have a lot of effect on sound. If they want you to hear them, they'll make sure you do, but if they don't, then they can manipulate the environment, just like they do with temperature, to muffle sound. Somewhere along the line, Gerty figured out that the more noise she made, the more people would come up to her floor to investigate. So, she muffles sound up there on a regular basis."

"You're telling me no one heard the gunshots?"

"Probably not," I said, straining to carry as much of Heath's weight as I could. He was starting to stumble and his lids were droopy. I was worried he was about to go into shock.

Olivera didn't say anything more as we got the back door open for him and eased him inside. The tank top I'd given him wasn't soaked in blood, but it had enough on it for me to be very worried. "I need to get him to the hospital."

"My car is equipped with a light box. Let me clear the way for you."

I nodded and was about to close the door when Heath lifted his head and looked at us. "Don't say you shot me."

Olivera and I both hesitated. "What?" we said in unison.

Heath pushed himself up with his elbow and closed his eyes for a moment, as if it was a strain for him to speak. "Don't tell anybody that you shot me, Detective. You'll be sent to a desk while IA investigates, and the case will get reassigned to a new detective. One that won't believe us either."

"I can't do that, Mr. Whitefeather."

I bit my lip but then nodded. I could see what Heath was talking about, and, much as I wanted Olivera to sweat out an internal investigation into the unarmed shooting of my husband, I knew that no good would come of it. Plus, reassigning the murder of Phil Sullivan and the theft of Oruç's dagger to a new detective would only delay tracking down the killer and the dagger—it was a one-way ticket to nowhere fast. And we *needed* to get that dagger back as soon as we could. Our lives depended on it.

Olivera's reaction was different, her mouth was actually agape. "You two can't be serious."

I pointed to the passenger side of the SUV. "Get in, Detective. I want to talk this through with you, but I'm not doing it at the expense of my husband."

To my surprise she got into the car without further argument, and I took it to mean that, even though she seemed a follow-the-rules type, she was fearful enough about the lasting consequences to her career if she reported that she'd shot an innocent man at a haunted house. I mean, she'd have to explain *why* she'd fired off thirteen rounds, wouldn't she? It wasn't like Hatchet Jack was leaving fingerprints or anything. Who the hell was gonna believe her?

I said as much to her on the way to the hospital, and I drove fast, zigzagging my way through traffic, barely pausing at stop signs and hitting the gas at all the yellow lights. We made it to the hospital without incident or a ticket, but I still hadn't convinced Olivera, so I stopped the SUV a block from the emergency entrance and said, "Get out."

"What?" she demanded.

"Get the hell out of this car, Detective. If you're not going to play along, then I need you to get out of this car. Now. Find your own way back."

"Mrs. Whitefeather, how are you going to explain your husband's injury?"

"Oh, for cripes' sake! Would you freaking call me M.J., and we'll come up with some excuse. I saw the wound up close. It could be from anything—a fall down the stairs, an accident with a power saw."

"We'll need to get our story straight, Em," Heath said from the backseat. "I like the power-saw idea. That seems manly."

I glanced over my shoulder. He still had his sense of humor, which made me feel he'd be all right after all. Turning my attention back to Olivera I said, "Well?"

"I'm a by-the-book type of cop," she replied, and yet her hand moved to the handle.

"Yeah, yeah," I said. "Tell it to someone who cares about your damn conscience, Detective. Much as I may not like it, we *need* you on this case. That spook back there, he's called Hatchet Jack. I dealt with him about six years ago. He very nearly killed me back then, and now he's come back, along with a few other friends." For emphasis I pulled down my scarf to show her the bruising I knew was still there. "This was courtesy of a spook named the Grim Widow. She nearly killed both me *and* Heath two years ago, and who knows when she'll strike again. The key is Oruç's dagger. We either get that back and lock it and all these damn demons down, or all manner of nightmare is going to start haunting this city. You're our only hope of figuring out what living, breathing person had a hand in all this, and I'm not going to give up that advantage if I can help it."

She considered me for a long moment, but then Heath gave a small groan of discomfort from the backseat and I think that decided it for her. "Fine," she said. "But get your stories straight before you talk to the ER staff. And go with the power-saw accident. I'll meet you in the lobby, M.J., just as soon as I check in with my precinct and make sure nobody else was injured from one of my bullets at that apartment house."

"It's abandoned," I told her. "Nobody lives there."

"Yeah, well, bullets can travel through walls and out onto the street. I want to make sure a stray didn't hit anyone else."

With that she got out of the car and went sprinting toward the door of a Starbucks that I'd inadvertently parked in front of. I figured she'd probably bum a power cord from someone long enough to charge her phone.

Good. For the moment, she was on our side.

Several hours and one hundred and fourteen stitches later, Heath and I were back at the condo. It'd been a rough afternoon and even rougher evening. The ER doc at the hospital had given us a hard time. She hadn't bought the whole "My power saw slipped" story. Quite frankly, I didn't blame her. She might have also noticed how careful I was to keep my scarf up around all the exposed skin of my neck. She sent for a police officer to talk to us—separately—but in the end Heath and I had both stuck to our story that he'd been working in the basement on a woodworking project when he'd tripped, knocked over the power saw, and cut his scalp to the bone. The cop had asked to see my neck, pointing out that I kept fiddling with my scarf, and I'd told him to stuff it. By that time I was pretty grouchy.

He let us go but gave each of us a pretty good lecture on the statistics of domestic violence and offered us the card to a marriage counselor. Heath had thanked the cop and politely taken the card, and I'd snatched it from his fingers and ripped it up in front of both of them. Okay, so maybe I was grouchy *and* hungry enough to shiv an old lady for a doughnut.

Before taking Heath home I stopped by our favorite Indian restaurant and picked up a carryout. My hubby had to take some pain meds and I didn't want him to do that on an empty stomach. Also, I didn't want to shiv any old ladies for their doughnuts, so I thought feeding myself might be a good idea.

I got Heath settled on the couch, propped up with pillows, and covered him with my mother's quilt; then I settled his plate on another pillow and told him to eat while I went to check on Gilley.

On the way down the stairs, I stuffed a naan into my gaping maw, chewed quickly, and approached Gil's door. I heard music on the other side. I knocked and waited, but no one came to the door. I knocked again, more loudly, but still no footsteps inside Gilley's place alerted me that someone had heard me.

I began to wonder if things were all right in there, and fished out my keys to let myself in. The moment I entered Gil's apartment I stopped dead in my tracks.

He was just coming out of the bedroom dressed in a beaded off-white silk flapper dress, complete with matching gloves, waist-length pearls, and a long black cigarette holder. He was also wearing false eyelashes, green eye shadow, and rose-colored lipstick.

Of course he shrieked when he saw me. I'll admit that I shrieked too, but probably for different reasons. "Nice getup," I said when I'd recovered myself.

Gil ran a hand along his elbow-length glove, tugging on the end to get it around his forearm. "I like it."

"I can tell," I said, coming into the living room to sit down. I realized that the loud music coming out of Gil's speakers was a familiar tune. "Where have I heard that before?" I asked.

"It's the theme to *Downton Abbey*," he told me, using his phone to turn the volume down.

My brow furrowed for a moment, and then I made the connection. "Sybil?" I asked.

Gil rolled his eyes and took a seat on the love seat opposite me. "Please. I'm clearly Lady Mary."

"Clearly. So . . . this outfit . . . is for what exactly?"

"Duh," Gil said. "The wedding."

I sat forward. "You're wearing *that* to the wedding?"

Gil appeared offended. "Yes, I'm wearing *this* to the wedding. What else would I wear?"

I tossed up my hands. "Gee, I dunno, Gil. Maybe a nice suit or a tux or something."

He rolled his eyes again. "Please. A suit to a nineteen-twenties-themed wedding. How gauche."

"Nineteen-twenties-themed . . . ?"

"Yes," Gil said.

"I thought you were going with a simple summer theme."

"Oh, that was soooo pre-Catherine Cooper Masters, M.J. She suggested a *Downton Abbey*–inspired wedding and I thought, *that's perfect*! For the reception line we'll have lots of pots of tea and those little tea sandwiches, and at the reception we'll have games of croquet and cricket!"

"Who in the wedding party knows how to play cricket?"

"Michel," Gil said immediately.

"And . . . ?" I replied.

"He can teach the others," Gil snapped. "What is it that you want, anyway? I tried to call you a couple of times today, but your stupid phone was turned off. All I got was voice mail."

I reached into my back pocket to pull out my cell and show him the display. "Completely drained," I said, dreading the next part of this conversation.

Gil leaned forward to hold out his gloved hand and I placed the phone in his palm. "Who'd you get too close to?" he asked me casually, but there was a nervous hitch in his voice.

I took a deep breath. No way could I keep what was happening from Gilley. It was too dangerous. "Hatchet Jack," I told him.

Gil dropped the phone and it clattered to the floor. "Please be joking."

"Sorry, honey. He paid us a visit."

"Where?"

"At Mrs. Ashworth's apartment house." I then went on to explain everything that'd happened on the fourth floor of that building, pausing only when Gil shrieked, "Heath was shot?!" and quickly explaining that he was okay, but currently laid up on our couch upstairs nursing a wicked-looking scalp wound.

"Did they shave his head?" Gil asked.

I frowned. Leave it to Gilley to concentrate on what wasn't important. "Only part of the one side near the wound. He's still got his long hair everywhere but around the temple of his left side." Discounting the big bandage covering Heath's wound, the new hairstyle didn't look bad at all. Of course, that could be because Heath was so freaking gorgeous, not much affected his overall sex appeal. "But that's not what's important here, Gil—"

"Said the woman who obviously let her hair air-dry today," Gil muttered.

I paused. Gil seemed unusually calm, given the fact that I'd just told him that Hatchet Jack had come back into the picture. Maybe he wasn't taking this as seriously as I thought he should because Jack had shown up clear across town. "Honey," I said. "You're right. I did let my hair air-dry today. But that had less to do with the fact that it was inconvenient and more to do with the fact that the Grim Widow showed up in my bathroom and tried to strangle me to death."

Gil's jaw dropped and for a long moment he simply stared at me. I saw goose pimples line the tops of his arms where the gloves couldn't hide them. "She . . . she came *here*?"

"She did."

"*Today?*"

"Yep." For emphasis I pulled down my scarf to show him the bruises on my neck.

Gil jumped to his feet and came over to me to put a gentle hand on my neck. "Ohmigod," he said. "Why didn't you tell me?"

I knew he was referring to our conversation from

earlier. "Because I didn't want to freak you out and have you pack a bag and leave town."

Gil swiveled away from me and marched toward his bedroom. "Where're you going?" I demanded, getting up to follow him.

"I'm packing a bag and getting the hell out of town!" he shouted, throwing his hands up in the air with a flourish.

"Gil," I said, but he continued to walk away from me. *"Gil!"*

"No way, M.J.! I'm not getting into another ridiculously dangerous ghostbust. I mean, it was one thing when some blanket went all poltergeist up in your condo last night, and more of another thing when Jack showed up on the other side of town, but when you tell me the Grim freaking Widow has actually *appeared* in your bathroom—one floor away from me—that's my cue to leave!"

I followed him to the bedroom and put a hand on his shoulder, but he tugged free and practically ran to his closet to pull out his suitcase. "I'll go to New York and hang out with Michel. He's staying at the apartment of some friends. It'll be a bit crowded, but we'll manage. I should stop by one of the shops in the airport and bring them a gift. Or maybe just send a gift to them and that way I don't have to bother with bringing it on the plane. A nice cheese selection or a good bottle of wine—"

"Gil!" I said loudly, standing in front of the closet so that he'd have a hard time getting past me to retrieve his clothes. "Don't go!"

"I'm going!"

"You can't!"

"I can!"

"What about the dagger?"

"Screw the dagger!"

"What about us?" Gil paused and I followed quickly with, "We need you, honey. I mean we really need you. We can't solve this thing without your techy help."

My best friend turned to me with ruby red lips all aquiver. "Come with me," he said, desperately grabbing my arms. "M.J., for once in your freaking life, don't get involved! Let's all just go away, spend some time in New York, and allow somebody else to solve it."

I sighed sadly. "You know I can't do that, right?"

His expression darkened and he let go of me. "Then you're on your own, sugar. I mean, if you can't see the insanity of staying here when Oruç, the Grim Widow, *and* Hatchet Jack come back for a little threesome, then I can't help you."

"I'm pregnant," I said. I hadn't actually meant to say that; it sort of popped out of my mouth before I could catch it.

Gilley's jaw dropped for a second time. "You're . . . you're *what*?"

"Pregnant. I found out this morning."

Gilley shuffled over to his bed to sit down and stare in stunned silence at me. Tears welled in his eyes. "You are?"

I nodded. "More than anything in the world, I want to go away and protect her, Gil. But as long as that dagger is out there, she won't be safe, no matter where I go. None of us will."

His gaze dropped to the floor and he seemed to consider that for a long time. "I'm going to be an uncle," he said, more to himself than to me. Then he lifted his chin to look at me again. "You think it's a girl?"

"I do. I know it. Abby Cooper thinks it's a girl too."

Gil nodded, like that seemed right to him as well. "You should think about naming her after your mama, M.J. She'd like that, right?"

Tears stung my own eyes. Gilley knew me so well. "She would, Gil. That's a great suggestion."

He sighed heavily then and pushed at the open suitcase on his bed. "Wouldn't be very uncle-y of me if I left you all barefoot and pregnant in your time of need, would it?"

I offered him a sideways smile. "Nope."

He sighed again. "Fiiiiiiine. But we need to fortify your condo. I mean, how the *hell* did the Grim Widow get into your bathroom, sugar?"

"That's what I need your help with, Gil. Today, when we were at Mrs. Ashworth's, I tested one of the spikes from my belt against a bottle cap, and there was no pull. The spike wasn't magnetized."

Gil eyed me skeptically. He was in charge of all our technical equipment and weapons. "If it was a spike that I gave you, it sure as hell was magnetized."

"This one wasn't."

"What about the others?"

"I haven't tested them yet."

"One dud spike doesn't mean a whole hell of a lot," he said.

I nodded, but something was really eating at me. "Gil, when Heath shrugged out of his gear and headed down the hallway with Olivera, he left his jacket and spikes on the landing. When I sent Olivera to retrieve his gear, it'd been moved down a half flight of stairs."

His eyes widened. "Someone came along and moved Heath's stuff?"

I bit my lip. "I'm wondering if it wasn't Gertie who did it. I mean, it was only moved half a flight away. If a person had done it, wouldn't they have taken it with them and hidden it altogether?"

"Okay, so Gertie moved Heath's stuff. Why are you focused on that?"

"Because she shouldn't have been able to get within ten yards of his gear. He had spikes, a lined jacket, and his boots had magnetized plates. How could she have fought through the field coming off all that to pick up and move his gear?"

Gil sighed. "I don't know."

"And the only thing that seemed to have an effect on Jack were my boots," I added, lifting one leg for emphasis. "I wear these pretty much every day, but Heath keeps his in the closet with all our other gear, so . . ." I let the rest of that sentence fall away. Gilley saw where I was going.

"Let's head up to your place," he said. "I want to test everything you took with you to Mrs. Ashworth's apartments."

"Did you want to change first?" I asked.

He looked down at himself. "Why?"

I stifled a chuckle and held out my hand. "Come on, let's go see why we can't seem to fend off the spooks lately."

Chapter 9

We found Heath in the same spot I'd left him, but with an ice pack held close to his temple. Gilley winced when he spotted him. "Nice look, dude."

"Back atcha," Heath told him tartly.

Gilley curtsied. "It's for the reception," he said, swishing the flapper fringe to and fro. "I've got a more elaborate gown for the wedding."

"I would've guessed you were a tux man myself," Heath said.

"That's what Michel is wearing," he said. "I wanted to make a statement."

"Mission accomplished," I told him, and Gilley beamed.

He then turned his attention back to Heath. "Heard you had a close encounter with an old friend of ours. And of course with a forty-five-caliber."

"Yep. I'm not sure which one was scarier either."

"Jack," Gilley said. "Jack's the scariest spook I've ever seen. Well, next to that thing from Ireland. And the Grim Widow. Although Oruç's demon was no picnic . . ."

"As much as I love this trip down memory lane," I said, reaching for Heath's belt with all of his spikes still firmly in place. "Mind taking a look?"

Gil took the belt from me and lifted out a spike. He looked around and walked it over to the hinge of the door leading to the bathroom. He knocked it against the hinge easily and pulled it away just as easily. "No. Way."

I went over to him and took up the spike, mimicking Gilley by tapping it against the hinge. There was no pulling sensation. Just metal striking metal. "Son of a bitch," I muttered, going back to retrieve the whole belt. Gil and I went through each spike and then on to the plates in Heath's coat, then in mine, then all the spikes and plates in my gear, and not a single magnet could be found. Except for the plates in my boots. Those were magnetized. And then I realized that my boots had been left at the office when Heath and I went on our vacation, not here in my condo.

"How is this possible?" I finally asked Gilley.

"I have no idea," he said, looking very shaken. Then he got up from the floor where we'd been testing the spikes with a screwdriver from my junk drawer and went over to the sofa, taking a seat at the end opposite Heath. "I magnetized all of these spikes and plates myself," he said. "I mean, I recognize them as the ones I bought and then magnetized."

"How do you magnetize something?" Heath suddenly asked him.

"With a magnetizer," he said simply.

"Seriously?" Heath asked. "That's a thing?"

"Yeah," I said to him. "You've seen him work with it on the set before, right?"

Heath moved the ice pack slightly. "I guess I have, but I never really took it in that that's what he was doing."

"You can buy one at any hardware store or online," Gil said.

"Okay, so how do you demagnetize something?" I asked next.

"With a demagnetizer," Gil said.

I looked skyward. Ask a silly question . . . "Okay, so where can you find one of those?"

"It's usually the same tool," Gil said. "I've got one downstairs, actually. There's a slot for magnetizing metal, and a slot for demagnetizing it. You just place whatever you want to magnetize or demagnetize in the appropriate hole."

"Sounds kinky," Heath said.

Gil and I both stared at him.

He held up his prescription bottle and wiggled it. "It's the drugs talking."

I turned my attention back to Gilley. "So, it's really that easy? You just stick the object you want to magnetize into the slot, and boom—you've either got a magnet or you don't?"

"Yep. It's really that easy."

"Could someone walk up with an improvised device

and demagnetize our stuff?" I asked. I was thinking that maybe Heath and I had worn our gear in public and maybe while we weren't looking, some perpetrator had zapped us.

Gilley shrugged. "I'm not sure, M.J., but anything's possible. What's weird is that Heath's boots were demagnetized but yours weren't."

That made me think of something; a few days after we'd left on vacation, Gilley had lost the key to our condo. I'd enlisted him to watch Doc and our place while we were gone, so I'd given him a copy of our house key. Not that I needed to, of course, because whenever I changed the locks—which was often—he'd sneak my keys away from me, make a copy, then come inside our place whenever the mood struck him. Trouble was, the mood was often striking Heath and me (if you get my drift), and there'd been more than one occasion when the situation had proven most awkward. "Gil," I said. "Do you remember that day that you lost your keys?"

"I do," he said. "Pain-in-the-ass day, that was."

"If I remember correctly, you lost them at the gym, right?"

"Yeah. I set them down next to this really cute"—Gil paused as he became aware of what he was about to say—"set of dumbbells."

"Cute set of dumbbells?" Heath asked.

"Dumbbells can be cute," Gil told him.

Heath smirked. "Apparently."

"*Any*way," Gilley continued, "I set them down and did my workout, and when I went to get them, they were gone."

"So somebody stole them," I said, feeling a cold prickle down my spine.

"Nooooo," Gil said defensively. "They were returned to the gym a few hours after I left. Thank God Michel was in town and could come to the gym with my extra keys. Lord knows what a pain in the ass it would've been to have to change our locks. Anyway, the gym called a little while after we got home to let me know someone had mistaken my keys for theirs and they'd turned them back in when they realized they weren't."

"Was our office key on that ring?" I asked him next, because I wasn't buying the "mistaken key" story and actually had a different theory.

Gil made a face while he thought about that. "No, I had that ring at home."

"So, on the ring that was taken from the gym, you had your car key, your house key, and ours, right?"

"Yes."

I looked around the room, then back over my shoulder to the kitchen. "Gil?"

"Yeah?"

"While we were away, do you remember anything in here being out of place?"

Gil's eyes widened. "Um . . . it's funny you should say that because about a week after you left I put your mail on the counter, and one morning when I came in, Doc seemed a little off and your mail just looked like it'd been re-sorted. I didn't really think much of it because I chalked it up to one of your friendly spooks paying a visit."

Every once in a while I'd get a visit from one of the

spirits I'd helped to cross over. They'd let me know they were around by moving little things, like a picture frame or my hairbrush. It was harmless and it always made me feel good that they'd stopped by to say hello. But I didn't think that's what'd happened in this case.

"You think someone made a copy of both of our condo keys before returning them to Gilley's gym," Heath said.

"Yeah," I told him. "I do."

"What?" Gil said. "No way, M.J. I mean, your TV is still here, along with your computer and one of mine in the spare bedroom . . ."

"They weren't after electronics, bud," Heath said. "They were after the dagger. And that's not kept here. When they didn't find it, they carefully and meticulously demagnetized our gear."

"But they were still after the dagger," I said. "Which we keep at our office, which has an alarm and a well-hidden safe." And then I thought of something else that didn't quite add up. "Gil?"

He was still looking about the room nervously. "Yeah?"

"This producer who called you; what was his name?"

"Bradley Rosenberg."

"Has he called you back yet?"

"No," Gil said, his brow furrowing.

"Did he contact you and talk you into putting the dagger up for display before or after you came in here and saw the mail had been re-sorted?"

"Uh . . . after. I think it was the next day even, if I recall."

"That's a pretty big coincidence, isn't it?"

Gil frowned and went over to retrieve his cell from where he'd placed it on the counter. Scrolling through his contacts, he placed a call, and a moment later we heard him say, "Bradley, it's Gilley Gillespie again. Listen, I really need you to call me back as soon as possible. We've got a situation here, and I just need to confirm a few things with you. Anyway, this is my number and you can call me back anytime, day or night." He clicked off and looked at me. "I agree it's a coincidence, M.J., but Bradley's legit."

"You sure, Gil?" I asked.

He rolled his eyes. "Yes. I mean, I called the studio and spoke to his assistant. Numerous times. He's legit."

I sighed, frustrated, because I'd been really suspicious that there was some kind of connection. "Okay, Gil. If you say so. But I think someone was in here and demagnetized our gear."

"But why?" Gilley said. "I mean, why risk breaking and entering just to demagnetize your gear?"

"To leave us vulnerable," I said. "Maybe not against Oruç or his cronies, but against anything we might face."

"Again, I gotta ask why," Gilley said. "You two are all but retired."

"Yeah, but who knows that?" Heath said. "We've never posted anything online definitively saying we're retired, Gil. Someone could've assumed we were still working and that we'd run up against something nasty, and, thinking we're protected, we'd get our asses kicked."

"And we have run up against something nasty," I pointed out. "Lots of somethings, actually." Shaking my head, I said, "I'm still not convinced there isn't a connection between whoever lifted Gilley's keys and the dagger being stolen."

"It'd have to be a pretty elaborate plan," Gil said.

"Agreed," I said. Then I thought about it and decided it really was somewhat ridiculous to think anyone would go to such lengths to cause us harm. Even to the point of committing murder. It did sound a little preposterous. "Okay, so maybe there isn't a connection and it's all a big coincidence. Still, we can't assume anything at this moment. We're on the defensive, and we have to get our act together here, quick, or we're not gonna make it to the end of the week."

"So what do we do?" Heath asked next.

"We start by remagnetizing all your gear," Gil said. "Hang here—I'll be right back."

"Wait," I said. Pulling off one boot, I set it next to Heath. It was the only working magnet I knew about in the house and I wanted him to be protected. "I'm coming with you."

"Why?"

"Because I can't be sure your gear wasn't tampered with either."

Gil visibly shuddered. Then he seemed to think of something. "My sweatshirt!"

Many years ago Gil had gotten the idea to glue a bunch of refrigerator magnets to the inside of a sweatshirt, which he'd then worn on all of our ghostbusts. The sweatshirt had been the prototype for the vests we wore on location while filming for the *Ghoul Getters* show.

With one heel higher than the other, I gimped after my best friend down the stairs and into his apartment. He went to his own front hall closet and pulled out his bedazzled black vest. Holding the screwdriver close to it, he let out an expletive and said, "He got my gear too! Ohmigod, I've been down here *exposed* all this time!"

I considered Gilley in his full 1920s attire. "I think you might've scared off the spooks for the moment, Gil."

"This isn't funny, M.J.!"

I snickered. "You know, I think it sorta is."

He glared meanly at me, then headed over to his spare bedroom, which was the only cluttered space in his entire condo. There were gizmos, parts of computers, cameras, and all sorts of other techy stuff scattered across a series of tables that Gil had in the room. He fished around until he came up with his little magnetizer, then went immediately into his bedroom and over to his still-open closet. After fishing through a few racks of clothing, he finally came up with a raggedy sweatshirt that sagged in many places and smelled like it could seriously use a wash. Holding the screwdriver to the shirt, Gil gave a triumphant shout when it clicked against one of the magnets. "Ha!" he said. "Didn't get to this one, did you, jerkhole?"

"Can we go back upstairs, now?" I said, anxious not to leave Heath by himself too long. Even with my boot, I didn't think I wanted him alone in a room with any of the spooks we'd encountered recently.

"Hang on," Gil said, taking a moment to throw the sweatshirt over his head. "Don't rush me."

I grabbed him by the arm and dragged him back to the door. We headed upstairs and found Detective Olivera at my front door, about to knock. "Oh!" I said in surprise. "You're here."

She turned to face us and her eyes nearly popped out of her head when she took a good look at Gilley. She then broke into a grin and tried to suppress a laugh.

For his part, Gilley narrowed his eyes, raised his hands in surrender and said, "Don't shoot!"

Olivera's humorous expression vanished and her chin pulled back as if she'd just been slapped in the face. I was hugely disappointed in Gil and gave his shoulder a shove. "Behave!"

"What?" he said defensively. "She shoots Heath and I get yelled at?"

"Gil!" I barked. "You're not helping!" We needed Olivera more than ever, and I hoped Gilley's rude remark wouldn't make her walk away.

He crossed his arms and continued to glare at her. "Whatever."

"Sorry," I told her.

She shook her head and held up one palm. "No, it's okay. He's right. I deserved that. How's your husband?"

I moved to the door and turned the handle. "Recovering. Please come in, Detective. We've got another development that I think you should know about."

I walked us inside and breathed a little easier when I found Heath snoring softly on the couch, my boot held to his chest.

Olivera stared at the boot cuddled in my husband's arms, but she didn't comment. I liked that she was learning at least. Gilley ignored Olivera and went right over to the pile of stakes in the center of my living room floor, and began the somewhat slow process of charging them one by one with a magnetic field. By the third spike, the tension in my shoulders had eased.

"What's this new development?" Olivera asked as I pointed to one of the counter chairs.

I told her what we'd discovered about the spikes and our gear being demagnetized, and about Gilley's keys being stolen from his gym.

"When was this?" she asked.

"A few days after we left on vacation, which would've made it about three days before Gil agreed to loan the dagger to the museum."

"This was planned out in advance."

"Or it's a huge coincidence."

"You believe in coincidences?" she asked me.

"Not really."

"Good. Me neither. So who knew about the dagger?"

I shrugged. "Any one of a number of people," I said. "There were people on that set in San Francisco who knew that the dagger was possessed and that some sort of demon was released. There was also the guy who used the dagger to commit murder. Maybe a few hotel guests. Ayden MacDonald, the detective on the case. Maybe one or two of the other detectives at his station . . ."

"So lots of people."

"A lot more than I'm comfortable with," I admitted.

"Okay, who knew that *you* had the dagger?"

"Only Ayden and us and our director, Peter Gopher. Peter supposedly told one of the producers about the dagger, and that's who called Gilley to talk him into displaying it, which means we don't know how many other people Peter might've told."

"Can't you call him and ask?" Olivera said.

"He's in the Himalayas, filming a documentary. He's unreachable."

"That's convenient," she said drily.

"It is," I agreed. "And even more of a coincidence that the one person who could help us identify the thief isn't available for us to talk to."

"You think maybe he's got something to do with it?"

Gilley snorted from his place on the floor amid all the spikes. "No way. Gopher's one of the good guys."

"You sure?" she asked me.

"We're positive," I told her.

"Okay. Is there another way to come up with a list of suspects?"

Gilley looked up from his task and said, "We need to go back to the museum, Detective. Besides trying to figure out how the thief overcame the alarms—which could yield us a clue—there might be some residual energy from him that M.J. could maybe pick up on."

Olivera looked at me and I looked in turn at Gilley. Was he serious? I wasn't a psychic detective. "M.J.," Gil said reasonably. "If Sullivan was murdered there, maybe he didn't cross over. Maybe he's wandering around the museum, and if you could talk to him, maybe he could point you in the direction of the killer."

I had to admit that was actually worth a shot. "Gil's right," I said. "We need to go back to the exhibit where Sullivan was murdered."

"You want me to let you sniff around the crime scene?" Olivera said.

"Yes," Gil and I said together.

She sighed, looking uneasy. "It hasn't been released yet. Bringing in outsiders could jeopardize the integrity of the case."

"You guys have had that scene for twenty-four hours. Why haven't you released it?"

"Because we still haven't been able to figure out how the perp got around the exterior alarm or the motion detectors inside. Until we have a clue how he did that, we're keeping the museum locked up."

"We had a theory about the motion detectors," I said.

"Which is?"

"We think that Sullivan hadn't turned them on yet because he was working late. He probably flipped the switch right as he was about to leave, which happened to be after the thief had already gotten inside and was upstairs in the exhibit about to steal the dagger."

"Huh," Olivera said. "That makes sense. But it still doesn't tell us how he bypassed the central alarm. We know that was on because it works on a timer, automatically turning on at eight p.m."

"Another reason we want to go back to the museum," I told her. "Gilley's a tech wizard. I bet he could figure it out."

I glanced at Gil and he smiled at Olivera and nodded. "She's right, Detective. I could."

But Olivera still seemed hesitant. "I'd get my butt assigned to desk duty if anybody found out I let you guys on the scene."

"I take it there was no fallout from today's events?" I asked, not so subtly.

Color tinged her cheeks. "None," she admitted. Then her gaze traveled to Heath. "Is he really okay?"

"He'll have a good scar," I said. "But no concussion. The bullet skimmed his skull for three and a half inches. A few millimeters to the right and it would've been a completely different story."

She then locked eyes with me. "I want to tell you how sorry I am," she said. "By rights you two should've had my badge."

I softened a little in my attitude toward her. She seemed very genuine in her apology. "I know you're sorry," I said. "But it's not enough. Gilley and I need to get a look at that exhibit. Something's not right here, and we're all in serious danger until we can figure out who's behind this and take back the dagger." For emphasis I removed the scarf from around my neck and laid it on the counter. She stared at my neck, then over her shoulder again at Heath.

"Fine," she said grudgingly. "But we'll have to wait for an hour or two. I know the beat cop who works that street, and I don't want to risk him seeing us. His shift ends at midnight."

We spent the next two hours helping Gilley remagnetize all the spikes and plates. Heath slept through all of it, which was both a relief and a worry to me. We'd be walking into that museum without the best ghostbuster I'd ever worked with, and in doing that, we'd also be leaving him here in my condo, alone and vulnerable. That in itself was a bit nerve-racking, but there was no way around it. I wasn't waking him up and forcing him to come with us after all he'd been through that day.

I did, however, call an emergency locksmith, and for three hundred bucks we got my locks changed and Gilley's too, in just under two hours. I left Heath his new key and a note to let him know where we'd gone and what we were doing just in case he woke up, but he seemed so deeply asleep that I doubted he'd stir until late morning.

I took the extra time to improvise some protective gear for Olivera too. She was taller and broader in the shoulders than me, so I let her wear Heath's vest. It was a little big on her, but at least she'd be protected. "How am I supposed to get to my gun if I wear this?" she asked, showing me her shoulder holster.

"You're not," I said, and leveled a gaze at her. "You can't kill a ghost with a bullet. They're already dead."

"Then why do you carry spikes?" she asked, pointing to my belt.

"Because the spikes carry a wallop of a blow to a spook. And, when driven into their portal, it can shut them down permanently. Until we find the dagger, however, all we can do is deflect their attacks."

Olivera shuddered. I wondered if she wasn't starting to really appreciate how little she knew about what we did, and how great our efforts were to keep the more dangerous spooks from doing major damage to innocents. "All this is so new to me," she said. "This morning I woke up and was absolutely convinced you guys were full of shit. Ghosts were like unicorns—fictional. Tonight it's like I just swallowed the blue pill."

"Red," Gil said, shrugging into his own bedazzled vest. "In *The Matrix*, Neo swallows the red pill."

"I thought it was blue," she said.

"Nope. Most people like blue over red, so they always pick their favored color when referring to the scene."

Olivera looked back to me. "Something else I learned today."

"The fun never stops," I said. Then I glanced at my watch. It was about ten minutes to midnight. "We should go."

When we opened the door to the condo parking lot, we received a nasty surprise. "Crap," Gil said, looking up at the steady rain that was coming down. Pulling out his phone from his backpack, he clicked on a weather app and turned his screen toward me.

I groaned. "We can't catch a break lately, can we?"

"What?" Olivera said, pulling up her coat against the rain.

"Rain is a bad thing," Gil told her.

Her brow furrowed. "Why?"

I pulled my own collar up. "It makes it easier for the spooks to reveal themselves."

"Why?" she repeated.

I let Gilley answer. I was tired of the twenty questions. "No one is exactly sure, but it's thought that rain enhances the electromagnetic field that most spooks put out. It allows their field to become more solid, and it also allows them to move with relative ease."

Olivera stiffened. "Wait, you think we're going to encounter more ghosts at the museum?"

"There's no way of knowing," I told her honestly. Then I pointed to her vest. "You're protected, regardless. Not much is going to mess with you as long as you wear that."

"How many times has a ghost messed with you while you were wearing this stuff?" she asked me pointedly.

I could've lied to her, but I had a feeling her bullshit-detection meter was pretty well calibrated. "A couple of times," I admitted. "But they always paid the price."

She wavered in the doorway, and while I couldn't exactly blame her, I really wanted to get to the museum to check out the crime scene, then back home to Heath. "We need to go, Detective," I said firmly. With or without her, I was determined to go to the museum and take a look at that exhibit room. And now that Gil had put the idea into my head, I really wanted to check for Sullivan's spirit too.

At last, Olivera nodded, took a breath, and followed us to the car.

Gilley drove, which was made easier by the fact that he'd finally changed out of his reception dress and into some jeans, a sweater, and enough magnets to bring down the ghost of Godzilla. He'd also brought along a few extras, like a metal ball which was completely magnetized and which he called a ghoul grenade, and one or two of the longest spikes I'd ever seen. Gil had told me that they could be pounded into concrete if the need arose. "One thing is still really bothering me," Gil said.

"Only one thing?" I asked, tucking my phone into the glove box. It'd be useless if a spook showed up, and I was sick of charging it.

"One thing more than all the others."

"What's that?"

"The dagger," he said. "M.J., when we tucked that thing into the office safe, it had enough magnets on it to lock Oruç and his demon down, but it also had enough magnets attached directly to it that, over time, it also should've become magnetized. The steel it was made from had a heavy content of iron ore."

I considered Gilley's theory and couldn't solve the puzzle. "So, you're saying that someone had to demagnetize the dagger the day the exhibit opened to allow Oruç or his demon to zap the lights and drain all the phones?"

"Yes," he said. "And that would've been super tricky given the fact that the place was full of witnesses and the dagger itself was sealed in the display case, surrounded by tons and tons of other magnets. Even if someone was able to demagnetize all the other magnets I installed, how the hell could they get into a locked museum case to demagnetize the dagger with everybody watching?"

"Would they have to get in the case?" I asked. "I mean, what if you just held a gizmo up to the glass? Would that do the trick?"

"No way," he said. "You'd have to be within an inch

or two for that to work, and with the glass and the position of the dagger within the case, there were at least eight inches of air between the top of the glass and the dagger at all times."

"What if someone constructed a more powerful demagnetizer?" Olivera said from the backseat.

Gil pursed his lips. "It's possible, but something that big definitely would've been noticed coming into the building. I can't imagine a security guard letting something like that through."

"What about before the dagger went into the case?" I asked.

He shook his head. "Nope. I was the only one that handled the dagger. And if it hadn't been so much money that the studio was willing to fork over to have me do it, I would've left it in the safe."

"You realize that once this is over, you owe me and Heath half that money," I said.

Gil pretended to ignore me. "As I was saying, the dagger was never out of my sight from the time it left your safe to the time I personally sealed it inside the case."

"What'd you wear while you were handling the dagger?" I asked.

Gil grinned. "I found these gloves online made of chain mail—oyster fishermen use them to cut open the oysters and they're heavy as all get-out, but I was able to magnetize them and handle the dagger without an issue."

"So how the hell did Oruç's ghost get out of that dagger and cause that scene the night of the exhibit?"

Olivera sat forward. "I'm still not clear on this whole

demon-in-the-dagger thing. How could a demon be *inside* a dagger?"

"It's not," I said. "Like I explained to you and your lieutenant yesterday, the dagger is a portal. I'd say that ninety-nine percent of all portals are fixed into large immovable objects, like walls or trees, or the sides of cliffs, castles, houses, and the like. Oruç's dagger was the first portable portal we ever encountered. It's truly unique."

"So wherever the dagger goes, so can the demon?"

"Exactly," I said. "Which is what makes it so dangerous."

Olivera was silent and I chanced a glance at her over my shoulder. She seemed rattled. "What?" I asked her.

"Since all this started, did you guys ever ask yourselves *why* somebody went to all that trouble to get the dagger?"

Gil and I exchanged a look. "Uh . . . no," I said. "I mean, we're currently assuming that it's got something to do with us. Somebody out there could have it in for us."

Olivera frowned. "But what if it's something bigger than just getting at you guys? What if it's to unleash hell in a public place and take out a bunch of innocent people?"

"Why would anybody do that?" Gil said.

"The same reason any lunatic commits a mass murder: to get noticed," Olivera said.

"Oh, shit," I said, feeling the color drain from my face. "If that's the case . . .

"Then we're all in *serious* trouble," Gilley said, finishing my thought.

Chapter 10

We got to the museum and circled the block, Olivera peering out both the front and side windows to make sure her friend the beat cop wasn't around. She needn't have worried; the area around the museum was all but deserted.

Still, we parked several blocks down and to the rear of the museum. That wasn't exactly on purpose—it's hell trying to find a parking space in downtown Boston at midnight. All the best spots are taken. And my SUV isn't on the small side either.

The three of us walked with purpose to the rear of the museum, and I wondered how Olivera was going to get us inside. She surprised me by punching in a code at the back door—which was locked by a techy-looking keypad—and voilà, just like that, we were inside.

I pointed to the keypad before passing Olivera on the way in as she held open the door. She said, "They reprogramed all the entrances to a code only BPD would have. That way we know that our crime scene won't be messed with, which is especially important if this was an inside job."

I wondered at her last words—what if this *was* an inside job? Maybe some disgruntled museum employee who didn't think he or she was being paid enough had seen an opportunity to steal a valuable dagger from an exhibit, only to discover that the dagger would control him or her in the end.

I quickly discarded that theory, however, because it wouldn't explain why Gilley's keys were stolen and then used to demagnetize our gear. A disgruntled museum employee wouldn't know that we'd be bringing the dagger to the museum ahead of time, and Gil's keys were stolen several days before he delivered the dagger. No, someone had done some careful planning with that, and that was the piece of the puzzle that I was most concerned about. Someone had it in for us, but who, and why?

Olivera led us into the interior of the museum, which was dimly lit by about every third light in the place. It was a sort of moody lighting, which allowed us to travel the hallways and rooms easily but lengthened the shadows and made the details of the science displays a bit muddled.

We moved in silence all the way to a large maintenance elevator, which Olivera paused in front of to press the button, but I stopped her. "Let's take the stairs," I whispered. "I'm not getting in anything that requires electricity to move."

She looked puzzled for a moment, and then I pointed to her phone and she seemed to understand. No way did any of us want to get stuck for the rest of the night in a maintenance elevator after some spook had shorted out the control panel. "The stairs are at the front of the building," Olivera said. "This way."

I followed the detective and Gilley brought up the rear. He whimpered once when the building's heat kicked on, but mostly he didn't protest, whine, or complain, which, for Gilley, was *huge.* "You okay?" I asked him over my shoulder.

He nodded, but his expression was grave. "I just want to get this over with and head back home. This place is creepy at night."

"Every place is creepy at night."

"Not ice-cream shops," he said. "Or doughnut shops. Or cookie shops."

"Cookie shops?"

"It's a thing," he insisted. "Mrs. Fields."

"Ah," I said. "I stand corrected. Okay, so cookie shops aren't creepy at night. What else?"

"Bookstores," he said. "They're pretty tame."

"Except the Stephen King section."

Gilley grunted in agreement. "Well, he's just disturbing. Candy stores, though . . . not creepy."

"I'm sensing a theme here . . ."

"Sugar, in any of its many comforting and delicious forms, is the cure for creepy."

"Right? Oh, also, your mama's kitchen. That's as uncreepy as it gets."

"Gurl . . . word," Gilley drawled. "By the way, I know what you're doing."

"What's that?"

"You're trying to take my mind off the fact that we're in this super-creepy museum where there may or may not be residual ghost essence present."

I glanced over my shoulder at him. "Is it working?"

"A little. But an actual dose of sugar in the form of a candy bar would work better. Got a Snickers or anything on you?"

"If I had a Snickers on me, I'd be eating it, honey."

By that time we'd reached the stairs, and we fell silent as Olivera led the way up. We climbed slowly and quietly, tiptoeing up the steps. There wasn't especially a reason for it other than I think we were all a bit nervous to be here for a multitude of reasons.

At last we reached the top floor and headed toward the exhibit, which had crime scene tape stretched across the doorway. "Most of the scene has been processed, but I can't risk you two putting fingerprints on something that didn't have them before," Olivera said, pausing at the tape to dig into her purse and retrieve a few sets of black rubber gloves. She handed those to Gil and me and we made quick work of putting them on. She then lifted the tape slightly to allow Gil and me to duck under. "Try not to disturb anything in the room," she said.

We nodded, and once in the actual exhibit hall, Gil and I fanned out a bit. I dug into the messenger bag I'd brought along, which housed a few extra spikes, an

EMF (electromagnetic frequency) meter, and a couple of flashlights. I took one of those out and handed another to Gilley, and we each headed straight for the display case, which had been smashed open. The display itself had been roped off from the public—out of reach for anyone who might've wanted to get too close to the glass. One section of the rope lay limply on the floor, probably left that way from when Heath had cast it aside after the lights were turned back on and he and I had checked on the dagger.

As we moved past the rope barrier, little bits of glass crunched under our feet. "Wow," Gil said when we stopped in front of the display.

The glass had been thick. Like, you'd need a heavy lead pipe or a hammer to punch a hole through it. "Was there an alarm on the case?" I asked.

"Only if it was lifted up off the base, but that was secured by a latch underneath, which was further secured by a padlock," Gil said. "The glass itself wasn't sensored, so it's not surprising that the alarm didn't ring when somebody broke the glass."

"What'd they break it with?" I wondered.

"We think a hammer," Olivera said, coming up to stand right behind us. "Which we also believe was the murder weapon."

I winced. "Not the dagger?" I asked.

"No," she said. "He suffered a skull fracture after three blows with something resembling a hammer."

"Huh," I said.

"What's 'huh'?" she asked.

"If the hammer was the murder weapon, that means

that Sullivan was probably killed before the murderer got into the case and stole the dagger."

I looked around again, my eyes noting a set of talon marks on the far wall that had ripped through the poster of us from the *Ghoul Getters* show. "What alarm was tripped in here?" I asked her.

"The motion sensor at the entrance to the exhibit," she said, pointing behind her. "It's one of only two in here, with the other one being in the glass case that housed the dagger."

We looked back at the case and studied the damage to it. It appeared to have sustained several blows, most of which were centered right above where the dagger had been displayed.

Gil bent to inspect the base and I cast my gaze all around the floor, seeing that the magnets I'd lain on top after the lights came back on had been removed and cast aside. All the other magnets adhering to the sides were still in place, though.

The base of the display itself was metal, and stuck to it were a dozen refrigerator magnets all with the *Ghoul Getters* logo on them. Gil studied the magnets, and as I watched him, I saw his brow furrow, and then he used his fingertips to pull at one of the magnets, which held tight to the display despite his efforts. "What the hell?" he said. "M.J., look at this!"

I squatted down next to him and saw what he was pointing to. Upon closer inspection I could see that the magnet wasn't even a magnet, just a piece of plastic with our logo glued onto what looked like cardboard, and that was glued onto the metal pedestal of the display to make it appear as if the base was covered in our magnets.

"Shit," I hissed, standing up and taking a long look all around. "Are any of the magnets in this room real?"

The exhibit had a ton of magnets all strategically placed around it. I could see that Gilley had gone to great lengths to make sure that Oruç's dagger was completely surrounded by them. By my estimation, there were several dozen in various sizes and shapes.

Gil stood up too, and after digging through his backpack to pull out a screwdriver, he moved with haste to the nearest wall to tap it against the first spike he encountered. It was a dud. Then he went to another, and another, and another. None of them pulled at the screwdriver's head. "How is this possible?" he asked me after he'd gone all around the room, testing at random, trying to find even one that held a charge. "I personally set this room up, M.J. I mean, how could someone come in here and demagnetize all of these in full view of the staff?"

"Are they all your magnets, Gil?" I asked, pointing to the ones on the display.

He turned back to the wall and lifted a metal spike away from the nails supporting it. "I can't be sure," he admitted. "I mean, our spikes are simple railroad spikes. You can buy them in bulk online and I never put anything distinctive on them, because why would I need to?"

Pointing to the tennis racket across the room strung with magnetized piano wire, I said, "What're the odds that's a duplicate?"

Gil headed straight for it. The racket had been placed on a shelf and Gil had to stretch to get it down, but the second he did I saw his expression darken. "Son of a bitch," he swore again. When he brought the racket to me, I immediately saw what he was so angry about. The racket wasn't strung with wire; it'd simply had its original nylon strings coated with silver metallic paint. Up close it looked sloppy, and obviously not part of our gear, but from the shelf, it'd looked real enough. "Somebody went through this entire display and carefully replaced every magnet with a dud to mirror your original setup, Gil," I said.

Gilley shook his head in disbelief. "*How?* I mean, M.J. . . . that'd take *hours.*"

"There's only one way," Olivera said. She'd been absolutely silent since we'd entered the room.

"How?" Gil repeated.

"With the cooperation of one of the staff."

Now, *that* made sense. Turning to her, I said, "Any theories as to which employee it could've been?"

"Not yet," she said. "Before I came to see you and your husband this morning, I'd been poring over the credit reports of all the museum staff. Nobody came back with anything suspicious, and while I haven't pulled financials for all the employees, there's nothing in any of their backgrounds to indicate that they would agree to risk their job over something like this."

I frowned. I felt like we were missing something. It was Gilley who sort of put it together. "Did you ever look into Sullivan?" he asked.

Olivera's eyes widened, and I knew immediately

that she hadn't. "No," she said. "There was no reason to. He was the victim of an apparent robbery in progress that went bad."

"He was also the one who set up the security system, which fed all the cameras to a laptop on-site," I argued. "And he was here late the night the dagger went missing. He'd also have access to every room in this museum, and could've let someone in to switch out all the magnets for dummy props."

Olivera's lips pressed together and she eyed the tennis racket in Gilley's hands. "But why kill him?" she said. "And for that matter, why smash the display case? Why not just get Sullivan to disarm the alarm for it and take it?"

"Maybe Sullivan argued with the thief," I said. "Maybe he wanted more money, or was experiencing a change of heart. Or maybe the murderer simply didn't want to leave a witness behind, and to make it look like Sullivan had interrupted him during the robbery, he'd smashed the case with the same hammer he'd used to kill the director."

Olivera crossed her arms and tapped her foot, thinking. "Sullivan's computer is still in his office," she said. "Downstairs."

Gilley turned to grin knowingly at me. There wasn't a computer in the world that could hide its user's secrets from Gil. "What're we waiting for?"

And that's the moment all the lights winked out.

Chapter 11

Gilley was the first to scream.

Okay, so maybe he was the only one who screamed, but he screamed loud. Like, *loud*. And with Gil, it's always a challenge to tell whether he's screaming in outright fright or because some spook has just taken him as a hostage. (It's happened before.)

For several seconds, I couldn't see a thing; my eyes were trying to adjust to the sudden loss of light—even our flashlights had died—but finally I saw a shape next to me and reached for it. Gilley screamed again. "It's me!" I hissed.

He responded by latching onto my arm and pulling me to him. He then wrapped himself around me like a koala hugging a tree. "Something's here!" he blubbered.

I wanted to shush him, but then I heard it. A beeping sound that sounded all too familiar. And it seemed to be coming from me, or rather my messenger bag. With a jolt I realized that the beeping was our EMF meter. And it was going off like crazy. Using my free arm, I dug it out of my messenger bag and clicked the back-light on the device. The meter was in the red zone.

"What the hell is that?" I heard Olivera ask. Her foot-falls told me she was coming toward me, drawn to the EMF meter as the only source of light in the room.

"It's a meter that measures electromagnetic frequen-cies," I told her. "It tells us when a spook is close."

I saw the shadowy figure of the detective stop in front of me. "I take it there's one close to us?" she said, a quaver sneaking into her voice.

"There's one right on top of us!" Gil shrieked.

"Gil!" I said firmly. His freak-out wasn't helping. "We're wrapped in magnets here. We should be fine."

Olivera moved even closer to me. I wondered if she was going to take up Gilley's koala pose. Meanwhile the EMF meter continued to go off, and it set us all on edge. "Can we get out of here?" Gilley whispered. "It's in here, M.J.! I know it!"

Although Gilley didn't identify the "it" he was refer-ring to, the hair on the back of my neck had risen high and goose pimples had already broken out along my arms. Gilley was right; something was in here with us. From the corner of the room there was a low rumbling. It reverberated off the walls, traveled along the floor, and vibrated under our feet and along our skin. My breathing was coming in quick pants. I knew that rum-ble. I knew that presence, and I also knew we were in deep, deep trouble. "Gil," I whispered. "Let go and get behind me. You too, Olivera."

Gilley scooted around to stand pressed to my back, his head knocking the space between my shoulder blades. He was trembling so much that I wondered if he'd be able to walk—or run—out of here. Olivera, however, hadn't moved other than to fumble with something at her waist. I knew that only because her elbow bumped me and I heard the slight rustle of clothing. "If you just took out your gun," I whispered, "I will leave you behind when Gilley and I make a break for it." I was serious too.

"What the hell was that?" she asked me. I could hear the chatter of her teeth as she tried to speak. She was absolutely terrified. Which meant she'd shoot first and ask questions later. Great.

"Detective," I said firmly. "Holster that weapon and get. Behind. Me."

For another few seconds I didn't think she'd comply, but finally she bumped my elbow with hers again and I knew she'd tucked the gun back into her shoulder harness. She then sort of shuffled backward a few steps, but she seemed reluctant to get behind me. I figured it was because she wanted a clear shot in case the demon across the room came at us. Which it was sure to do unless I did something first.

Very slowly and carefully I reached into my messenger bag and felt around until I had what I wanted. Gripping it tightly, I pulled it out and held it at both ends. "Listen to me, you two," I began, keeping my voice low and steady. "I'm going to set up a distraction. The second my distraction hits, we bolt for that doorway and go until we're out of here." Neither Gil nor Olivera replied. "Tap my shoulder if you understand," I said. I felt two taps. Good. They were on board. "Gil, get your spikes out. If that thing comes at us, throw all you've got at it. I'll be right behind you." When motivated, Gilley could outrun me. He wasn't often motivated, except at times like these. Or when the smell of freshly baked doughnuts scented the air.

I tightened my grip on the thin tube in my hands and said, "We'll go on three. One . . . two . . ."

Just as I was about to shout three, a high-pitched roar filled the room and was so deafening that it nearly knocked us all over. The three of us staggered back, Gilley pulling me along as I tried to hold myself upright. And then there was a sort of pounding of feet heavy enough to compete with an elephant. Olivera screamed. Gilley screamed. Even I screamed. On reflex I tore at the top of the tube I was holding and threw it at the approaching monster. The darkness shrank as the road flare I threw at the demon blossomed into red bubbling sparks that shot outward and hopped along the floor. Within the light of the flare was a creature at least nine feet tall. Beady, recessed, glowing red eyes focused on our quivering forms, and a snout as long as my arms, with fangs that dripped black sludge, inched hungrily toward us.

Oruç's demon had just crashed our party.

"We are so screwed," I heard Olivera whisper.

At the sound of her voice the beast charged forward

on two legs, with limbs that resembled a human's, but the skin of the beast was thick and gray, gnarled with bumps and ridges. The arms of the beast were thin and elongated, as were its three fingers, each tipped with what looked to be razor-sharp talons.

The sight of Oruç's demon coming at us was enough to take Gilley's screams to a pitch high and loud enough to pop my eardrums.

Olivera also screamed, and out of the corner of my eye I saw her go for her gun again. With one hand I hit her hard across the forearms and wrenched the spike clutched in Gilley's fist away from him only to then throw it right at the demon. It struck and stuck in the beast's snout, and that stopped its charge long enough for me to grab both Olivera and Gilley and wrench them to the right and over toward the exit.

Gilley kept screaming the entire time. I barely noticed. I was too focused on the six-inch fangs of the beast and the razor-sharp talons swiping at us as we dashed by it. We got by unscathed, although I could see Olivera kept reaching for her gun, and I kept reaching for her arm, which made it impossible for me to draw out another spike. Gilley gained the lead and darted ahead of us out into the open room leading to the front stairwell. The spike in his right hand was still firmly gripped, which did us no good.

Olivera kept looking over her shoulder as she battled my attempts to thwart the drawing of her weapon, and at one point she stumbled and fell down. Here's the part where I admit that I almost left her. The fear coursing through my veins at that moment was so intense and the instinctual urge to run from a massive predator and leave anyone else in my wake was nearly overpowering. Reason returned, however, and with a snarl I stopped, retraced my steps, and grabbed her under the arm. *"Get up!"* I roared.

With my help, she did, and we barely escaped the downward swipe of the demon's claws.

By now, Gilley had gained the stairs, and I saw his head disappear as he hurtled down them. I let go of Olivera because holding on to her was slowing us both down, and we raced after him. She had much longer legs than me, but I'm a serious runner, and we reached the top of the stairs together. It was so dark that it was impossible to see the steps individually, but that didn't stop me from launching myself down them. Breaking a leg was nothing compared to possibly being ripped apart by talons and fangs.

Behind us the beast kept coming. I didn't dare look back; I was too focused on my feet, trying to guess where each step was. Gilley reached the bottom while we were still in the middle of the stairwell, his screams echoing throughout the massive front hall of the museum. In the back of my mind I wondered if someone outside might hear him and call the cops. Then I realized that if the demon caught one of us, it would likely shred us within a matter of moments, and then the police would have to deal with it, and how were they supposed to handle a demon that couldn't be killed, with talons that could tear apart human flesh?

"This isn't happening!" Olivera suddenly blurted out. "This can't be happening! That thing can't be real!"

"Keep moving!" I shouted. No way did we have time to argue whether or not the nine-foot monster currently shaking the stairwell with its footfalls was real or not. It was friggin' real enough!

The messenger bag on my hip bounced and jostled, and I desperately wanted to pause long enough to reach into it and pull out a fistful of spikes, but that was a risk that I couldn't take on the stairs.

At last we reached the bottom and I took off after the sound of Gilley, who was still screaming his head off. The first floor was even darker than the rooms upstairs, and navigating them was tricky to say the least. Olivera kept calling my name, and I kept answering, "Here!" to keep her with me. I had no more flares, and the flashlights weren't working, and the demon had the advantage here, because it's a known fact that demons can see in the dark.

Gilley had no such gift, however, and in the next moment his shrieks were cut off by a loud *thwack!* and then the sound of a body hitting the floor. *"Gilley!"* I cried. I didn't know if he'd hit a wall or if someone had hit him.

He replied with a whimper and a groan.

Behind me the beast growled low and terrible.

There was a sort of scrambling noise and Gilley must've gotten to his feet again, because his screams resumed and echoed through the hallway, definitely getting farther away from us.

By now I was nearly out of breath. The adrenaline that had fueled the first part of our flight was wearing off, and the toll of the run out of the exhibit hall, down the stairs, and through the museum at an all-out sprint was taking its effect. My lungs were yelling at me to slow down. The frosty breath on my neck from the demon behind me, however, was encouraging me to speed up. I settled for simply maintaining the sprint.

Gilley's shrieks zigzagged through the halls, and Olivera and I did our best to follow him with the demon hot on our heels. At one point I swear Gil changed direction, and then there was another *thwack!* and a sudden halt to his shrieks, but he seemed to recover from that a bit faster than from the last one.

I hadn't realized what a maze the first floor was until we were running for our lives through it. I also wondered at Gilley's ability to keep shrieking, because I could barely draw breath. Olivera was having a somewhat easier time of it, I thought. And really, I shouldn't have been so out of breath; I mean, I run my ass off, train for marathons and such.

But then it dawned on me. I was pregnant. Of course I'd be out of breath. And then it *really* dawned on me. I was *pregnant*, and the demon was currently threatening the life of my unborn child.

That's the moment when my motherly instincts kicked in and I came to an abrupt halt, pulling free a spike from my bag and taking what I hoped was careful aim. I threw it straight in front of me and there was a god-awful screech. "Ha!" I shouted. "Take that, you son of a bitch!"

Olivera's hand gripped my arm, and she pulled me back hard, just as I felt the air next to my nose move sharply—the demon had just taken a swipe at my head and I'd escaped having my head lopped off by less than an inch. *"Are you crazy?!"* she shouted.

I didn't answer. I just ran.

We bolted toward the back of the museum, moving in a zigzag pattern, always chasing the sound of Gilley's fading shrieks. It took me a little while to realize he was simply lost and acting like a panicked rat in a maze, darting down any corridor or into any room that might lead out.

"He's . . . lost!" I wheezed to Olivera.

"He's not far off the mark!" she yelled back. And then, as if in answer to a prayer, one lone light bulb ahead of us came on, illuminating the darkness and showing us exactly where we were.

It didn't give us an advantage over the monster still hot on our heels, but at least it evened the odds. I chanced one glance over my shoulder at Oruç's demon. I'd thought it was scary upstairs in the pink glow of the flare—that was nothing compared to the shadowy figure it cut as it bared its teeth and seemed to surge forward toward me. It gained on us and I faced forward again, concentrating on pumping my legs and arms as fast as I could.

As we dashed past the overhead light that'd illuminated the area for us, it winked out, but another light turned on to our left and we headed straight for it. Then it winked out and another light farther down the corridor winked on.

I suddenly realized that our way out was literally being lit up for us. "Gilley!" I shouted with all the air I could spare. "This way!"

His screams abruptly changed direction—maybe he'd seen the lights too?—and he came racing toward us. Trouble was, the demon wasn't letting up on the chase, and I didn't think I had it in me to keep ahead of it to the end of the museum. The harder I pumped my legs and arms, the less air I could draw into my lungs. And I needed air, desperately. Olivera pulled ahead of me and then Gilley showed up just down the hall from us. He didn't even look behind him; he just ran toward the lights winking on, then off.

We were all so focused on them that I don't think any of us noticed that the hallway we were in ended at a closed door. And it sure didn't look like an exit out of the building to me. Olivera and I probably realized it at the same time. She faltered slightly, but I kept running. If I had to run through that door like Wile E. Coyote, then I would. Anything to escape the clutches of the demon that was closest now to *me*.

Gilley kept running and screaming, and at last he noticed the door too. He didn't stop; he ran right to it and tried the handle, but it wouldn't budge. He proceeded to pound his fists on the door and tried again and again to turn the handle, but it appeared to be locked. In front of me, Olivera faltered again, and I knew she was considering doubling back and taking her chances. One glance over her shoulder, however, seemed to shelve that idea. She shrieked, faced forward, and ran straight for Gilley.

I was so fatigued and out of breath that I thought I might pass out. I once fainted on an eighteen-mile run. It'd been a very hot day, and I hadn't taken along nearly enough water. I have no memory of passing out, only waking up in the grass as another female runner attempted to come to my aid. The light-headed woozy feeling I did remember right before losing consciousness was what was happening to me at that moment—just ten yards away from the door. Which wouldn't open. Which Gilley kept pounding on.

With what was left of my ability to think, I sent up a prayer. *Please,* I said in my mind, which, trust me, in that kind of situation is pretty much all you need. With five yards to go the door handled turned and Gilley heaved the door open. He darted inside with Olivera right on his heels. I strained with everything I had and reached the door a second later, careening through it just as Olivera yanked it closed.

As I crashed into Gilley, collapsing into his arms, I heard the click of the dead bolt, followed by a terrible crash that shook the entire room. The demon had hit the door. Hard.

I sucked in as much air as I could, gulping it down in great heaves. Gilley was panting almost as hard, but he was trembling from head to toe too. Other than the sound of our labored breathing, the room was deathly quiet. And then a light came on, and we all turned to see that a Tiffany lamp, perched on a desk, had magically illuminated the room.

I noted that we were in someone's private office, tastefully decorated with art on the wall, a Turkish rug on the floor, a mahogany desk, and a comfortable leather chair with matching footstool in one corner.

On the desk was a laptop. My gaze was drawn next

to my two companions. Gilley had two large welts on his forehead but seemed relatively okay, and Olivera looked frightened beyond reason, but at least she was blinking and looking around. I hoped that we could all collect our wits and our breath without further incident, but that hope was short-lived when the silence was shattered by a tremendous slap at the top of the door and then what I can only describe as a terrible metallic raking sound.

It was the most grating, terrifying noise you can imagine. Think of a velociraptor scraping its talons down the face of a chalkboard and you've got some idea of what it sounded like, and this was taking place mere feet from us on the other side of the door, starting from the top and slowly gouging its way down the length of the door. We all huddled together and cringed while we waited for it to be over, but as soon as the raking reached the bottom of the door, another slap at the top started and the slow slide of talons over steel began again.

Pushing away from Gilley, I staggered to my feet and stumbled forward to the door. Placing my hand on it, I felt the cool touch of metal along with the vibrations from the talons on the other side. "M.J.!" Gilley said hoarsely. "Get away from there!"

Ignoring him, I dug into my messenger bag and pulled out a spike, which I slammed against the door right at the center of what I hoped was the demon's paw. The beast screeched and the grating sound stopped abruptly. I then reached for another spike and slammed that against the door, then another and another, until I was all out of spikes. I turned and looked at Gilley, and he came forward tentatively to hand me all his spikes too. I added them to the rest, effectively creating a solid barrier against the demon.

As the last spike went on the door, Olivera said in a hushed whisper, "Can it come through the walls?"

Gil and I looked at each other. He shrugged and I had to admit I really didn't know either. "Technically, it probably could," I said. "But the walls look like they're concrete block, so it'd be tough for the demon to bring it's full form through that kind of density. And once it started to do that, we'd be able to stab the hell out of it with a spike."

"What does that even mean?" she asked. I noticed that she'd scooted to the farthest corner in the room, well away from the door.

It was Gilley who answered her. "The demon took on as close to a physical form as it could," he explained. "That requires energy. A lot of energy. It'd take significantly more energy for it to move through a wall, and after giving us chase and getting zapped by our magnets, no way does it have enough juice left to push its way through concrete block quickly. It'd have to squeeze through slowly, and we'd be able to attack it from this side with all of our spikes."

I had to hand it to him; he sounded very sure of his conclusion.

"So we're safe in here?" Olivera asked.

"We are," I told her. I wasn't a hundred percent sure, but I didn't see the sense of worrying her more than she already was.

As it happened, for the next several minutes, we heard nothing from the demon, and not long after that a dim light lit up under the door. I tried the switch next to the door and the overhead lights blazed on. I then looked at my companions in the stark white light and knew that I looked just as freaked-out, exhausted, and shaken as they did. Olivera was the first to speak. "What . . . *the fuck* was *that*?"

"Oruç's demon," I said simply. "And now you know, Detective, *exactly* why we have to get that dagger back."

Chapter 12

Olivera stared wide-eyed at me. I knew that her brain was currently attempting to marry the reality she'd always known with the one that'd taken place tonight, and she had to be struggling under the weight of that.

Gilley had a hand to his forehead, as if he had a terrible headache, and he also appeared quite shaken. "Hey," I said. "You okay?"

"No," he said, his lip quivering. "*Why* did you have to bring me here?"

I put a hand on his shoulder. "Honey, I'm so sorry. I really needed you, and I had no idea that demon would show up."

"It came after us, M.J.!" Gil whined. "I mean, with the amount of magnets we had on, it should've gone in the other direction."

"That's one powerful demon, Gil," I reminded him.

"Which is why I've had that dagger locked up in my safe all these years."

Gil's shoulders slumped with guilt. "I forgot how freaking strong it is," he whispered. "I really thought that, with enough magnets placed around the dagger, there'd be no way it could get loose."

"He wouldn't have if someone hadn't sabotaged the exhibit," I reminded him. "But now the genie is out of the bottle, and we gotta do everything we can to put it back in. And I'm still going to need you on this case, honey. For this one, it's all hands on deck."

Gil bit his lip and wiped his eyes, but he also nodded a little. "Got any Tylenol?" he asked.

"No. Sorry," I said with a sigh, moving away from him a few feet to a box set against the wall. Taking a seat on the box, I motioned to the desk and said, "Maybe there's some in there?"

Gil shuffled over to the desk and pulled open a drawer. It stuck a little and he had to tug on it, then root around inside. "Aha!" he said triumphantly when he came up with a small bottle of Excedrin. "Who's got water?"

I shook my head and Olivera did too. That didn't stop Gil from popping back two pills. He gulped audibly and plopped down in the desk chair to sit back and sigh wearily. His gaze then traveled to the computer screen, which was emitting a faint glow against Gil's face. I figured the computer had come to life when he'd jostled the desk looking for some pain-relief medicine. As I watched Gil watching the screen, he suddenly jolted forward in his seat to exclaim, "M.J.!"

"What?"

"Come here!"

With fatigued effort I got up from my box and moved to stand next to him. "There's a camera feed coming into the computer," Gil said, pointing to the screen. "It's from a camera at the back door."

I looked at Olivera. "I thought you said that all the security cameras had their feeds sent to a laptop that was stolen."

"They did and it was," she said, coming over to the desk to look as well.

"All except this puppy," Gil said, tapping the screen. "It's the only one that feeds to this laptop."

"Why?" I asked.

Gil shrugged. "Don't know." He was about to say something else, but at that moment the camera showed the door to the back opening, and the blurry image of a figure dressed in dark clothes emerged and darted quickly away out of the sight of the camera.

"Who was *that*?" I said.

Gil shook his head. Of course he didn't know.

"How the hell is someone able to exit the museum without tripping the alarm?" Olivera snapped as she leaned forward to peer at the screen. "We're the only ones who have the passcode!"

"Obviously not," Gilley said. "And even if you guys did erase all the other access codes to put in your own, there's still a master code that could override all attempts to lock it out."

"What're you talking about?" Olivera asked.

"Well, to every electronic lock, there is always a

master code. It's the one that would allow the person at the top access, even if the recently fired IT guy decided to take his revenge out by locking everyone out of the system. It was created specifically for those types of scenarios, actually."

"Who would've had that kind of authority?" Olivera asked him.

Gil shrugged. "I can only think of one person, Detective, and he's dead."

"Sullivan," she said.

"Aren't we missing the point here?" I said, pointing to the screen again. "That was clearly the murderer and our thief escaping the museum. The only way for Oruç's demon to have shown up here tonight is if the dagger was close by."

Olivera's eyes widened again. "Shit! You're right!" She raced to the door, intent on giving chase, and Gilley shot out from the chair and reached her just as she was starting to turn the dead bolt.

"Hold on!" he said, wrapping his hand firmly around her wrist. "You can't just go chasing after him!"

"Why not?" she and I said together.

Gilley turned to me and said, "Really, M.J.? I have to explain it to you too? That guy could've just left with Oruç's dagger. The one that houses the demon who tried to play tag with us tonight. You really wanna go chasing down a dark alley after him?"

Olivera stopped trying to pull her wrist free of Gilley's grip. "Good point," she said.

I squinted again at the computer screen. There appeared to be a steady drizzle coming down. "It's still raining out," I said, as if that absolutely decided it. "Gil's right. It's way too dangerous to give chase at this point."

"So what do we do?" Olivera asked. "I mean, if we can't catch or confront this guy, how the hell are we supposed to get you two the dagger back without encountering the demon?"

Gil let go of her hand and looked to me as if I should know. "We'll have to figure out who the hell the murderer is," I said. "Then we'll need to approach him armed to the teeth, and in broad daylight. It can't be raining that day either."

Gilley made a face. "Then we should make plans to go on vacation for a week, because it's supposed to rain for the next several days."

"What?" I said. "No way!"

Gilley motioned me back over to the computer with him and pulled up a weather map with a giant system currently headed toward the East Coast, as well as another giant system just offshore in the Atlantic, which must've been where all the rain of the past two days had come from. "These two weather systems are supposed to collide sometime around three p.m. today, right over Massachusetts, Rhode Island, New Hampshire, and New York City. It's then supposed to park itself there until next Tuesday."

Tuesday was four days from now. "How did I miss this?" I muttered.

"It's been all over the news," he said.

I sighed and went back to sit on my box. "Guess I picked the wrong time to stop watching the news, huh?"

"So what do we do?" Olivera asked again. She seemed close to panic at the revelation that we'd have to wait for a sunny day to confront the person behind all this.

"We identify the killer," I said again. "And once we do that, we figure out how to proceed."

Gil pointed to the laptop. "This might help," he said.

"How so?" I asked.

"It's Sullivan's computer."

I looked around. "This was his office."

"Yes," Olivera confirmed.

"Can we take the computer?" Gil asked.

Olivera bit her lip. "I'd feel more comfortable handing that over to one of our techs," she said. Gilley and I exchanged a look and I decided to be honest with her. "Detective—," I began.

She cut me off. "Please call me Chris."

"Um . . . okay. Chris. Gilley is actually one of the best computer geeks you'll ever meet. If this computer has any kind of information relevant to the case, he'll find it."

"It's the not-relevant-to-the-case information that I worry about," she said. "Sullivan could have personal information on that computer that I'm certain his family wouldn't want a stranger digging through."

To this, Gilley rolled his eyes. "Oh, please. If I really wanted to uncover personal information on Sullivan, not having access to his computer wouldn't stop me."

Olivera studied him for a minute. "You're a hacker."

Gil flexed his fingers. "One of the best."

She sighed. "I'm not just at risk of losing my job

here, guys. I'm probably at risk of being arrested for obstruction if I let you take that computer."

"We'll put it back," I told her.

She rubbed her forehead, as if she too had a headache. "No," she said firmly. "Sorry, but it can't leave the scene. I could have to swear in court that the physical chain of custody remained intact, and I'm not going to lie on the stand. See what you can find out between now and when we're ready to get out of here."

Gil sighed, but he seemed to accept her decision. "Fine," he said, and then he held up the bottle of Excedrin. He'd noticed her squinty expression and the rubbing of her forehead too. She nodded; he tossed her the bottle, then sat down to start typing on the keyboard.

"Don't leave a trace," I told him. The last thing we needed was for one of the techs at BPD to figure out that we'd been snooping in Sullivan's computer files.

Gilley made a face but never took his eyes off the screen. "Gurl, pleez," he said. "Who do you think you're dealing with?"

"Sorry," I told him. "You know what's odd?" I said next.

"Your fashion sense?"

I glared at Gil. "Funny," I said flatly. "And no, what's odd is why the killer thought to take the computer that the other cameras fed to, but not this one."

Gil paused in his typing and looked at Olivera, as if she might have the answer. "That's easy," she said. "The office was locked."

Gil turned to me. "That's true," he said. "When I first got to this office, it was totally locked."

"I was meaning to ask you how you managed to get it open," Olivera said.

Gilley pointed at me. "It was probably someone from her crew."

Olivera eyed me quizzically. "What's he talking about?"

"The lights that turned on to illuminate our path," I said. "That was probably one of the spirits that watches over me, and that same spirit likely managed to unlock the door." I had a very strong sense that Sam had once again come to my rescue, but I didn't want to go into a lot of detail about who he was, et cetera, for Olivera, who would probably only ask me a bunch of irrelevant questions.

"One of the spirits that watches over you?" she asked.

I shrugged. "I'm a medium. I work with a lot of souls who've crossed over. Occasionally, one of them does me a solid."

"Huh," Olivera said, like I'd just given her the solution to a complicated math problem. "That's either wicked cool or wicked creepy."

I smiled. "Let's go with cool, lest we offend them."

"Right," she said, and eyed the ceiling nervously. Then she moved over to Sullivan's leather recliner and sat down heavily. "Anyway, can we talk about what the hell happened here tonight?"

"What's there to talk about?" I said, knowing I needed to be frank with her. "We came to investigate the scene; the killer found out about it and set Oruç's demon loose to kill us."

Gilley shuddered and paused his typing. "Jesus, M.J., did you get a *look* at that thing in the light of your flare?"

"I did," I said. "I got several more looks at it too."

"How did you even think of bringing a flare?" Gil asked. "That was kind of genius."

I moved another box that seemed to contain books over to rest my feet on it and leaned back against the wall. "Thanks. It was actually Heath who gave me the idea. He got me a roadside safety kit a few weeks before we went on vacation, and when I saw the flares, I thought they'd be a great backup on a bust should our flashlights ever fail."

"It was a great idea," Gil agreed. "I wish I'd thought of it, actually."

"We should probably retrieve it before someone finds the flare stub," I said. Both Olivera and Gilley looked at me like I was crazy. "No *way* am I opening that door until morning," Gilley said.

Olivera stared uneasily at the door too. "You think the demon is still out there?"

Gilley shrugged. "It could be," he said. "I mean, all the killer would have to do is leave the dagger out in the hallway and wait for us to come out."

"I highly doubt he'd leave the dagger behind," I said. "Not after all the trouble he went to to get it in the first place."

"Do you know that for sure?" Gilley said. "Seriously, M.J., are you willing to bet your life and the life of your baby on it?"

I yawned. Man, I was tired. And I kept thinking

about Heath, alone, at home, but I also had to admit that I didn't know if the dagger was still at the museum and taking the chance that it had gone along with Sullivan's murderer wasn't something I was prepared to do. I went over to the phone on the desk and called Heath's cell. It rang four times and he finally answered. "M.J.?"

"Babe, are you okay?" I asked without preamble.

There was a pause, then, "Yeah. Yeah, I'm okay. Where are you?"

It was my turn to pause. If Heath hadn't spied the note yet, then it might be best to go light on the details. The last thing I needed him to do was to come in search of me at the museum. "I'm out, doing a little legwork with Gil and Detective Olivera."

"What time is it?" he asked. His words were slightly slurred. The effects of the drugs and the fact that I'd woken him up.

"It's early, sweetheart. I just wanted to call and check on you."

"That was nice," he said. "Do you need me to come help you?"

"No. No, no. We're wrapping it up here. Why don't you go back to sleep and I'll be home before you know it."

Heath made a muffled sound of agreement and I crossed my fingers. "Wake me up when you get in, okay?"

"Promise," I said. He told me he loved me and clicked off, and I breathed a small sigh of relief. "He's fine." I looked up at my companions. Gilley's fingers were flying over the keyboard. Olivera was reclined in the leather chair, and exhaustion apparently had taken over, because her eyes were closed and her breathing was deep and rhythmic.

Gil paused his typing to glance at her; then he reached down to his backpack, fished around for a second, and pulled up a flash drive. With a finger to his lips at me, he inserted the drive into the USB port and began to download the contents of Sullivan's computer. I smiled and offered him a thumbs-up.

I then leaned back against the wall and closed my own eyes. I really wanted to sleep, but I didn't feel like I could just yet. I wanted to figure out what the hell was going on. So far we'd been stalked and attacked and our homes had been broken into. This wasn't just Oruç and his demon getting revenge. This had taken careful planning by someone living. Someone who had it in for us. But who?

"Gil?" I said.

"Yeah?" he replied distractedly. He was very focused on his task of rooting through Sullivan's computer.

"The thing with the magnets. Not a lot of people know about how magnets affect a spook."

"What's your point?" he asked.

"My point is, someone went to a lot of trouble to ensure that, once they set the demon free, it could cause maximum harm. Here. At the museum."

Gil paused to look at me. "Whoa," he said. "Are you saying what I think you're saying?"

"I'm saying that I think whoever our thief was knew enough about our ghostbusting techniques to neutralize any attempt we might have made to stop Oruç's demon from appearing. I'm also saying that I think the killer had something big planned for opening day at the exhibit, but when Heath and I showed up with our gear from the closet in my office—the gear that was still fully magnetized—we might've thwarted that plan."

Gilley sat with that for a moment. "I'll bet you're right, M.J.," he said.

"And you know what else keeps going around in my head?" I asked him.

"What?"

"It's to your earlier point about the fact that not a lot of people know about the effect magnets have on a spook. Sure, we've highlighted that in a show or two, but the dagger isn't just a haunted relic—it's a portal, Gil. A gateway, and one of the things that's intriguing about the theft of the dagger is that the body count isn't higher."

"One dead isn't enough for you?" Gil said drolly.

I ignored that and went on with making my point. "Oruç hated women. He lusted for killing them, and yet, the only person dead is a man, who wasn't even killed with the dagger. That suggests to me that someone knows how to control the portal and is opening and closing the gateway at will."

Gil's jaw dropped. "Ohmigod," he said. "You're *right!*"

"Only someone with a hell of a lot of experience would know how to keep Oruç under wraps like that. Someone's clearly keeping Oruç under tight control but allowing the demon to run free, and that could only be done by someone with hands-on experience. Handling demons is no joke, you'd be safer trying to handle a rabid lion, so whoever did this is orchestrating things on a level of a fellow ghostbuster. Somebody who knows a lot about electromagnetic frequencies and how they can affect, specifically, a portal, and also, how to handle a demon well enough to put the genie back in the bottle when necessary."

Gilley studied me in a way that suggested he hadn't really thought of all that. "Shit," he swore. "You think it's one of our competitors?"

"Who else could it be?"

Gil wiped his face with his hand. "That's certainly one way to narrow the pool of suspects," he said. "Okay, let me try searching Sullivan's computer for any sign of someone in our industry. Maybe there'll be an e-mail or a reference to a name I recognize."

And then that thing that'd been bugging me since this all began surfaced in my mind again and I said, "Gil, can you look for a connection between Sullivan and that producer, Bradley Rosenberg?"

Gil's fingers paused on the keyboard. "Why?"

"Because I just don't trust this whole setup," I said. "I mean, we've been advertising the fact that we'd have an exhibit here at the museum for a couple of months now, and we all spoke about what we'd contribute to it on the fan site, but then all of the sudden, just when Gopher, me, and Heath are out of the country and unreachable, *you* get a phone call from some mysterious producer we've never heard of, telling you that Gopher—someone we trust—supposedly told him about Oruç's dagger and how it'd be the *perfect* thing to add to the exhibit. This Rosenberg guy never tried to call me or Heath about it . . . just you. And he offered you a lot of money, right?"

"Twenty thousand," Gilley said meekly.

I whistled. "Twenty grand to pony up an old dagger? I mean, when you really think about it, it's absurd, right? Bradley represents an industry literally *built* on props, but suddenly he's got to have you bring the real thing here to the museum? And," I added, "as of today, you haven't received said check, correct?"

"He said it was in the mail," Gil said, even more meekly.

"Of course it is," I said, my voice dripping with sarcasm. "And even if it were, Gil, think about it; you haven't heard back from good ol' Bradley after leaving him a voice mail telling him that the dagger he paid twenty thousand dollars for has just been stolen. Don't you think that's a *little* suspicious?"

"But, M.J.," he protested, "like I told you, I've called his business line. Several times. I've spoken to his assistant. He's legitimately *from* the studio!"

I crossed my arms, tapping my finger to my biceps. "Call the office number he gave you now," I said. "I'd like to hear his legitimate assistant's voice mail."

Gil glared at me and lifted his phone from his backpack. After several attempts to turn it on, he muttered in irritation, dug again through his backpack, and came up with a charger. Plugging his phone in, he waited a moment for it to charge enough so he could access his contacts and, with a triumphant tap, placed the call and turned on the speaker function.

It rang twice before the error message broadcast through the phone. "The number you have reached has been disconnected or is no longer in service. Please check the number and try again."

Gilley made a barely audible squeaky noise, and he stared unblinking at his phone.

"Yep," I said. "That's what I thought."

But Gil wasn't giving up. "It's gotta be a mistake," he said, thumbing through his contacts again. "I'm calling Bradley's cell again." He left the speaker function on when he made that call too, and sure enough, another error message came on suggesting that the voice mailbox for the person he was trying to call was full.

Gilley's eyes misted with tears. "No," he whispered.

"Sorry, Gil. You were set up," I said. I had very little satisfaction in the revelation. I hated that he'd been duped, and hated even more that the end result was that one man had already died, and the dagger was now in the possession of some lunatic willing to commit murder just to get noticed.

"Oh, God, M.J.! What've I done?!" Gilley moaned.

"What's going on?" Olivera asked groggily. We'd woken her up.

"Nothing, Chris. We're just putting pieces together."

"Wanna fill me in?" she asked.

I took a few minutes to do that and she eyed poor Gilley with a measure of sympathy. "I see smart people get played all the time," she said. "Don't take it so hard."

"I have to take it hard," Gilley said miserably. "Because of me, the dagger is loose and some asshole is opening up the gateway at will for every spook we've ever sent to the lower realms to have another crack at us. M.J., what if the demon from Heath's pueblo in Santa Fe comes after us? Or the one from Ireland? Or"—he gulped before he said the next name—"the Sandman. I mean, what if they all come after us at once? No *way* can we survive that!"

I got up and went over to lay a gentle hand on Gil's shoulder. "You're right," I said to him—there was no sense lying. "But we're not gonna let that happen, Gil. We're gonna put a stop to this before it gets that far. We'll track down the sons of a bitches responsible for this mess, and take back that dagger. You have my word on that."

"But how?" he said pitifully. "I mean, we've got nothing to go on! Bradley could've been anybody, and his admin also could've been anyone."

"True, but if we start putting together enough of what we *do* know, maybe the trail will lead back to one or both of them." I then eyed Sullivan's computer pointedly.

Gil followed my gaze and squared his shoulders. "Got it," he said. "Gimme a few hours."

Chapter 13

Only half an hour into his hacking, Gilley had gained access to Sullivan's bank account. "Why people do their personal banking on a work computer is beyond me," he said. "Okay, here we go. Five thousand dollars was wired into his account the day after Bradley got me to agree to display the dagger."

"Does it show the source?"

"Someone named Todd Tolliver."

"That sounds like a made-up name," I said. "And five grand doesn't sound like a big enough bribe to let in someone looking to sabotage an exhibit at the risk of losing his job."

"It was probably only the down payment," Olivera said, making sure to frown at the fact that Gilley was rooting around in Sullivan's bank accounts. "A show of good faith. He was likely promised that he'd get the rest after the dagger had been stolen."

"Gil and I were talking while you were sleeping, Chris, and we think that the dagger being stolen was only part of it. We think that whoever set all this up was planning something big at the exhibit's opening day, but then Heath and I showed up with gear that had been at our office and was still fully magnetized, and we thwarted his plans. I believe that this guy then came back to get the dagger after hours, not knowing that Sullivan was here in his office working, and when he tripped the alarm, Sullivan surprised him, and maybe he and the killer got into it, which is how Sullivan ended up dead."

Olivera nodded. "Sounds like a reasonable scenario," she said. "What big thing do you think the killer was planning?"

"Well," I said, "unleashing a demon like we saw tonight into a crowd of innocent bystanders makes for a pretty big statement, don't you think?"

Chris's expression turned grim. "To what end, though?" she said. "I mean, this guy is obviously smart. He's careful. And he's plotted this whole thing out expertly. What would he have to gain by doing something like that?"

Gilley and I exchanged a look, and it was Gilley who answered. "We think, given his knowledge of how magnets affect a portal, and his knowledge of the dagger and its history, that he's a fellow ghostbuster. Someone who's had extensive experience working with spooks, and even demons."

"Huh," she said. "Okay, so who in your line of work could pull off something like that?"

Again I looked at Gilley. "Nobody named Todd Tolliver; that's for sure," he said. "But there is one guy who comes to mind."

"Rick Lavinia," I said, and Gilley nodded as if he'd been thinking the very same thing.

"Who's Rick Lavinia?"

Gilley scoffed as if he couldn't believe she'd never heard of him. "He's a ghostbuster with his own cable show too. He started about two years before we did, and he was haunted TV's most popular ghostbuster until Heath came along." My brow furrowed indignantly and Gilley shrugged and added, "You're super cute and all, M.J., but most people tune in to watch that hottie you're married to. I know that's why I watch the show."

"Can we get back to the point here?" Chris said.

"Yes," I said firmly, with another irritated look at Gil. "Rick has, on a few occasions, publicly dogged our show. He's the guy who likes to stomp around haunted locations and yell at the spooks, daring them to come out and show themselves. He got hurt pretty bad a year ago when one such spook picked his ass up and tossed him down the cellar stairs."

"It was epic!" Gilley said with a giggle.

"Which is exactly what Gilley tweeted right after the episode aired. He tagged Rick in the tweet, which wasn't his smartest move . . ."

Gilley rolled his eyes. "That douche bag had it coming."

". . . and Rick went off on a tirade about our show and how fake it was and how lame we were. It was kind of embarrassing to watch."

"So you two are competitors," Olivera said.

"We are," I said. "But it's one-sided, more so from his perspective than ours."

"Why's that?"

Gil and I exchanged a knowing look. "We got the movie deal," he said simply. "And all the fame and fortune that follows that. They'll be airing reruns of our show till the cows come home and we'll get royalties from the show and the movie for a long time to come."

"Meanwhile," I said, "we heard through the grapevine that Rick's show is on the bubble."

"On the bubble?"

"Likely to get canceled," Gilley told her.

"But what would stealing Oruç's dagger get him?"

"Ratings," I said. "Rick likes to call himself the demon slayer. He learned from us that magnets can bring down even the nastiest spooks, and he's actually locked up one or two of the nastier ones. If he unleashed Oruç's demon here and caused a panic, he could swoop in and be the big hero. Especially if he had possession of the dagger itself."

Olivera nodded. "Okay, so we've got motive. What about opportunity? Where's Rick Lavinia based?"

Gilley smiled. "Right here in Boston, baby."

"Is he in town right now?" she pressed.

Gilley began typing on Sullivan's computer, and we waited for him to say something, but after a few moments all he did was drop his jaw. "No. Way."

"What?" I asked.

Gil swiveled the screen around. "There's no mention

of where Rick is right now," he said. "But his Instagram posted *this* from him yesterday morning."

I moved over to look closely at the photo. My heart began to thud in my chest when I saw that it was a photo taken from fairly far away of a building we'd been in the day before and knew intimately. The caption read, "Got notice that this abandoned apartment house is crazy haunted. Might have to check it out soon."

"Ashworth Commons," I said, honestly shocked that Rick would be so brazen.

Olivera had stepped forward to look at the photo too. "Now, *that's* interesting," she said. "But also odd, don't you think? I mean, he says that he got some sort of notice about it. That place *is* crazy haunted. Could someone have tipped him off about it?"

I shrugged. "It's possible, but isn't it sort of too big of a coincidence? I mean, Rick has means, motive, and now we know he's had opportunity. What more do we need?"

"A smoking dagger would be nice," Olivera said. "Okay, I'll dig into his background a little in the morning, see if I can't find out where he is at the moment at least."

Turning back to Gilley, I said, "Is there anything on Sullivan's computer connecting him to Rick?"

"None that I could find," he said. "He had his personal e-mail on here as well as his corporate one, but nothing looks suspicious, and I sifted through his deleted e-mails too."

"Then do you think everything was arranged by

phone?" I asked, hoping maybe Olivera could get Sullivan's phone records.

"It looks like . . . ," Gilley began, before his voice trailed off and he stared off into space for a moment. "Hold on," he said. Typing furiously again, he said, "Well, would you look at that!"

"What?" I said, moving toward the desk to peer at the screen he'd just swiveled around to me. "It's a draft of an e-mail."

Gilley nodded. "Yes! But *read* it, M.J.!"

I did—out loud so that Olivera could hear it. "Come at midnight. You'll have the place until five a.m. I've turned off the motion sensors. Use the back door. My code is seven-two-one-four." I cocked my head after reading it. "That's it for the message, but I'm not sure how this points us to the perp. Sullivan never sent the e-mail."

"He didn't have to," Gilley said. "The draft was last saved a week ago. All the killer had to do was log into this e-mail account and look up the draft. Sullivan could've easily edited the draft later to something totally innocuous and no one would've ever been the wiser."

I squinted at the screen again. "There's an address in the 'To' field. Two-kittens-and-a-canary at gmail dot com."

"That's Sullivan's mother's e-mail address," Gil told me. "Again, the museum director was really careful. If anybody peeked into this file on his personal e-mail account, they would've thought it was just some random message to his mom, or, if they were suspicious, he could've claimed he'd been drafting an e-mail to his mom which got interrupted and he never sent it out."

"Wow," I said. "Gil, do you think Sullivan would've thought this up on his own?"

"I doubt it," Gilley said. "His computer skills weren't the greatest. I think it's more likely that someone told him how to set it up. And Rick Lavinia is fairly savvy on the computer. He's got all the social media accounts up and humming, and he monitors and posts them himself. I also think that, at one point in his past before he started ghostbusting, he was a graphic designer, so this communicating through a draft on an e-mail wouldn't be a big leap for him."

"Is there any way to back-trace exactly who logged in to Sullivan's e-mail remotely?"

"I can try to trace it through the IP address," Gil said. "It could work."

"Cool." Leaning my head back against the wall and closing my eyes, I thought I'd just get a few minutes of sleep.

"M.J.?" Gilley suddenly said.

"Yeah?" I said, jolting awake again.

"Come here and look at this!"

I got up and moved to the desk, and Olivera did too. Gil had pulled up the draft of the e-mail again, and the former message was gone. The one there now was being typed out even while we watched.

I will destroy you. I will destroy everything you love. Everything you hold dear. Everything you are. Everything you wanted to become. You will all die and there's nothing you can do to stop me.

And then the cursor on the page moved to the top of the e-mail and clicked the delete button, and the draft was gone.

Hours later I crept through the door to my condo on tiptoe. Gilley was doing his koala thing again, his hand planted squarely on my back as I unlocked the door with my new key. He'd refused to go home to his condo, insisting on staying with me until we got the dagger back. Truth be told, I was a little happy he was sticking so close. It was one less person I had to worry about if they were out of my sight.

Heath stirred as we came through the door. "Em?" he said groggily as I walked over to the sofa where he lay.

"I'm here," I said, sitting on the floor next to the sofa to drink in the sight of him. Banged up though he was, he was still the most gorgeous man I'd ever seen.

"What time is it?"

"It's early."

Heath sat up and cupped the side of his head with his hand. "Ow," he said, then blinked in the light that Gilley had just turned on. "Hey," he said to Gil. Then, "Those are some mean-looking welts on your forehead, buddy. What happened to you?"

Gil shook his head. I'd told him to let me do the talking.

Heath's brow furrowed and then he turned to look at the clock on the cable box. It read five a.m. He then focused on me. "Em?" he said, smoothing a lock of my hair. "You look like you had a rough night too. How about you don't spare me any of the details?"

I laid my head on the sofa cushion. I'd gotten maybe half an hour of sleep. I was so tired I didn't think I could force out a paragraph, much less a long story with all the details. "Can I tell you in a few hours?"

Heath stroked my hair. He didn't say anything and I had a feeling he was looking at Gilley like he needed to start talking.

"She needs some rest," Gil said. "And so do I, but I can give you the highlights after M.J. goes to bed."

I picked my head up. Letting Gilley tell Heath about the night we had was super risky. He tended to over-exaggerate the scary parts, and I didn't want Heath to freak out that we'd come so close to getting ourselves filleted alive by a nine-foot-tall demon. "It's better if I tell you," I said wearily.

Heath stared at me for a good minute. "Which demon came at you tonight?"

"Oruç's."

"Shit, Em!" Heath said, sitting straight up and looking like he was ready to take on the demon all by his lonesome. "Where?"

"The museum," Gil said. "Olivera took us there to check out the crime scene."

The muscles along Heath's jawline bunched and he visibly looked like he was trying to control his anger. "You guys went there without me?"

I sighed. "It's not like you could've contributed anything, babe. I mean, you *did* get shot in the head and all."

"You couldn't have waited?" he asked me. His tone wasn't accusing; it was more . . . disappointed.

"No," I said. "We couldn't. We had to check it out, and honestly, I'm glad we did, because now we know what we're dealing with."

"What?" Heath said.

"Someone who wants to hurt us really, really bad."

"We didn't know that before?"

"Oh, we did, we just didn't know the lengths he was willing to go. Anyway, we're okay, we learned a lot, and we'll fill you in just as soon as I've had three hours to sleep."

With that I pushed myself to my feet and shuffled to the bedroom. I wasn't surprised that Heath followed right behind me. I shrugged out of my jeans and my sweater and crawled under the covers in the shirt I'd worn to the museum. Screw it. I was too tired to get into my pj's.

Heath went around the bed and got in on the other side, scooting over to wrap me in his arms. I fell asleep in seconds.

The next thing I knew it was eleven a.m. I jolted awake, took one look at the clock on the nightstand, and groaned. Then I looked around the bedroom for my husband. Heath wasn't there, but I heard hushed voices coming from the kitchen. "Dammit!" I swore. I just knew that Gilley was flapping his gums, freaking out my husband and making himself look like the hero.

Quickly I got into a pair of sweats and rushed out to the kitchen. Gilley stood at the counter, serving Heath a huge omelet complete with hash browns and toast. My stomach grumbled. "Traitor," I said looking down at it. Where was a good bout of morning sickness when I needed it?

"Hey!" Gilley said, spying me in the doorway. "You're finally up."

I shuffled over to the kitchen and reached for a coffee cup. "Ah-ah," Gil said. "No caffeine for you! I brought up some of Michel's green tea from downstairs. You can have a cup of that."

I glared at Gilley. Hard. "Why're you so chipper?"

He held up his coffee mug and smiled meanly. "I've had my coffee."

I was tired and cranky enough to kick him in the "coffee cups" but settled for snatching up the green tea and moving to the sink with my mug.

"Gil told me what happened," Heath said. I felt the tension in my shoulders ratchet up another degree.

"Great," I muttered.

"I didn't embellish," Gil said. "I just gave him a few highlights. Like, I told him that the demon appeared while we were in the exhibit, but that we were packing so many magnets that it shrank back from us and we chased it all the way across the museum with our spikes before we saw it vanish, and then we saw a guy we couldn't identify leave the building out the back door. That's when we found the door to Sullivan's office and let ourselves in."

My grumpy mood lessened, and I offered Gilley a grateful smile. "Thanks for filling him in," I said.

"Yeah, like I believe Gilley's version," Heath scoffed.

I cleared my throat. "For once, Heath, Gil did not embellish."

Heath considered me skeptically, and I knew he thought I was hiding something, but I wasn't about to elaborate. "Is that as far as you got in the telling of what happened last night, Gil?"

"No, I told him all the rest too."

"Ah," I said a little disappointed. "So, we're all up to speed."

"Unless there's anything you want to elaborate on," Heath said.

I took my brewed cup of green tea out of the microwave. "No. I think we're good."

Gilley set a plate down at the counter and pointed to it. "Eat," he ordered. "I made you a salmon, spinach, feta cheese omelet—all great pregnancy foods."

I sat down next to Heath, ready to tuck into my omelet, but the smell of it hit me and in a moment I was running for the bathroom. As soon as I was done having my little bout of morning sickness, I wandered back to the counter, where both Gil and Heath were staring at me in alarm. "You okay, babe?" Heath asked.

"I am now," I said, tucking into the omelet with gusto. I'd gone from totally nauseous to totally famished in about six seconds. Flat.

I ate with relish, consuming the entire two-egg omelet almost without pause. When I was done I sighed contentedly and pushed my plate away, only to find Heath and Gilley once again staring wide-eyed at me. "What?"

"Nothing," Heath said, averting his eyes to focus on his coffee.

Gilley inched forward and slowly removed my plate. "Thanks for leaving the china," he snickered.

"I was hungry!" I snapped. Then I realized I'd spoken rather harshly. Lord, was I really going to turn into one of those pregnancy clichés? Feeling bad, I tried to form an apology, but my gaze landed on the remains of Heath's breakfast still on his plate. "You gonna finish that?"

He scooted the plate over to me with a chuckle. "Have at it, darlin'."

I polished off Heath's breakfast, then had Gilley make me a smoothie. While I sipped at it, we discussed the case. "Are we really considering Rick Lavinia for this?" Heath asked me.

He had none of the same animosity for Rick that Gilley and I held. I'd thought Rick was a pompous jerk and disliked his "techniques," and Gilley of course had gotten into it with him in their online feud, but Heath had always had a note of sympathy for Rick. Maybe it was a "bro" thing. "I honestly wasn't sold on him as the killer until I saw the photo on his Instagram of the Ashworth Commons," I said. "That's just too big a coincidence for me. And, it'd be just like Rick to taunt us with something like that."

"Did you see him at the exhibit the night of the premiere?" Heath asked.

"No," I said. "But we were a little distracted, remember?"

"Yeah," Heath said. "But if he was there, don't you think one of the fans would've noticed him? Rick's pretty recognizable."

Rick was a good-looking guy, and he had very distinctive hair, black roots with white tips, and he wore it spiky. "He could've been wearing a hat or some kind of a disguise," Gilley said. "I mean, our fans went to the exhibit looking for stuff related to us, and when you two showed up, they only had eyes for you. It wouldn't have been too difficult for him to blend in and go unnoticed if he put on glasses and a hat."

"Plus," I added, "Rick would know how to impersonate a Hollywood producer well enough not to raise Gilley's suspicions."

Gil nodded enthusiastically. Using air quotes he said, "'Bradley' really sold it with the name-dropping and studio-speak. He sounded legit."

"Is Rick even in town, Gil?" Heath asked, obviously still skeptical.

"Olivera is going to check into it," Gil said.

Which reminded me of something. "Were you able to trace the IP address for the person who logged into Sullivan's e-mail account?" I asked Gil.

He nodded. "Yes. It routed to an address here in Boston. I sent a text to Olivera to call me as soon as she got up, but she hasn't yet."

That made me a little nervous. "We sent her home with plenty of magnets, right?"

"We did," Gil assured me. "She's probably still sleeping, M.J. Don't worry. She'll call."

I'd worry until she called, but I didn't say it. "What about Ayden?" I asked. "Have we been able to get in touch with him to see how he's doing?"

Gilley eyed his watch. "It's eight forty-five his time," he said. "Think that's too early to call his hospital room?"

"Nah," I said. "No one can sleep well in a hospital. Let's call."

"Right," Gil said, and pulled out his cell. After placing the call, he laid the smartphone on the counter and hit the speaker function.

"Hello?" a gravelly voice sounded after the third ring.

"Ayden?" I said. "It's M.J."

"Hey, lady," Ayden said. "You okay?"

"I'm better than you, apparently," I told him, wishing he were closer so that we could visit him.

"Yeah, somebody got the drop on me," he said. "The son of a bitch."

"How're you feeling?" I asked.

"Great," he deadpanned. "Never better."

"We heard you had some cracked ribs and a punctured lung," Gil said.

"Hey, Gilley," Ayden said. "Yeah. The lung was just a small puncture. Doesn't even hurt anymore, but the son of a bitch really did a number on my ankle. It got twisted up pretty good. They think I tore a ligament and they've been talking surgery all morning."

I winced. As a runner, I knew that tearing a ligament was sometimes worse than breaking a bone. "Sorry to hear that, buddy," Heath said.

"Is that Heath?"

"It is," he said. "We're all here."

"Wish I was there with you," he said. "What's the word on the dagger?"

"It's still out there," I said. "And someone has unleashed the kraken."

"Oh, man," he said. "I was afraid of that. Anybody hurt?"

Heath, Gilley, and I exchanged a pensive look. Finally I said, "No. Still only the one dead."

"And you're all okay?"

"We are," I said.

"Barely," Gilley muttered.

"So Oruç's demon came after you," Ayden said. He'd heard Gilley.

I shot Gil a stern look and said, "It did, but we handled it. The bigger problem we're dealing with right now, Ayden, is that Oruç has apparently opened up a portal big enough to let through at least some of the other spooks we've managed to shut down into the lower realms over the past few years. We've had encounters with three other nasties in just the past twenty-four hours."

"Which ones?" Ayden asked. I'd forgotten that he'd been following our cable show for years.

"The Grim Widow, Hatchet Jack, and I'm fairly certain another spook named Sy the Slayer paid me a visit two nights ago."

"Plus Oruç's demon?"

"Yes," I said.

Ayden sighed. "What a time to get mugged," he said. "You guys need me and I'm stuck in this hospital bed."

"I'm not sure what you could do here," Gilley told him. "Except run for your life, and with that bum ankle . . ."

I shot Gilley another stern look.

"What?" he said.

I made a dismissive motion with my hand. "Anyway, Ayden, we think someone planned this whole thing starting about three weeks ago. It looks like the producer who called Gilley to arrange for the display of the dagger was an impostor. It also looks like there was at least some cooperation between the killer and the victim. We think we've found evidence of a five-thousand-dollar payoff in exchange for access to the exhibit hall to swap out all of Gilley's magnets, and that led to the killer having access to the alarm code that would let him come back to steal the dagger."

"Were you able to trace where the payoff came from?"

"Yeah," Gil said. "Some guy named Todd Tolliver. We're convinced it's an alias."

There was silence on the other end of the line, and then Ayden said, "Son of a bitch."

"What?" Heath and I said together.

"Just a little over three weeks ago I took a case investigating a hit-and-run for a couple of parents who lost their nineteen-year-old son on his way home from Stanford. His name was Todd Tolliver."

I blinked. We all did, taking that in for a second. "Did anybody know about the case you were working?" I asked.

"Yeah," Ayden said. "Probably lots of people. I was able to track down the car and the person responsible, and the news did a story on it."

"So if this guy knew about the case you were

working on, Ayden, then maybe you weren't mugged at random. Maybe someone wanted to cause you permanent harm."

"That's what I was just thinking, Heath," Ayden said.

"He's playing with us," I said. "Taunting us. He's letting us know that he's one step ahead of us at every turn. If we start digging, all we'll find are the many ways he's already outmaneuvered us." I then explained to Ayden our theory about the killer and thief being Rick Lavinia.

"You know he called me not long after your show started, right?" Ayden said.

"Wait, what?" I said. "He's spoken to you?"

"Yeah. You two were credited with helping to solve the murders at the Drake Hotel, and I think Rick was looking for some dirt on you. He wanted to expose you as a couple of frauds, but he got nothing from me but high praise."

"That's how he knew about the dagger!" Gilley said. "He was researching the Drake murders and figured it out!"

Heath caught my eye. He offered me a look that suggested he apologized for being skeptical of Rick Lavinia as the primary suspect. "He probably wanted you out of the way, Ayden, because you would've remembered that phone call and probably pointed us right to him as a suspect."

"Still," Ayden said, "it doesn't explain how Rick stole the dagger, murdered Sullivan, then made it all the way to San Francisco to get the jump on me."

"He had help," I said. Then I turned to Gilley. "Hey, didn't you say that you spoke with Bradley's assistant a couple of times? Maybe he's part of this too."

"The assistant was a woman, M.J.," Gilley said.

"Ah," I said. "Any chance the person who attacked you was a woman?"

"Maybe a woman gorilla," Ayden said with a chuckle. "All I remember is getting hit by someone *big*."

"Doesn't mean that Lavinia doesn't have more than one accomplice," Heath pointed out.

"True," Ayden said. "Still, that kind of thing takes money. Does he have the cash to support all this?"

I glanced at Heath and Gilley. They both shrugged. "We don't know, Ayden. Maybe?"

"It'd be worth checking out his financials, but you'd need a warrant to dig into them, and for that you'd need some pretty compelling evidence that Lavinia is your guy. Right now, I don't think you have enough," Ayden said. It sounded like he was about to say more, but at that moment there was the sound of other voices in the background. "Crap," he said. "Listen, the doctor's here to talk about my ankle. I gotta go for now, but call me if anything new develops, okay?"

We promised we would and said our good-byes.

"I seriously think we should ditch this whole thing and go on an extended vacation," Gil said into the stunned silence that followed.

Heath eyed him seriously. "If I thought that alone would keep us safe, Gil, I'd be the one buying our plane tickets."

Gil's phone rang and I thought it might be Ayden

again, but it turned out to be Olivera. "Did you have a chance to check out Rick Lavinia?" I asked her.

"I did," she said. "But I don't have a lot of info. He's got one arrest on his record for a drunk and disorderly. He got that in Georgia last year, probably while filming for his show. I can't find an address for him in Boston; his last known here was three years ago, and there's someone else living in the apartment he once rented. If he owns property, it could be in a trust and I'd be unable to locate it unless I had the name of the trust, or, if he lives with someone, then the house could be in their name. His driver's license still lists the old address, though. The only point of contact for him is his agent, and when I reached out to him, all he'd tell me was that Rick was in town on an investigation which is supposedly a tightly guarded secret, and he was unwilling to share the address with me unless I had a subpoena or a warrant."

"Wow," I said. "The agent's a little touchy."

"He is but it might be for good reason. His agent said that a few of Rick's fans have tried to crash his locations before by posing as the police," she said. "He said he wouldn't tell me anything over the phone but he would relay a message if I wanted to leave one."

"Did you?" Heath asked.

"Nope. I figured it'd be better not to tip our hand that we're looking for him."

I drummed my fingers on the counter. "Don't you think the agent will call Rick anyway and tell him that you called?"

"He might, but maybe not. He made it sound like

Rick was totally unavailable to anyone for the next forty-eight hours."

"That's more than long enough to unleash hell on us," Gil moaned.

"It's also more than enough time to track his ass down and get the dagger back," I countered.

"Anyway," Olivera said, to get us back on track, "Gil, I can't find the paper that I wrote down the residence on for the IP address you gave me. Can you give it to me again?"

"Sure," Gil said, lifting the phone to consult it. After a moment he said, "Four-ten Forrest Street."

"Great," she said, "I'll check it out. You guys stay put."

She hung up abruptly, and once again we were all left to stare at one another. "She's crazy if she thinks we're not going to meet her there, right?" I said.

"What?!" Gil exclaimed. "No way, M.J.! Rick might be there, lying in wait!"

I nodded. "Yes, Gil . . . *with* the dagger!"

"Oh, shit," Heath said, sliding off his chair and moving around to the kitchen. "We gotta go!"

Gilley stood there with his mouth open, as if he couldn't believe we were dashing off to meet Olivera. "Are you people *crazy*?"

I shoved his magnet-lined vest into his chest. "Get dressed or stay here and take your chances with whatever might show up, Gil."

He paled. "I'm moving you to the table at the back of the reception hall with Michel's crazy uncle Max and his flighty sister!"

I flashed him a toothy smile. "Promises, promises."

Heath tapped my shoulder as Gilley and I glared at each other, and I got busy getting ready. Gil could come or he could stay, but Heath and I had to get to Olivera before she went all guns-a-blazing again.

As I was pushing my foot into my boot, I saw Gilley angrily duck into his vest. He was muttering pretty good under his breath too. "Maybe you should drive," Heath said to me.

I grabbed the keys from the dish by the sink. "Good call, honey."

We arrived at the address that Gilley had tracked to the IP address from Sullivan's computer and I was surprised to find a nice, fairly well-kept house with yellow siding, freshly painted shutters, and a wreath on the front door. "This the place?" I asked Gil as I pulled the SUV to a stop in front of the house.

"Yep," he replied. "At least, according to the address I got from Sullivan's computer."

I looked around for Olivera, but there was no sign of her. The driveway did have a car parked in it, though.

We stared at the residence for a little while, waiting and watching in silence as my windshield wipers swiped back and forth against the steady rain that'd be with us for the next couple of days. "Think someone's home?" I said.

Gil pointed over my shoulder. "There's a light on in the front. And a car parked in the drive. Odds are pretty good that someone's home."

The door to the house suddenly opened, and an elderly woman with a hunched back, blue hair, a housecoat, and brown slippers stepped out. Opening up an umbrella, she proceeded to walk down the front steps. As she shuffled along, she eyed us a little suspiciously before heading to her mailbox to retrieve the mail.

"Wow," Heath said drily. "Rick looks taller on TV."

"Ha!" Gil chuckled. "And younger. The miracles they work with stage makeup."

I frowned. "Seriously, you guys, will you quit it?" We needed to keep our focus, because even though this old woman had come out of the house, it didn't mean someone else wasn't inside with Oruç's dagger. "Gil," I said, thinking of a possible connection between the old woman and our prime suspect. "Did Rick ever mention his mom?"

"Not that I know of. But I never watched past the third season, which, frankly, was beyond boring after Rick got his ass tossed down the stairs." Gilley chuckled again at the memory. "So epic!"

"Shhh!" I told him, staring at the woman. Her body language seemed off to me, but that could've been because we were parked across the street from her house, engine running and watching her every move.

Before heading back inside, the old woman made a point to pause and frown at us.

"Come on," I told the boys as I got out of the car to trot over to her. "Excuse me," I said, holding my arm up over my head to block the rain. "Do you live here?"

"I do," she said, clutching the handle of her umbrella.

"I'm sorry to disturb you, but we're looking for someone. Does anybody else live with you?"

Her eyes narrowed. "Why do you want to know that?" she asked me. I realized that I probably should've introduced myself before asking about who lived in the house with her.

"Sorry. I'm Mary Jane Whitefeather, and that's my husband," I said, turning to point to Heath, who was coming up behind me. "And that's my best friend, Gilley, in the car."

She shrank a little away from me. "I don't know who you are," she said. "And I don't know why you're asking about who lives here."

I tried to think of a quick explanation as to why we needed to know but couldn't readily think of one. "A friend of ours is in trouble, and he gave us this address to pick him up, but I don't see him anywhere around."

"He gave you my address?" she said, utterly confused.

"Yeah," I said. "I think he was just trying to text me an approximate location. He must've seen your house number and used that to let us know where he is."

"I haven't seen him," she said.

"Maybe someone else in your home saw him?" I said. "I mean, if you'd like to go in and ask the other members of your household if they've seen a guy, about five-ten, with brown hair, walking around . . ."

The old woman backed even farther away from me. I'd spooked her.

In desperation I said, "Does Rick Lavinia live here?"

"I think you should go," she said, pointing to my car. "This is private property and you're trespassing."

"Okay," I said, holding up my hands in surrender. "I'm really sorry to have disturbed you. Thank you, ma'am."

With that, I turned and grabbed Heath's hand. He hadn't heard most of the conversation, thank God, because I'd really botched it. "Does she live alone?" he asked me as we headed back to the car.

"I can't tell," I said. "And now I've spooked her."

"So what do we do?" he asked.

"We head back to the car and wait to hear or spot Olivera."

As we were just about to get into my SUV, another car pulled around us and into the driveway. I glanced at it, wondering if it was Olivera, but the person who got out of the car wasn't her; it was a man in his mid-forties or thereabouts, with thin brown hair and a mustache.

For two seconds I wondered if we were wrong about Rick, and this was the guy who'd been behind the theft and the murder, but then something else about him caught my attention. I knew him.

Heath motioned with his chin toward the man. "Isn't that . . . ?"

"Murdock," I whispered. "The security guy from the museum!"

At the same moment we recognized him, he must've recognized us, because he paused as he was walking toward the house, did a double take, then quickly fumbled his keys, which fell to the ground.

"Yo!" I said, as I thought about what he'd done, the danger he'd put innocent lives in, and especially the danger his actions represented to my unborn child. "Murdock! Where's the dagger?"

Murdock hastened to bend over and retrieve his

keys, but they slipped again from his grasp, and all of a sudden he just left them there and bolted. Heath took off after him like a rocket, and I gave chase too.

The three of us tore down the street, getting pelted by the rain, which made it tough to see. Murdock had a good lead on us, but Heath runs like he was born to it. I watched him pull away from me, his stride so smooth it looked effortless. His arms pumped steadily, his legs moved so fast they were a blur, and he quickly closed the distance between him and Murdock. A few more strides and he'd tackle him, I was sure, but the security guard had a trick up his sleeve neither one of us saw coming. He wheeled to the side, grabbed an empty garbage can that was left at the curbside, and hurled it at Heath.

My husband must've been focused only on closing the distance between him and Murdock, because he was slow to react, and the garbage can struck him in the shins. With a grunt of pain, he went down. I cried out because Heath had hit the pavement hard, but he rolled to the side, grabbed his knee for a moment, then struggled to his feet. I reached him just as he took one limping stride forward. "Ohmigod! Are you okay?" I asked, coming up next to him.

"That *asshole!*" Heath growled through gritted teeth.

Meanwhile, Murdock was regaining his lead, and he ran as fast as he could down the street, taking a sharp right at the corner. Heath took another sort of limp-hop and groaned.

"Honey! I think you're hurt!"

"I'm fine!" he told me, hopping a few more steps as

he tried to walk off the pain, and then he began to jog a little as I kept pace with him. We were still losing ground to Murdock, but at least we were keeping him in our sights. "There!" I said, pointing to Murdock as Heath began to pick up speed.

At the moment that Heath began to regain his stride, edging away from me, a car came around the corner and pulled up next to me. "M.J.!"

I turned to look and was shocked to see Olivera behind the wheel and Gilley sitting next to her.

I pointed ahead of me toward Murdock. "He went that way!"

"Get in!" Olivera yelled.

I slowed as she did and yanked open the back door even before she'd come to a stop, which, honestly, she never really did. By this time Heath had worked through the pain of his fall and was sprinting all out after Murdock, who had just ducked down a side street lined with commercial-looking buildings.

Olivera pressed down hard on the accelerator and took off after him. We caught up to Heath, who was baring his teeth and running with a speed I'd never seen from him. He appeared mindless of the three of us in the car and just kept chasing the security guard.

At one point, Olivera had to punch the brakes to allow Heath to cut in front of her and chase Murdock down the alley behind the commercial buildings. "Don't lose him!" Gilley yelled at Olivera.

"Shut it, Gillespie!" Olivera said, turning the wheel forcefully to get around Heath and follow Murdock without hitting my husband.

As we made the side street, the car bounced hard—the alley was unpaved and heavily potholed. Olivera had no choice but to slow her speed or she'd wreck her frame, and Heath passed right by us as he gained even more ground on Murdock. The alley then narrowed and it became impossible to pass Heath. We had to settle for driving behind him and trying to follow Murdock's movements.

At last Murdock reached another alleyway that cut back through to the commercial side of the street, and he turned sharply once again. Heath was maybe twenty yards behind him. We pulled up to the narrow alleyway and considered our options.

For me, it was a no-brainer. I popped the lock and pushed my way out of the car, rounding to the back of it, then chasing after my husband. Behind me I heard the roar of an engine. Olivera was going to try to go around the building and cut Murdock off on the other side. Good.

Heath blocked out all signs of Murdock racing away from us, so I just followed Heath and waited to see him launch himself at the guard to bring him down. But abruptly, Heath stopped and pulled open a door to the building on our right. I determined that Murdock must've gone inside to try to evade us. The door banged shut after Heath went in. I reached it five seconds later and pulled on the handle. It opened and I dashed inside.

I quickly discovered that I'd run into an auto mechanic's garage and nearly came up short when I saw all the mechanics who'd stopped their work to watch as first

Murdock ran past them, then my husband; and then they all turned to look at me.

Murdock seemed to have a good understanding of the layout of the place, because he zigzagged around cars, carts, and tires to reach the front door and pull that open too. Heath weaved, dodged, and jumped over the same obstacles as Murdock, but he was slowed by them more than Murdock had been.

I stopped gawking and gave chase again too, following right behind Heath and trying to mimic his route.

Heath reached the front door and pulled it open to head back outside after Murdock, but as I watched, I saw my husband go down *again*! And then I realized that that son of a bitch Murdock had put another trash can in his path, right in front of the doorway.

I silently vowed to strangle Murdock with my bare hands if Heath needed medical attention. When I reached him he was on his side, clutching his hip. "I'm gonna *kill* that son of a bitch!" he groaned as I kicked the can out of the way and bent to help Heath.

"Babe," I said, panting for air. "Can . . . you . . . walk?"

Heath let go of his hip and stumbled to his feet. He lifted his chin and stared at Murdock, who was running steadily and without slowing toward a building across the street. One I recognized. "Oh, *shit*!" I swore.

The building in question was none other than Ashworth Commons. I hadn't realized we were so close to it, but Murdock appeared to know it well. He didn't waver as he crossed the street, heading right for the side entrance.

At the moment he leaped from the street to the sidewalk, Olivera's car rounded the corner with a screech. She hadn't beaten Murdock, who'd taken the shortcut through the garage, but she did see where he was going. An oncoming car stopped her from turning left and cutting Murdock off, and he made it to the side entrance of the building before any of us could really react. Once he got inside, I just knew that all hell was certain to break loose.

Literally.

Chapter 14

Olivera pulled up next to Ashworth Commons as I finished helping Heath limp across the street. "You've *got* to be kidding me!" Olivera said when she got out and stood looking up at the building.

"This day just gets worse and worse!" Gilley whined as he too stared up at the four-story building.

"Why the hell did he go in there?" Olivera demanded, rounding on me and Heath. She seemed genuinely angry to be back here. I figured it was a coping mechanism, because she had to be freaking scared. Just like I was.

"I think the dagger is hidden here," I said. "Somehow, Murdock heard about this place and decided it was a good idea to stash the dagger here."

"Did you post about this site on our fan page?" Heath asked Gilley.

Gil copped a defensive attitude. "I needed some new

material!" he snapped. "You guys weren't doing anything interesting for the longest time, and this was the only thing I had to work with!"

"Great," Heath said, turning away from Gilley dismissively, which was a bit unlike him. Heath was usually more patient with Gil than I was.

"Let's focus on the problem at hand," I said loudly, trying to remind everyone here about the mission to get the dagger back. "If Murdock got into the building, we can assume he's headed for high ground, which is probably all the way up to the fourth floor. Between all of us, we've got enough armor to go in after him without exposing ourselves to any undue harm."

"Can I just remind you of the *freak show* that took place at the museum last night?" Olivera snapped. "That demon *thing* came after us, and you two were covered in magnets!"

"True," I said. "But what choice do we have, Detective?"

Her lips pressed together and she stared at me for a long moment. To show her I wasn't backing down, I squared my shoulders and began to move toward the side entrance. "Anyway," I said over my shoulder, "we've got even more armor with us today, so lock and load, people!"

Heath fell into step next to me and I waited nervously for Olivera and Gilley to come with us. I wasn't completely convinced they would, but we had no choice. Our only chance of getting the dagger back was to apprehend the person who'd stolen it. If we let him get away, then none of us would ever be safe and the body count would only rise, and it was likely to include someone I loved.

Heath and I marched steadily forward, and finally, as we reached the other side of the street, out of the corner of my eye I saw Olivera come even with me. And then I felt Gilley's hand on my back.

Olivera put her hand out to stop us, however, right as we reached the side entrance and Heath pulled his set of keys from his inside vest pocket. "I think I should call for backup," she said. Her skin was pale, and her eyes wide. She was seriously scared, and it was no wonder; she'd had only two encounters with the supernatural, and both of those had nearly been deadly. For a cop who was taught that she could fell any threat with good aim and enough bullets, this new reality had to be insanely intimidating.

"No backup," Heath said to her, subtly tucking his long hair behind his ear to show her the bandage covering his head wound. "You can't call a bunch of cops in here and expect them to resist the temptation to shoot up the place once a demon appears, Detective. They'll do way more harm than good."

Olivera was breathing heavily now; I felt she might be on the verge of panic. Reaching for her hand, I put two of my spikes in it and said, "These work. They do, Chris. You're going to go in there and likely face a knife fight, but it's one you can win. Keep one of those clenched in your fists at all times, and if something comes at you, then stab it for all you're worth. Otherwise, stay behind Heath and me. We'll be on point."

Olivera gripped the spikes in her fists, her knuckles

whitening around them. "Yeah," she said. "Okay." And then she seemed to think of something else. "My uncle's a priest," she said. "I could call him."

If the situation weren't so dire I would've laughed out loud. "He won't be able to help us in there," I said to her. "Exorcisms need to be conducted by priests seasoned in the ritual and who know what they're doing. Otherwise, heading in there with only a cross and some holy water is likely to get your uncle killed."

Olivera gulped audibly. "Jesus," she said.

"We'll be okay," I assured her. "We will."

I then turned away before she could think of some other plan to stall us from going inside. We needed to get to Murdock before he spent too much time in the company of the dagger. Heath inserted his key into the door. It unlocked and he held up a finger as he inched his torso forward through the doorway to look around. Then he motioned for us to follow him.

We walked into the first-floor hallway and I was brought up short by the feeling of the place. Malice permeated the very air of the building, and I swore I hadn't felt it until I'd hit the fourth floor the day before. "They've taken over," I whispered in Heath's ear. He nodded.

Goose pimples lined my forearms, and the hairs on the back of my neck stood on end. Wicked things haunted these halls.

Heath took the lead again and motioned for us to follow him single file. He walked us over to the stairwell and I felt the evil energy ratchet up a notch. My heart pounded as we began to climb the stairs, all of us on tiptoe. On the landing of the third floor, my palms started to sweat and my breathing became labored. I paused and tugged on Heath's vest to stop him. He turned and I pointed to myself so that he could see I was struggling to keep my fear in check.

Fear is a really bad thing when you're going up against a demon. It's not just that it can make you panic and do something stupid, like freeze in place, or run into a wall as you're trying to escape. It's more that fear is like blood in the water, attracting all manner of man-eating monsters directly to you.

If you ever come up against a nasty spook in close quarters, don't be scared—which I know sounds ridiculous, but you'd be doing yourself a solid to calm the hell down before getting the hell out.

To calm myself down, I flattened myself against the wall of the stairwell and took deep breaths. Olivera was looking at me like I was nuts, but I pointed to her and whispered, "We need to set aside our fear before we face them."

She was trembling from head to toe by now, and her own breathing was heavy and quick. She shook her head at me. No way was she going to be able to set aside her terror. And by the looks of Gilley, who was clutching at least ten spikes to his chest, neither was he.

At last I'd taken enough deep breaths to feel a bit less freaked-out and was about to push away from the wall when I felt something drip onto my forehead. I wiped at it and happened to look at my fingertips, which were smeared with blood. "Oh, no," I whispered, slowly lifting my gaze up and up to the fourth floor.

All the effort to calm myself vanished as I startled at the sight of Murdock, pressed against the railing of the stairwell, his eyes sightless and his torso dripping blood down onto me.

Perched above him on the railing itself like an ugly raven was the Grim Widow, gleefully snickering at me as I took in the sight of both her and the dead security guard. She licked her black lips and revealed jagged teeth when she smiled wide.

"Em?" Heath said softly. I felt his hand on my shoulder. It was all I could do to point up the stairs toward Murdock's body, my hand shaking hard enough to cause tremors throughout my entire body.

Heath's head tilted up and he sucked in a breath at the same time as Olivera.

Gilley was the last to notice, and I know that because a full three seconds after Heath and Olivera reacted, Gilley began screaming.

That's when the Grim Widow launched herself off the railing and into the air. She spread her arms, and the rags for clothing she wore fluttered out while she fell down toward us like a giant, horrifying bat. Heath shoved me against the wall and put himself directly in her path. I saw him raise a spike as the Widow descended, hissing loudly as she came and baring her jagged teeth.

As I watched in stunned silence, his body tensed just before impact and she landed with a triumphant scream right on top of him, taking him down to the floor. I screamed too, because the sound of their crash was loud. The Widow covered Heath, her arms and legs thrashing and kicking at him. I was so shocked by what'd just happened that for a moment I couldn't move, but then Olivera darted over to the Widow and started driving her spike into the center of the spook's back.

The Widow screamed and her bony arm lashed out, striking Olivera so hard she flew back into the wall. Anger replaced fear in the center of my chest and I dived for the Widow. I got her around the waist and unleashed my rage. She rolled off my husband and took me with her, shrieking as I stabbed her with the spikes but cackling with hysterical laughter as well. It was maddening.

We rolled three times before I realized she was taking me toward the stairs. Too late I tried to stop the momentum she'd created and we fell onto the first stair together, with my head taking a terrible blow against the hard surface.

Gritting my teeth, I just continued to stab her, plunging my spikes into her bony back for all I was worth. I had no idea how she could take that much abuse, or how she could possibly hold on to me so tightly, as I was covered in magnets from head to toe.

We hit another stair and I took it on the shoulder. It was a slow roll down to the third, which was on my back, and then the fourth, which was on that same shoulder. I cried out and my right arm went numb with pain. I'd only gotten my breath back when we landed on yet another stair, which hit me in the ribs.

I didn't think I'd make it to bottom of the staircase before I blacked out from the pain. The strikes were too intense to bear, and just as I saw stars from yet another blow to the head, I felt something brace against my back, stopping the roll down. A moment later the Widow was doing a whole lot of screeching and not much cackling. And then she let go of me and scrambled away.

With stars still popping behind my eyes, I looked up to see Gilley there, teeth bared and a ferocious look on his face. Channeling his inner Sigourney, he roared, *"Get away from her, you bitch!"* It was then that I noticed him holding up his dukes, which were covered in steel-lined gloves, and in his right hand was one of his longest spikes.

The Widow spat at him as she backed away up the stairs, moving on all fours like a spider. I did my best to get to my knees without falling farther down. My head was pounding from the beating, and my sore ribs were protesting all the extra air I needed.

Somehow I managed to perch myself on my haunches next to Gilley while he continued to focus on the Widow.

She stopped backing up and hissed again, then darted a little forward, but Gilley got in a right hook and jabbed with the spike at her. She spun away hissing and screeching but began to come around again. That's when Gil stomped his foot and yelled, *"Do it and I'll gut you like a fish!"*

The Widow's eyes narrowed. She seemed to be considering his challenge. She reversed direction and backed up a few steps before stopping, that sinister smile reappearing. She now had the high ground, and I knew she was gonna come at us again. With significant effort I forced the numb fingers on my right hand to reach for the spike at my belt and shouted to Gil, "Brace yourself!"

No sooner did I get those words out than the Widow launched herself right at us. My entire focus was on her, but the synapses in my brain were firing at the speed of light. We were midway down the stairs to the second floor. She'd hit us with enough force to send us tumbling. One or both of us could end up with a broken neck.

Somehow I got to my feet before she hit, and grabbed Gilley's arm to pull him out of the way. The Widow landed on the stairs exactly where we'd just been, and she whipped toward us like a scorpion, with barred teeth and outstretched hands, ready to rip us to shreds. I raised my arm to strike at her with the spike, but I had no idea if I'd be fast enough to block her lunge.

And then . . . and then . . . in that pinnacle moment right before she struck, there was a sound that I cannot fully describe. It was primal—yet familiar—and when it reached my ears, my chest filled with hope and courage. It was one note . . . one beautifully rich, sweet note that seemed to blast to the farthest reaches of the building. Filling the space with its essence, it banished the cold, sinister atmosphere the deadly spirits that had come to haunt Ashworth Commons had brought with them. It was like sunshine after a storm, and my eyes misted in witness to its purity and strength.

I didn't realize at first where the source of the sound was, until my husband appeared high above us, in midair, descending the staircase after making a giant leap, and from somewhere deep inside him came a war cry that awakened his ancestors, who appeared from nowhere and everywhere. They lined the stairs, surrounded us, and closed in on the Widow.

She shrieked and tried to turn away, but Heath reached her before she could get far; landing on her as she had landed on him, he drove her into the stair where she stood and rode her down the rest of the steps like a skateboard. Not once did his voice break off from that one beautiful note.

I watched in awe as his long hair fluttered behind him, that distinctive white streak he'd gotten a few years back on another deadly encounter waving at me in triumph.

The Widow's density was starting to wane. She'd been as solid as any living soul only seconds before, with superhuman strength, but in the face of so many of Heath's ancestors, who effectively cut her off from her power source, she was no match.

She struggled underneath his weight, flailed her arms and legs, but she couldn't shake him. He rode her until they stopped. And then Heath's war cry went up one octave and I saw his elbow jerk and his fist went high and he plunged his stake into the center of the Grim Widow's chest.

And just like that—she vanished.

For many moments afterward, no one moved. Gil and I simply stared at Heath, whose chest was heaving and posture was stiff like that of a great warrior after a tremendous battle. He looked down to where the Widow had been, as if daring her to make a reappearance, but the change in atmosphere was so distinct that I knew he'd sent her back, somehow, to the lower realms.

"What. The hell. Was *that*?" Olivera said from the top of the stairs.

All three of us turned to stare up at her. She was looking down at us, but also all around the stairwell. "*That*, Detective, was my husband," I said, my heart bursting with pride and relief and even joy.

Heath smiled sideways at me as he came up the stairs. He was bleeding from a few various scratches, and the bandage covering his wound had come off, exposing his stitches and a little blood there too.

He reached us and came right to me; cupping my head with his hand, he said, "Are you okay?"

I nodded at first, but then shook my head and started crying big wet tears and tried to brush them off. "Pregnancy hormones," I said with a forced chuckle while wiping my cheeks.

The truth was, I was moved beyond words. Heath was this magnificent creature, this thing of absolute beauty, grace, and power. He was also kind, and good, and thoughtful, and sweet. He took care of me in a thousand ways, little and big. He understood me like no one else could, and shared an intuitive talent so rare that it set us apart from almost every single person we knew. And this magnificent person was mine.

He was just . . . mine.

I loved him with a magnitude that felt greater than something that could ever be quantified. It filled me and lifted me and moved me to tears that I couldn't hide and

I couldn't stop. They dribbled down my cheeks and my lip trembled and I had a hard time looking up at him because it almost hurt to feel that much for anyone.

"Aw, babe," he said, throwing down the spike in his hand to cup my face with both of his. "I know. Me too." And then he kissed me, and I shed myself in that moment. I left behind M. J. Holliday, the tough, serious, fiercely independent single person who just happened to be married, and I became half of something so much bigger and a thousand times more powerful.

And then Gilley cleared his throat. "Geez, you guys. Get a room."

Heath laughed and then so did I. He pulled me into his arms and held me tight, and so much of the past few minutes already felt more distant.

I heard Olivera's shoes on the stairs and I lifted my head from Heath's chest. "I'm glad you guys are having a laugh," she said, "but we've got a problem."

I sighed. "I know. We haven't gotten the dagger back yet."

She seemed puzzled by my response and pointed up. "No," she said. "Him."

With a jolt I remembered Murdock, and I lifted my gaze to the fourth floor, where the security guard's lifeless body was still pressed up against the railing.

"Crap," Gil said. "What the hell are we gonna do about him?"

"You'll have to call it in," I said.

"And say what, exactly?" Olivera asked me. "That after chasing a person of interest in the murder of Phil

Sullivan into an abandoned building, I found him murdered by a ghost?"

I squinted up and took note of the blood on Murdock's torso. "It might not have been the Widow who murdered him," I said, letting go of Heath to start heading up the stairs. "Her modus operandi is to strangle or drown her victims. She usually doesn't draw blood."

We ascended to the fourth floor without speaking. Although the air was no longer thick with a sinister essence, we were still mindful that a person had been murdered, and that carried its own solemn energy.

I was the first to reach Murdock, but I didn't touch him. No one did. Well, except for Olivera, who checked him for a pulse and then stepped back to look over his body for several moments, eventually leaning over the railing to get a better look at the wounds on his chest. "He's been stabbed."

"I was afraid of that," I said. "If he's been stabbed, then it probably wasn't a spook who did it."

Olivera pointed down the stairwell. "That freak show looked like she could wield a knife," she said.

"I don't think she would've," Heath said. "Like M.J. said, the Widow prefers snapping necks, or strangling or drowning her victims. And even if she had murdered him, then why didn't she use the blade against us?"

Olivera frowned and scanned the ground around Murdock's body again. "No sign of the weapon," she said.

"You won't find it here," I told her.

"How do you know?"

"Because the killer took it with him, and I'm guessing the weapon he used to kill Murdock was Oruç's dagger."

"So Murdock wasn't our guy?" Gilley said.

"It doesn't look that way," I replied.

"Then how was he involved?" Heath asked.

"The same way Sullivan was probably involved. Another accomplice. If the IP address led back to Murdock's house, then the killer could've asked to use Murdock's Wi-Fi, right, Gil?"

Gilley nodded. "Yes. Easily."

"What I can't figure out," I said next, "is why he thought to come here after Sullivan was murdered. I mean, he headed right for this place like he knew the killer was hiding out here."

"I'm guessing he came to warn the killer," Gilley said.

"There's one problem with all of this," Olivera said. "I checked Murdock's accounts today after you guys gave me the address, and it came back to the one Murdock listed when we interviewed him. He's got fifteen hundred between his checking and his savings accounts and nothing deposited other than his biweekly paycheck."

I thought about that for a minute and remembered the old woman from the house where Murdock had pulled up. If Murdock really did live there, could that old woman have been his mother? "Chris, I think you should do another search on the financials for the woman Murdock was living with. If that was his mother, he could've easily set it up with the killer to deposit it in one of her accounts to avoid exactly this type of suspicion."

Olivera nodded. "You're right," she said. "I'll look into it, but we still need to decide what to do with Murdock's body. I mean, I *have* to call it in, and given the encounters we've had here in just the past two days, I'm not sure I want to risk a paramedic's life when he comes to collect the body."

"You should all be safe for a little while, Detective," Heath said. "There's no threat to you or anyone else here right now."

"How can you be sure?"

Heath pointed to the top of the stairs next to us. There, lying in plain sight, as if it'd been there all along, was a large snowy white feather. "Where did that come from?" Olivera asked, looking up and around as if she expected to see a bald eagle hanging out on the banister.

"My ancestors set it there," Heath said simply. "And they're going to keep us all safe until we get out of here. But I'd make that call soon. Their protective energy can't be sustained indefinitely."

Olivera cleaned up all the shell casings expelled from her gun from the day before. Then she made the call and tried to get us to leave so that nobody would ask us too many questions. "No," Heath told her firmly after she all but insisted. "If I leave, so does your protection. We'll hang out downstairs, Detective, but I'm not leaving you alone in this building."

She relented, and I swore I saw relief in her eyes.

Still, I felt I had to leave before anyone arrived. I was away for about two hours, after making an emergency appointment with my ob-gyn, who, luckily, was only fifteen minutes away.

She'd been my doctor for more than ten years, so she'd seen me covered in bruises before and knew the type of job I had sometimes got a little physical. This time, I was much more worried about the baby after that tumble down the stairs, but after she'd checked me over thoroughly and performed an ultrasound, she said the baby was just fine. Still, she did make the suggestion that perhaps for the next seven and a half months I should probably find a new line of work.

I took the printout of the baby—no bigger than a bean!—back to show Heath, but when I got back to the building, which still had a number of crime scene techs there working, Heath was in a sort of deep meditation up on the second floor. Choosing not to disturb him, I went in search of Gilley, who filled me in on the details of what'd happened while I was gone. "Some other detective—I think his name was Smith—showed up," he said. "But Olivera was able to deflect attention off us and back onto the dead guy. Then the medical examiner showed up and I overheard him say that whoever had stabbed Murdock to death had probably done it by taking him by surprise.

"He also said," Gilley continued, "that the first wound was to Murdock's stomach, which he thought meant the killer had hidden the weapon, moved in close, and stabbed Murdock, who then fell to his knees and then was stabbed several more times on his way down to the floor. The ME said that all he could really tell was that the killer was right-handed."

"That's not much to go on," I said. "Is Rick Lavinia right-handed?"

Gil pressed his lips together. "No," he said. "I already checked while you were gone. Rick's a leftie."

"Dammit," I swore. "Well, that doesn't mean he didn't stab him with his other hand. Maybe he had something else in his left hand and used it to distract Murdock while he stepped in close and stabbed him."

"Maybe," Gilley said, but he sounded skeptical.

We fell silent then, waiting for everyone to finish up. I wasn't sure what Olivera had said to her peers to allow us to remain in the building while they investigated the crime, but when I'd gotten back to the building, all I'd had to do was tell the beat cop standing guard at the entrance my name and that I was with Olivera, and he'd let me head inside.

Around us the techs were starting to clean up and pack up their cameras, evidence bags, et cetera, and my gaze traveled back to Heath, who was leaning against the wall with his eyes closed and a serene expression. "He's been like that since you left," Gil mumbled out of the side of his mouth.

"He's meditating," I told him. "He's helping his ancestors hold the energy here."

"What do you think will happen to this place when we leave?" Gil said next.

I looked around the hallway we were in, brightly lit by the police spotlights, and thought about the absence of all that energy. "I think it'll go straight back to hell, Gil."

Chapter 15

It took another half hour for the police to wrap it up. Still, by that time, beads of sweat had broken out on Heath's forehead and he'd visibly paled. When I pulled him out of the deep meditation he was in, he actually had trouble walking.

We got him to the car and Olivera told us she was headed over to the house where Murdock lived. She wanted to talk to the old lady.

"We'll call you later," I said as I got into the car next to Heath in the backseat.

"Great," she said. "Stay safe, M.J.," she added, and I smiled. We were turning into friends after all.

We headed out, and Gilley drove while I sat with Heath's head in my lap, and in moments he was asleep.

I felt bad that I had to wake him once we got to the condo. He shuffled inside and went straight to bed. I knew he'd be all right, but still, it was hard to see him so drained.

After making sure Heath was settled, I came back out into the living room to find Gilley on the sofa just staring at the floor, as if in a trance. "Gil?" I said a bit warily. He'd once been possessed by Sy the Slayer, and my heart ticked up a beat, wondering if the evil spook had once again entered my home.

But Gil simply sighed and said, "I'm so tired of this, M.J. I'm so sick of battling things that shouldn't even exist. They're worse than my worst nightmares, and they give my worst nightmares fuel."

I went over to sit next to him and took his hand. "If I thought that sending you to New York to hang with Michel until this thing was over was the answer, Gil, I would've done that on day one."

He squeezed my hand. "I know," he said. "But I'm talking about more than just right now. I never, ever want to do this again."

I swallowed the lump that formed in my throat. "You're moving after the wedding," I told him. "And Heath and I are retiring from ghostbusting."

He turned his head to smile sadly at me. "That's just it," he said. "You and Heath can't seem to help yourselves. You guys get embroiled in these things like there's a target on your back that only evil spooks can see, and because I love you, I come running to help. I don't know how to say no to you the next time you guys need me on some bust that you pinkie-swear is the last one you'll ever do."

I bit my lip. That stung. Mostly because he was absolutely right, even though in this instance, it was mostly Gil's fault. "Gil," I said. "It's different now."

"How is it different, M.J.?"

I put my free hand on my belly. "*I'm* different," I said. "Literally. And when my daughter comes into this world, she'll be my greatest vulnerability. Some demon is gonna figure that out someday and go for her. The *only* way I can protect her is to say no the next time some evil spook is causing all sorts of trouble and my phone rings with a plea for help."

"But, sugar, how're you even going to avoid going to their aid? I mean, it's almost like you've had a beacon on your back everywhere you go, and evil spooks seem to abound here in Boston." Gilley stared at me as if he was pleading with me to keep my word.

I swallowed again, but this time for courage. "Gil . . . Heath and I are moving to Santa Fe. We'll be close to his family. His tribe. And his ancestors, and today you saw how effective they are at intervening. They'll protect us, and they'll protect Madelyn when she's born."

Gil's eyes misted some more. "You're moving to Santa Fe?"

"Yes."

"How soon?"

"Right after your wedding."

Gil's face registered a series of expressions that each broke my heart. "How come you didn't tell me?"

My own lip trembled, and in a quavering voice I said, "I didn't know how. You've been with me as my best friend . . . my brother since I was eleven. How do I tell someone I love so much, who's so important to me, and who's been such a part of my life all these years, that I'm heading to the other side of the country?"

Gilley looked down at our joined hands. "I felt like I was betraying you when Michel and I made the decision to move to New York."

"I know *exactly* what you mean."

We were silent like that for a while, just holding hands and tearing up. It's like there were no words to describe how much we loved each other, and how much we'd meant to each other, and how very much we'd miss each other. Finally, I broke the silence by saying, "We're planning on building a guesthouse, you know."

Gil looked up at me hopefully. "Yeah?"

"Yes. It'd be a real favor to me if you'd come and decorate it once it's complete."

His brow rose a little more. "I can come to visit a lot, you know. Especially if you need help with the baby."

I let go of his hand to wrap my arms around him and hug him fiercely. "I'm counting on it, sweetie. I'm counting on it."

Late in the afternoon Heath shuffled out of the bedroom, still looking drained and exhausted. I patted the seat next to me on the sofa as Gilley busied himself in the kitchen cooking up a storm.

I'll hand it to Gil: He's one hell of a good cook, and he was making us a feast of salmon tacos with homemade pico de gallo and guacamole. The scents coming from the kitchen were mouthwatering. "Smells great,

Gil," Heath said, plopping down on the sofa next to me.

Gil picked his head up at the sound of Heath's voice. "Oh, good. You're up. Dinner in ten minutes, people."

My stomach gurgled. I was insanely hungry. Heath raised an eyebrow at the sound. "Wow. Our kid's loud for someone so small."

I chuckled. "Yeah. She's pretty gabby."

"How're you feeling?" he asked me, stroking my arm affectionately.

"A little sore, but no real damage done."

"You sure?"

"I'm sure," I said, thinking of the printout of our little bean in my messenger bag. I decided to show him that when we were alone. "The doc says the baby is okay, and everything looks good. I'm scheduled for a follow-up in two weeks." Squeezing his knee, I added, "How're you feeling?"

He rubbed the side of his head that hadn't been grazed by the bullet. "I think she knocked some sense into me," he said with a grin.

"Oh, yeah?" I chuckled. "What kind of sense is that?"

"That we need to get out of the ghostbusting business. It hurts too much."

I laughed again. "I was just saying that to Gilley a little earlier. What I don't understand is how the hell these spooks are overcoming our magnets so easily. I mean, the Grim Widow was freakishly strong today, and by rights she shouldn't have been able to attack us like she did. I mean, she held on to me as we rolled down the stairs, and I was covered in magnets."

"I spoke with my ancestors about that in my meditation," Heath said. "Whitefeather told me that the dagger itself had gained a considerable amount of power as a portal. He said that there was something amplifying its energy, but he couldn't tell what."

From the kitchen Gilley said, "I think I might know."

I hadn't thought he'd been listening. "What, Gil?"

He wiped his hands on a kitchen towel and came around the counter to us. "To magnetize or demagnetize something you need a charge. Electricity. When you demagnetize something, you change the electromagnetic frequency around the object. So, in theory, if our thief stole the dagger and placed an improvised demagnetizer on it with, say, a battery pack to supply the power, you'd be amping up the wattage of whatever spook came through that portal in a big, bad way."

"Wow," I said. "That's not good."

"Nope," Gil said, turning to go back to the kitchen. "And you know what else isn't good?"

"What?"

"The fact that I need a little help here and neither one of you has volunteered."

Heath and I smiled at each other and he began to get up but I pushed him down. "Sit. I'll help bridezilla."

"I heard that!" Gil snapped.

Ignoring him, I said to Heath, "You rest and I'll bring dinner to you."

With my help, we had a hearty meal ready within the next five minutes, and we'd no sooner settled ourselves comfortably in the living room with full plates balanced on our laps than the doorbell rang.

I think the three of us sighed collectively. "I'll get it," I said with a groan.

Setting my plate on the ottoman, I got up and answered the door. Chris Olivera stood there looking nearly as exhausted and worn-out as Heath. "Hi, M.J.," she said.

"Chris. Good to see you. Please come in."

She came into the kitchen and immediately stopped in her tracks. "I'm interrupting your dinner," she said. "I can come back."

"No, no," I said. "Would you like to join us? There's plenty."

I heard Gilley clear his throat, but I ignored him. I knew I'd be giving away his chance for seconds, but Chris was on our side now, and there was no sense being rude to her.

She licked her lips but held up her hand. "No, that's really nice of you, but I don't want to impose."

I waved her comment off. "Oh, please," I said. "It's fish tacos. Gilley made them and I can tell you from experience, they're amazing. Go sit in the living room and take the plate on the ottoman. I'll bring you a glass of iced tea, and I'll fix myself another plate."

Chris wavered for another moment, so I just got right to making myself another plate, and she took the cue and headed to the living room.

I joined her there with the last of the fish tacos and ignored Gilley's barely veiled frown. "Oh, my God," Chris said after she'd taken a bite. "These *are* amazing!"

Gilley's frown vanished, and thereafter he was the

epitome of the polite host, offering Chris extra help-
ings of guacamole and pico de gallo.

We ate without discussing anything about the case,
which I think was an unspoken agreement among us.
It was an unnerving topic, and no sense spoiling a
delicious meal with talk of death and mayhem.

Finally, though, we'd finished the meal and Chris
politely took each of our plates to the kitchen, then
came back and sat down. Folding her hands in her lap,
she said, "I looked into Murdock. The elderly woman
he lived with was his mother. He had power of attorney
over her finances, and when we looked into her bank
account, we discovered a pattern almost identical to
Sullivan's. Five grand deposited about two weeks ago,
but he got an additional five grand the day after Sullivan was murdered."

"Do you think he murdered Sullivan?" Gilley asked.

She shook her head and shrugged. "My gut says no."

"Did you find any link between Rick Lavinia and
Murdock?" I asked next.

Chris shook her head. "No. Murdock's mother
wasn't exactly a fountain of information. She thinks
we murdered her son."

"Yikes," I said. "Is that going to spell trouble for you,
Chris?"

She shrugged again. "I spent a lot of the afternoon
going over the incident with Internal Affairs. They don't
like the fact that I chased a suspect into an abandoned
building, and, out of my line of sight, he was murdered
by an unknown assailant who then got away."

"Are you still on the case?" Heath asked.

"Yeah. For now," she said wearily.

He considered her for a few moments before he said, "Your dad was a cop too, right?"

She blinked in surprise. "How'd you know that?"

"You guys share the same first name," he said without answering her directly. "He's really proud that you're carrying on the legacy. He also thinks that the move to the new house in Cambridge was terrific. He's glad your mom didn't talk you out of it."

In an instant, Chris's eyes glistened with tears. "How are you doing that?" she said breathlessly.

Heath smiled kindly at her. "It's what I do. Your dad is asking for a favor, Chris. He'd like you to make his mom's pasta dish. He keeps showing me a bowl of spaghetti and he keeps connecting it to the number twenty-four."

She barked out a laugh and wiped her cheeks, which were now wet with tears. "His birthday is on the twenty-fourth of this month, and my grandmother's spaghetti Bolognese was his absolute favorite dish. He used to tell me that I was the only person who could make it like she did."

"I thought it was something like that," Heath said. "Anyway, he's really, really proud of you. And he says that you're smart to keep yourself in such great shape. He says you learned from his mistakes, and by that I think he means that he didn't take great care of himself. He died from heart trouble, right?"

Chris's lower lip trembled and she put her index

finger against it to stop the quivers. Unable to speak, she simply nodded. My heart went out to her, because she clearly missed her dad, and I knew exactly what it felt like to lose a parent.

"He's pulling back now, but the last thing he just told me is that he wants you to take the captain's exam within the next year or two. He says you'll pass it and get your own precinct by the time you're thirty-six. A little before he was able to do it."

She sucked in a small breath and stared at him wide-eyed. "My dad got his first precinct at thirty-seven," she said. "He was the youngest in our family to get that far that fast. I come from a long line of cops."

Heath sat back with a sigh and said, "Sorry for that impromptu reading. Your dad was knocking on my energy from the minute you came in the door."

"What does that even mean?" she asked him, a look of wonder on her face as she picked up her iced tea and took a steadying sip.

I answered for Heath. "Sometimes when a deceased person sees a chance to communicate with a loved one, they work really hard to get our attention. We call it knocking, because it sort of feels like that. It's sort of a tap-tap-tap on our energy; not a sound really, just a sort of pressure tapping at the edge of our personal space."

"That was amazing," Chris said. "Like, really, Heath. That was amazing."

He blushed. "M.J.'s just as good," he said.

She looked at me, and there was a hint of newfound respect in her eyes. It was immensely satisfying. "Getting back to Murdock," I said, because I knew we really did need to focus on figuring this case out, "is there anything more you can tell us?"

"Well, I did get a few things out of the mother. Beginning two weeks ago a man came to her house to speak with her son. She said she didn't like him, but Charlie—that's Murdock's first name—told her that he was a friend and he was doing a job for him.

"I showed her a picture of Lavinia, but she said her eyesight is bad, and she couldn't say for sure that it wasn't him."

"Crap," I muttered. "Is that enough to get a warrant and maybe do a search of Rick's financials to see if the deposits made to Murdock and Sullivan correlate to any of his accounts?"

The detective shook her head. "No. And because I'm desperate, I even ran it by the lieutenant, and he all but laughed in my face. We need something solid to connect Lavinia with Murdock and Sullivan—something that we don't need a warrant to prove."

We all were silent while we thought about how to go about doing that, but without even knowing where Rick Lavinia was, there didn't seem to be much of a place to start.

Finally, Gil said, "Was there anything else that Murdock's mom said? Any other clue she gave?"

Chris sighed and set her glass of iced tea aside. "The only other thing she gave me about this mystery man was that he showed up wearing a cape, and she remembers that because it was soaking wet and he refused to take it off, so it dripped on her carpet. I checked a couple of Google images for Lavinia, and he seems to be a T-shirt-and-jeans kind of guy. There's no image anywhere of him wearing a cape."

I stared in stunned silence at Chris. She looked back at me, furrowing her brow. "What?" she said.

I turned to look at Gilley, and he stared at me with an equally shocked expression. "No. *Way!*" he gasped. "No, *freaking* way!"

And then he jumped up and ran to his backpack to pull out his computer.

"What's happening?" Chris said as we all continued to stare at one another, shocked to our toes.

"We know who the killer is," Heath said to her.

"Rick Lavinia?" she guessed.

"Nope!" Gil said, bringing her his laptop. "Count Chocula!"

"Captain Comb-Over," I added. "He *always* wears a cape."

She looked first at Gil, then at me, then at the computer screen, which is when her jaw dropped. "*That guy* is the killer?"

"Yep," I said, getting up to go over and look at what I assumed was the image of Bernard Higgins. "In a million years I never would've thought him capable of something like this," I said.

Gilley took his laptop back and sat on the ground to type furiously. "Bernard Higgins," he said, while his fingers flew over the keyboard before pausing so that his eyes could focus on the screen, "is a world-renowned medium. At least that's according to his Web site. He's a medium to the *stars*, or so it says here."

"He looks like a joke," Chris said.

"That's what we've always thought," I told her. "But apparently, we've *way* underestimated him. A couple of years ago, Heath and I were paired with him and some other woman who looks like Elvira—"

Gilley gave a tiny gasp. "Angelica Demarche!"

I snapped my fingers. "*That* was her name!"

"She and Bernard were married in twenty-thirteen," Gil said, his gaze darting back and forth across the screen.

"No way!" I exclaimed. "You're kidding me."

"Nope, not kidding," Gil said. "And you know what else, M.J.?"

"What?"

"Bernard—Bradley; Angelica—Angela."

"Who's Angela?" Heath asked.

"Bradley's assistant. The one I spoke to at the studio when I called his business line."

"She's a part of this," I guessed.

"Has to be," Gil said.

"Okay, I'll give you that all this is starting to add up for Bernard," Heath said, "but I mean, Gil, that guy really didn't seem smart enough to pull something like this off. There was a lot of tech stuff involved here."

Gilley looked up from the computer long enough to say, "According to Bernard's bio, he was an electrician until nineteen ninety-five, when an electrical shock gave him the powers to speak to the dead."

"An electrician could certainly figure out how to demagnetize our equipment," I reasoned, wondering how I could've underestimated Bernard so fully. It must've been a bias I formed at our first meeting, when he focused on my cleavage and only my cleavage. Also, he just looked silly parading around in that cape. I hadn't really considered that there might be a whole lot more substance to the man.

"Plus, he's from San Francisco," Heath said, pulling me out of my thoughts on Bernard. "And he was there at the hotel when the dagger first appeared. He definitely could've known all about it."

"He also could've followed the Drake murder case," I said. "He could've put two and two together and figured out that Ayden had given us the dagger to keep it safe."

"And remember," Gilley said, "he and Angelica were fired from the *Haunted Possessions* cast. He was pretty steamed about that."

"So he's carried a grudge against us all this time?" I said. It never would've occurred to me to hold on to something like that for so long.

"M.J.," Gil said, "from the *Haunted Possessions* show, you and Heath got your own thirteen-episode cable show; then you got a movie deal. Of course he held a grudge. In his eyes, you probably stole his big break."

"We probably stole Angelica's too," Heath said.

"Plus, as a medium, he'd know all about portals and such."

"He would," I agreed.

"So, this Rick Lavinia . . . ," Chris said. "He had nothing to do with this?"

"Oh, I'm guessing he did, but I'm also guessing he didn't know he did. Gil, remember that Instagram photo he posted? The caption said that he was sent that image, right?"

"Something to that effect," Gil said.

"I'm thinking Bernard sent Rick the image in the hopes that Rick would post it and we'd get thrown off Bernard's trail."

"It worked," Gil said.

"It did. That bastard."

"Okay, so what do we do?" Chris said next. "Should I put out a warrant for him?"

"No!" Gilley and Heath said together.

"He's got the dagger," I reminded her. "And I doubt that, if he's in Boston, he's staying anywhere under his real name. Plus, this guy's been dogging us from the beginning. He's been stalking us and unleashing the demons at us at will. I think we should use that to our advantage."

"How?" Heath asked.

I bounced my eyebrows because I knew *exactly* how we'd find them. "By making them come to us, baby."

Chapter 16

"How exactly are we going bring Bernard and Angel-ica to us?" Gilley demanded.

"Well," I began, "if I had to guess, I'd say that Bernie and Angie really want to get noticed, right? Their goal is probably to get on camera and show off their skills by saving the day. But in order to do that, they'd need to be in control of the spooks, because, let's face it, as mediums, those two suck."

Gil snorted. "Angelica in particular was just god-awful," he said.

"She was," I agreed. "So, if we post something online suggesting that we're going to be busting a haunted apartment house and filming it to show off our skills to those people who might think we're big fat fakers, how could Bernard resist showing up with the dagger and unleashing his little demon horde at us? It's win-win for him, especially if one or all of the demons kill us. He'll get to make his grand entrance on camera as a gifted medium who felt a disturbance in the force and came to save the day."

"Wait," Gilley said, his expression alarmed. "You *want* him to open up Oruç's portal?"

"No," I admitted, feeling a sense of dread in the pit of my stomach. "But I don't see how we can avoid it. Bernard has the dagger. He's in control of the portal. The only way to get to him is to survive the gauntlet."

The room was very quiet after that, and I knew that they all saw that I was right. "I don't like it, Em," Heath said.

"Me neither, sweetheart, but what other choice do we have? It's too big of a risk to hope that Bernard doesn't choose some other crowded event to unleash the dagger so that he can garner some attention."

"You think he'll be lured to a concert or a mall or something over our little get-together?" Gil said. "I mean, he'd have a *much* bigger audience."

"True," I said. "But he'd also have a hell of a lot more risk with it. He already tried to orchestrate a big disruption at our event, and that failed miserably."

Chris took a deep breath and raised her eyes skyward as if she were sending up a prayer. "I'm in."

"You *are*?" Gilley asked her. "Sorry," he added quickly. "I mean . . . you are?"

She grinned. "Yeah. I figure if my dad sees me making captain someday, then I'll probably survive the night. You guys also need all the help you can get, so tell me how to fight these spooks and I'll do it."

I sent her a grateful smile, then turned to Gilley. He

rolled his eyes. "If you weren't pregnant, M.J., no *way* would I walk into an ambush like that."

I let out the breath I'd been holding. "Thanks, Gil," I said.

He scowled irritably at me but picked up his laptop again and began to write the post I'd mentioned to our fan page. "If that kid turns out to be a boy, or if you ever have a boy, you'd better name him after me," he grumbled.

"That goes without saying," I said, ignoring the sharp look I got from Heath. Our children could have more than one middle name.

At last I turned to Heath. There was no question that he'd join us, but I did wonder if he'd put up a fight to exclude me in the brawl with the spooks. I gave him a few moments to think about it before I said, "You can't do this without me, and I wouldn't let you even if you could. We either use everything we've got to get the dagger back and put Bernie behind bars, or we're chased by these spooks for the rest of our lives."

Heath sighed. "For the record, I wasn't going to try to talk you out of it. I just want us to use every available precaution, and I'm worried about the timing."

"What do you mean you're worried about the timing?" Chris asked.

"We barely have time to prep, let alone set a trap."

Gilley finished typing, then leaned forward with interest. "Trap?"

Heath nodded. "You don't think I'd let us walk in there without orchestrating how it's gonna go down, do you?"

I smiled. "I'll get some paper and a pen. Let's map this puppy out."

Several hours later, we were huddled in my kitchen, going over the plan from start to finish. It'd been a herculean effort to bring it together. Gilley especially had really come through for us, and he'd so cleverly thought of a way to hide the trap that I felt less trepidation than I probably should've about how things would unfold.

Olivera had left us only to go home and grab some extra clothes. She was dressed in them now—and they covered her thin form rather well. She wore a baseball cap with the brim pulled low and an oversized Windbreaker that hid her Kevlar vest.

She was wearing the bulletproof stuff for a reason, and that was that she'd insisted on bringing her gun. "Bernard's got a knife," she told us. "You don't bring a spike to a knife fight if you want to win. You bring a big black gun."

I had to give her points for coming up with that argument. Also for the fact that she was probably right: If we spotted Bernard, he'd be dangerous. The spirit of Oruç could take hold of him in a heartbeat, and the Turkish warlord wasn't going to give a crap if Bernie lost his life. He'd find some other hapless person to possess and do his bidding.

Still, I'd insisted that Chris pack some extra magnets inside her vest and her boots. Oruç could as easily possess Chris as he could Bernard, and the last thing I needed was for the lone person with a gun to become possessed by a murderous, psychopathic ghost.

As for Oruç's demon and his merry crew of spooks of Christmas past, Gilley had spent the entire evening crafting a weapon that we hoped would level our playing field.

The idea actually came from Chris's argument that you don't bring a spike to a dagger fight. You bring a gun. That sparked a very creative idea for Gilley, who began to draft a design on paper, and then spent the next few hours tinkering.

In the end we all marveled at his genius. "It's perfect," I said, hugging his arm.

"It's not," he insisted, that worry line in his forehead creasing deeply. "If all the batteries drain, we're dead in the water."

"Then we should house them in magnets," I said. "And, we'll have to hope that luck is on our side."

Chris picked up the movie camera—which was actually a fake. The outside was simply a housing for a large magnetizer locked away inside. "How is this gonna work, exactly?"

"Like a gun," Gil said. "If you point it at something made of metal, it'll magnetize the crap out of it."

As a demonstration, Gilley took the camera from her and pointed it at my utensil drawer. He then pulled the trigger on the handle of the movie camera. A moment later we all heard a series of clinks. I opened the drawer and took out several forks, which were stuck together. "You are so freaking cool!" I said to Gil.

He beamed and returned the camera back to Chris. Using air quotes, he said, "You're going to be our 'cameraperson,' so you've gotta make it look like you're recording M.J., Heath, and me. If M.J.'s right, and Bernard shows up with the dagger, he'll unleash the demons first, but he shouldn't be too far away. While we're all dealing with the monsters, you've gotta track down Bernard and fire that thing straight at him."

"Will it take him out?" she asked.

Gilley snorted. "Not hardly. It won't have any effect on him. But if you keep your finger on the trigger, it should neutralize or even kill the portal housed in Oruç's dagger. What I'm banking on is that his demagnetizer will have required a really big charge to open the portal and supply the spooks coming through it with lots of wattage. That takes away from his gadget's ability to keep the dagger demagnetized, and as my gizmo is *only* focused on magnetizing the dagger, he'll run out of juice long before we will. Once that portal is shut down, the spooks won't be able to draw power from it, and they can be neutralized. We've got enough magnets and spikes to do that."

I nodded as Gilley spoke. I liked our chances, but Heath didn't seem nearly as enthused as I felt. "What?" I asked him quietly.

He shook his head. "Everything depends on Chris finding Bernard in time," he said. "And we haven't even accounted for Angelica. What if she's going to provide him with backup?"

"Is there another way?" I asked him. "I mean, because if you can think of something better, honey, I swear I'm all ears."

Heath pressed his lips together and shook his head. "I can't think of one, and I've been trying to all night."

"Then we just go in there with all we've got and keep our fingers crossed, okay?" Heath gave a reluctant nod and I turned my attention back to Gilley, who was speaking.

". . . should split up the backup batteries for the camera. We can't have Chris carry all of them."

"Why not?" she asked.

I said, "Because if you get zapped with a power drain, or if the magnets protecting the batteries get demagnetized before you get to Bernard, and a spook then drains all of them, then we're totally screwed. Everything depends on Gilley's gizmo. And it takes a big charge. If we don't have power to feed it, we've got no hope."

Chris turned a little pale. "No hope of what? Overcoming Bernard? Taking out the spooks? Making it out alive?"

"All of the above," I told her, and there was no humor in my voice. I was dead serious.

"Great," she said, tucking the tightly packed batteries into the top of her vest. "No pressure on me to get the batteries switched out fast or anything either."

"Practice," Heath told her firmly. "On the way to the Commons. You have to be fast, Chris, and you can't mess up."

She glared at him a little. "Like I said, thanks for not putting pressure on my role in this thing."

"You volunteered," Gilley said drolly.

I thought we might be ganging up a little too much on Chris, so before she could snap at him, I said, "You'll do great, Chris. You will. I have total faith in you."

She attempted a smile, and it was almost convincing. Taking a deep breath, I pointed to the clock. "It's nearly midnight. We gotta go."

Grabbing our gear, which was no small feat, as we were bringing as much as we could carry, we headed down the stairs single file and without a word. It was like that on the drive over to Ashworth Commons too, except about ten minutes into the drive, Heath, who was at the wheel, said, "Someone's following us."

I almost turned to look over my shoulder, but Heath reached for my hand and said, "Don't. They'll know we know."

"It's gotta be Bernard," Gil said from his spot in the backseat. He was still fidgeting with the giant spikes he was bringing along.

"Good," I said. "Let him come to us." After another slight pause I added, "Chris, when you get out of the car, make a big show with the camera. Pretend you're filming the building so that Bernard can see we've come to record.

She said, "I could make a call and have him pulled over in less than three minutes."

"No!" the three of us said at once. I explained, "If you have a couple of beat cops pull him over, one of two or both of these scenarios is likely to go down: Bernard unleashes the demon from Oruç's dagger and you have a couple of filleted cops, and/or he unleashes the demon *and* he lets Oruç take possession of him, and you have a filleted cop and a stabbing victim."

"He could also let Oruç take possession of one of

the beat cops," Gilley said. "He could save the demon for us and turn one cop against the other."

I shuddered and snuck a peek over my shoulder at Chris. She was mimicking my body language. "Sweet Jesus," I heard her whisper. "Fine, no extra manpower."

About ten minutes later we pulled up in front of Ashworth Commons. The rain hadn't let up all day, which made the atmosphere perfect for taking out some spooks.

When we got out, Chris did a great job of pretending to film the exterior of the building while we grabbed our gear and made our way to the side entrance. Heath led the way and held the door for us as we all filed in.

Once inside he pointed to the stairwell. "We need to take the high ground. Fourth floor, you guys."

"What about Gertie?" I asked.

"She'll have to hide in one of her apartments. We can't worry about placating her tonight. We gotta keep the top floor so Bernard and Angelica can't get above us and trap us between two sets of demons."

"Okay," I said, falling into line to head up the stairs.

"Where do you want me?" Chris asked as she brought up the line.

Heath said, "Stick behind me until I clear a path for you through whatever's gonna come up those stairs. Once I do that, you head down and start clearing floors, looking for Bernard. Once you find him, point that camera at him and don't stop firing until you run completely out of juice."

"What about the backup battery that M.J. has?" Chris asked.

I patted my right chest pocket subconsciously. The battery was safely tucked into my vest and was itself covered in magnets.

"If you need it, send up a war cry before you have to use your last battery," I told her with a slight grin at Heath. "I'll come find you. Don't you worry about it."

"Where am I?" Gilley asked as we crested the second-floor landing.

"You'll be behind M.J., supporting her with that bag of tricks, buddy," Heath said. "If she gets in trouble, you get her out of it, you get me?"

Heath had said that a little forcefully, and Gilley and I exchanged a look of surprise. I'd almost always been the one to protect Gil, not the other way around, but then I realized that Heath was asking Gilley to step up more than he ever had. Gil didn't get it, though, and he said, "I have to bail her out of trouble?"

Heath paused and rounded on Gilley. Poking him in the chest, he said, "Gillespie, you're braver and stronger than you think, man. Don't you remember earlier today when you fended off the Grim Widow? You always sell yourself short, and I'm sick of it. And what's more, we don't have time for it. You gotta step it up, dude. That's my *wife*," he added, pointing to me. "And she's carrying my kid, and if anything happens to her or the baby, I will never, ever, ever forgive myself. So I'm counting on you to come through for me just like you did today. Understand?"

Gilley stood there blinking for a good ten seconds.

At last he said, "Okay, okay. I hear ya. I've got her back, Heath."

Heath turned again toward the stairs and marched up past me. I looked back down at Gilley, who seemed a little rattled, and when he caught my eyes, I mouthed, *Wowsa!*

That got him to grin, and I was relieved. Gilley was a certified genius, like, Mensa smart, but when he got rattled or really scared, he mentally shut down. That was the last thing we needed tonight.

We reached the top floor and Heath and I felt out the space. Gertie poked her head out of Apartment 4C and glared at us. "Gertie, you'd best head back into that apartment and stay there," I told her. "We'll be making some noise out here, and I'm sorry for that, but we mean you no harm and we'll leave your floor alone after tonight. Deal?"

She seemed to consider that, and then the head sticking right out of the door faded in front of our eyes. "Sweet Jesus," Chris repeated from behind me. "How the hell do you guys ever get used to that?"

I shrugged and set my duffel on the floor. "We've seen a whole lot worse. Enough exposure to the nastier spooks and not a lot of the milder ones freak you out anymore."

Chris shuddered. "What do you think is going to come at us tonight?" she asked.

Heath and I exchanged a look. We'd purposely avoided talking about that because we hadn't wanted to freak out either Chris or Gilley.

But then I considered that there wasn't a point to

keeping it from them any longer. What would come, would come, and we were here, so they might as well be prepared for the worst. "Heath and I think that our main threats will be Hatchet Jack, Oruç's demon, Sy the Slayer—whom you haven't met yet, Chris—and we're hoping that's it."

Chris gulped. "Who else could come, though?" she asked with a quaver in her voice.

I sighed. "We dealt with a spook in Santa Fe that made Oruç's demon look like a cute, cuddly puppy. And a guardian shadow spirit in Ireland that, if he showed, alone would have the power to take us all out. Quick."

"What about the witches?" Gil asked, referring to some determined and deadly ghosts from Scotland we'd dealt with a few years back.

I shook my head. "Nope. They at least won't show. That I know."

"The Grim Widow again?" he asked, and he shivered at the mention of her name.

"God, I hope not," I said. "Heath and his ancestors took a lot of her firepower out today on the stairs, so we'll see. I'm hoping she sits this one out, because even weakened she's a freaking nightmare to deal with."

"The . . . the Sandman?" Gil said with a gulp.

I shuddered involuntarily. "God, I hope not, Gil."

"How long?" Chris asked next. I noticed that she'd lowered her voice to barely above a whisper. The anticipation and the anxiety were both building for her. For all of us, really.

"Could be awhile. Could be any minute," I said, setting down several canisters of metallic dust. Another one of Gilley's ideas, and we'd barely managed to find a source before the stores all closed, but we now had a dozen small canisters of the stuff, and the dust carried a lovely magnetic charge. I passed two each to Gilley and Chris, then instructed Chris in how to use them. "These are your last resort, Chris," I said. "They're like a grenade. You set one off, it'll buy you some time to get the hell out of the building. One is to get you to the ground floor. The other is to get you through the door and outside, where you will run as fast as you can until you can't run anymore."

She considered the canisters gravely. "What do I do with them? Just toss one and bolt?"

I pulled up on the top and showed her the insides. "Flip the top, toss the contents directly *at* the demon or spook that's coming for you, and run like hell."

"Why are these a last resort?" she asked me next, taking the lid from me and putting it back on the canister.

"Because they may or may not stick to the spook. We've never tested them before, so we don't know. Worst-case scenario, they'll simply create a magnetic cloud that the spook will have to pass through on its way to you, and that's not going to be anything a ghost or even a demon will want to do. It'll wait for the dust to settle, so to speak, before giving chase."

"Can't it just chase me outside?"

I pressed my lips together. She'd asked me the one question I hadn't wanted her to. "Yes. But we're hoping it won't."

She palmed the canister and studied it for a long

moment. "I hate that plan," she said at last. "Let's make sure we don't have to use it."

"I hear ya."

We took the next several minutes to get set up, and then we heard something downstairs. The four of us stood straight and rigid . . . listening.

No other sound came to our ears, but I pointed to Heath and mouthed, *Action!*

"So, what I'm thinking," Heath said in a loud voice, "is that M.J. can sort of kick the door closed, and if it's dark enough, then we can film it so that the audience thinks there's a ghost behind the door. I'll jump a little when it happens, but make sure that the angle doesn't get her in the shot so the audience won't suspect anything."

"Got it," Chris said, also in a loud voice.

Gilley had written us out a script to help egg Bernard on. He figured that if Bernie suspected that we were big fat fakers, he'd feed that by having us pretend to stage a ghost shoot.

Again there was a sound from downstairs, and Heath rolled with it. "Hey, maybe you can capture some of the sounds from this old building, and we'll tell the audience that the spooks are letting us know they're around. We can turn up the volume when we edit so that it looks to the audience like the sound was much louder."

"They'll believe anything you tell them," I said with a laugh.

"Right?" Heath agreed. "Suckers!"

We each made a show of giggling, but it was all fake.

I knew that my friends were just as nervous and scared about what was coming as I was, but it was important to set the stage.

"I wish we'd had some of that afternoon action on tape," Gilley said. "Man, did we show that bitch spook something or what?"

"We did," I agreed. "She wasn't no thang," I sang. "Easy peezy."

As I taunted the Widow and we all laughed again, there was a distinctive sound from below. I knew it well and barely resisted the urge to tremble. It was that same slow, grating sound . . . talons on a hard surface.

Chris gave a small startled squeak, and Heath took her by the arm and sent her far down the hall behind him. Gilley shuffled down the hall too, taking up a stance on my side of the corridor, about six feet farther back than Chris. Before leaving my side, however, he'd handed me one of his extra-long spikes, and I'd seen that he'd put on his metal gloves again.

Once I saw that Gil and Chris were set, I turned to nod at Heath to show him I was ready. He nodded back and picked up the crossbow he'd brought with him. We'd gotten that little number on the way back from getting the metallic dust powder. He had several arrows knocked into place, each one tipped in steel. Magnetized, of course. When Gilley had first seen it, he'd said, "That's gonna leave a mark."

I was just glad my husband knew how to shoot it. We waited like that in the hall near the landing, watching the top of the stairs for anything that might come at us.

Lucky us, we didn't have to wait long . . .

Chapter 17

It came at us from behind, and we never saw it coming. We were so intent on watching the stairwell that none of us considered that the elevator was also a way to access the fourth floor.

I was standing in a defensive posture, hands loaded with spikes, canisters of metallic powder ready to hurl at any spook that got too close, when I heard a *ping!*

Instantly I knew what that sound was. I stiffened and turned my head to Heath, who looked at me and said, "Oh, *shit!*"

He and I couldn't whirl around fast enough. Out of the elevator rushed three of my worst nightmares, and they hit Chris and Gilley first.

Hatchet Jack was all but a blur as he bulleted his way toward Gil, who screamed and had no time to get his spike up. To make a very bad situation a thousand times worse, Gil had been at least fifteen feet behind me. I couldn't have possibly gotten to him in time. That didn't stop me from trying, but Hatchet Jack had already landed on Gilley and was dragging him by the throat toward the elevator.

Gilley beat at Jack, his hands flying wildly, which turned out to be the wrong move, because both his heavy gloves slipped from his fists and flew to each side, taking the spike he was holding with them. Jack barely flinched and simply tightened his grip on Gil's throat, hauling him farther away from me with freakishly terrifying speed. I ran as fast as I could, but Jack moved quicker.

Meanwhile, Chris was overrun by Sy the Slayer. He was much like Hatchet Jack in build and evil grin. He grabbed Chris by the hair, but she managed to swipe at him with her spike and he backed off a fraction. "I can't get a clear shot!" I heard Heath shout as I kept trying to get to Gilley.

I realized that Heath's crossbow was of no use to us as long as Gilley and Chris were in his line of fire.

Waiting at the door to the elevator was Oruç's demon. It stood there with its three long-taloned paws, hideous face, and gleaming white teeth, as if it were simply waiting to be fed.

Judging by the looks of things, Gilley would be its appetizer.

Desperate and terrified for him, I screamed with fury and reached for one of the canisters. Pulling at the lid, I sprinkled a little of the metallic powder on myself before managing to throw it at Hatchet Jack. It covered both him and Gilley, and I realized that I'd been wrong.

In their current form, the spooks were solid ectoplasm, as real and dense as any living person, but they weren't alive, just held together by a substance that science had no explanation for.

The metallic powder clung to both Gilley, who was covered in magnets, and Hatchet Jack—who screamed in fury and pain as the dust coated him.

Almost immediately he let go of Gilley, who'd been choking out a small scream the whole time. That was the moment I lunged for his hand, reached him, and pulled him back toward me. I hoped that perhaps Hatchet Jack was done with the fight.

He wasn't.

He came at me in a furious rage, but I was still tangled with Gilley. Jack's bony fingers grabbed my hair, and he jerked my head back so hard my feet tingled. I was knocked off my feet and onto my back, expelling all the air in my lungs as my bruised ribs hit the hard floor. I tried to reach for a spike or another canister, but I couldn't get my limbs to move fast enough.

All around me were shouts and screams. Chris sounded like she was in real trouble, and Heath kept yelling at her to get down.

My own situation was quickly deteriorating. Jack was all over me. The dust still clung to his form, but his anger fueled renewed strength in him. He rained down blows that were as painful as getting punched by a real one-hundred-and-seventy-five-pound man. Somewhere in the background I heard Heath roar, *"Gilley! Get out of the way!"*

And then there was a sound, like a *thwack!*, and

instantly Jack was off me. Another *thwack!* and Jack screamed. I barely managed to focus my eyes enough to see the third arrow strike him. He reeled backward, his arms pinwheeling as he tore at the arrows. His form began to disintegrate, and he left long trails of ectoplasm on the floor and the walls.

Gilley appeared at my side as Jack melted even more, his body becoming transparent, which allowed the arrows to slide out of him and hit the floor. But the damage from the dust and the arrows was enough to do him in, and the last of his hideous form disintegrated at the foot of Oruç's demon.

Meanwhile, Sy continued to pull Chris down the hallway, dragging her by the hair with one hand while his other arm draped around her neck. He paid no mind to Jack, or what happened to him; he simply dragged Chris toward the elevator doors. I knew he'd either feed her to the demon or take her prisoner before we could get to her. In the hope that she'd survive the latter long enough for us to get to her, I shouted at my husband, *"Heath! Shoot the demon! Shoot the demon!"*

He'd been aiming at Sy, but without even looking at me, he immediately changed his aim and let loose another arrow. It hit the demon midchest, and that beast roared loud enough to shake the walls. I cringed and clung to Gilley, who clung to me as well.

Heath then unleashed a whole volley of arrows, but only one more struck the demon before it vanished into thin air. Heath didn't have a chance to reload before Sy had Chris on the elevator, and the doors began to close. I staggered to my feet and raced down the last twenty steps of the hallway, trying with everything I had to get to her before the doors closed.

I was five feet from her, staring straight into her terrified eyes, when the steel doors slid shut, and she and Sy vanished too.

Heath got to me only a moment later. "Dammit!" he yelled.

I was panting and out of breath but managed to point to the stairs. "We have to get her back!"

Heath tore off down the hallway toward the stairs, and to my surprise, Gilley followed. I took a few steps but couldn't catch my breath. My ribs hurt so bad, the pain was blinding, and I wondered if Jack had cracked at least one of my ribs. And then I put a hand to my belly, remembering the baby. Had I been punched in the stomach? Was the baby all right?

Using a hand against the wall to support myself, I carefully felt around my belly and decided that all the pain was coming from my right side, because I'd been lying on my left side when Hatchet Jack had hit. I didn't think he'd struck me where the baby was, but it was a very close call and one I was determined wouldn't be repeated.

Limping down the hallway as I hugged my ribs, I paused only as long as it took to pick up the camera, which Chris must've dropped as she fought with Sy; then I gimped after Gilley and Heath, but I didn't know which floor they'd gone too.

I listened carefully but at first didn't hear any sounds. And then I did hear sounds. Screams. Several from my husband.

I cried out myself and shot down the stairs, mindless of my own pain, to the second floor. What I saw there brought me to my knees. Heath was dangling in the air, four or five feet off the ground, clawing at his neck, where Oruç's demon held him. On the ground next to the beast was the crossbow, empty of its arrows.

Gilley was also on the ground, about ten feet away from Heath. His arms and legs were pinned down by Sy and by the Grim Widow, who cackled happily but looked even bonier than she had earlier in the day.

Worst of all, coming down the hall from the elevator were Bernard and Angelica. Chris was being marched in front of Angelica, her arms raised, and it was obvious that the gun she'd brought to the knife fight had ended up in the wrong hands. Bernard had a sinister look in his eyes that wasn't all human. It was far, far creepier, and I knew it to be Oruç himself, currently possessing Bernard.

He held the dagger aloft, and it was wrapped with tape and a small contraption held to it. The demagnetizer. Bernard as Oruç snickered when he saw me. He had something in mind. Something I was quite sure would destroy me to witness.

"My pet is hungry," he said, while my mind raced to find a way to save them all. My gaze darted from Heath, whose complexion was quickly turning blue, to Gilley, who was being slapped around by Sy and the Widow, to Chris, who looked like she couldn't believe what was happening.

"We'll sacrifice the short one first," Bernard said,

indicating Gilley. "Then we'll do the camera girl and Whitefeather. We'll save Holliday for last."

I was shaking from head to toe. He had me. He had all of us. There was nothing I could do. If I tried to save Gilley, who was closest to me, Heath would die. If I went for Heath, the demon would snap his neck right in front of me. And if I tried to save Chris, then Angelica would likely shoot her, then me.

But then I heard Heath's grandfather whisper to me in my mind, and suddenly I knew what to do. "You beat us," I said to Bernard. "You really did. But I can still let our audience know what an asshole you are, and what you've done here tonight." With that I raised the movie camera and pointed it at Bernard. Chris snapped her head in my direction, and I knew she was ready to make a move.

Bernard stopped his slow trek down the hall toward me, studying the camera. I had a feeling the part of him that was still in control of his mind was intrigued about being filmed. It was all the hesitation I needed. Taking a few quick steps toward him to get within range, I pulled the trigger on the camera several times, pulsing the magnetizer as I went. I stopped when I was about ten feet from him.

At first there didn't seem to be any effect at all, and I wondered if the battery had been drained, but when I looked at the monitor, it still registered a charge. And then Bernard's expression seemed to change. He shook his head slightly, as if coming fully awake, and looked around, and what he saw seemed to terrify him. "Now!" I shouted at Chris, and she reacted by whirling in a half circle with crooked elbow, striking the arm that Angelica was using to hold the gun on her. Angelica never had a chance to pull the trigger, and the gun went flying. Chris then leaped on top of her and wrestled her to the ground, while I went right for Bernard, taking two giant leaps before raising my leg high and striking him midchest with it.

He shot backward and the dagger also went flying. As fast as I could manage, I grabbed the dagger, tore off the batteries fueling the gizmo, and plunged the whole thing into one of the inner pockets of my vest, where it would be completely surrounded by thin magnetic plates. Then I whirled around again and looked toward Oruç's demon, which seemed genuinely confused. But only for a second or two. In the next moment it became very, very angry and began to shake Heath in a way that surely would break his neck.

It was Chris who came to Heath's rescue when she threw a canister of metallic powder at the demon and covered it in gray dust.

It shrieked and dropped Heath, who crumpled to the ground and tried to crawl away on his forearms. He wasn't going to get away fast enough, it seemed, so I yelled to Chris, "Help Gilley! I've got Heath!" and ran toward my husband. Just as I got an arm underneath him, however, I was delivered a blow that knocked me all the way across the hallway. I hit the far wall and slid to the ground, and the world spun. Heat exploded along my shoulder, and as I dizzily gazed down at myself, I saw a thin stream of red snaking its way down my arm. "M.J.!" Chris cried out, but I couldn't get my chin to lift up from where it rested on my chest. I could only move it from side to side.

I felt the demon approach when the ground underneath my legs vibrated with its steps. The demon, which I'd locked out of its portal, would kill me well before the last of its power drained away.

I tried to get up from the wall, because I knew if I didn't, I'd be dead in about ten seconds, but my limbs refused to respond. I could feel my guide, Sam, urging me to get up, but I just couldn't do it.

At last I managed to lift my chin, and I saw Heath, on the floor ten yards away, reaching out to me helplessly, a look of anguish on his face, and I felt so sad that he had to watch the demon kill me. It wasn't at all what I'd wanted.

Finally, I looked up at the demon itself, and I refused to show fear. It would kill me as I had attempted to kill it, but my soul would be free, unlike its soul, which would always be bound. At least there was that.

The demon raised one of its giant paws, tipped with talons, and prepared to bring it down on me. "Fuck you," I told it. I tried to say it loudly, but it mostly came out as a mutter.

And then the hand descended, and I closed my eyes, waiting for the deathblow.

But it never came.

Instead there was a loud shout from my right, and then a tremendous percussion of sound. I sank to the side and onto the floor, managing to open my eyes and see the strangest sight: the demon had a crutch sticking out of its eye. It roared in pain and wheeled backward, swiping at the crutch, but then a shadowy figure stepped clumsily over me, making a loud thud on the floor as it did so, and it swung the other crutch it held right at the demon's head.

To my astonishment, the head of Oruç's demon caved in slightly, and it began to bleed ectoplasm. Again, the shadow struck. And again. And again.

The demon continued to wheel away, blinded in one eye by the crutch and unable to fully focus with the other. It ended up tripping over its own feet, and that's when the shadowy form who'd saved me began to beat the demon with determination. By the tenth or eleventh blow, the fight was over. The demon disintegrated. Well, everything but its talons, which clicked to the ground harmlessly.

Meanwhile, Chris was working to free Gilley, and she was doing a tremendous job of it. She'd already dispatched the Widow with the one can of metallic dust she had left, and she used Gilley's own spike to strike the center of Sy the Slayer's chest. He backed away as the demon had, with much noise and clumsiness.

He fell right next to Heath, in fact, and my husband wasted no time dispatching his ass back to nothingness with one final spike to the head.

And then . . . all was quiet, save our labored breathing and Angelica's moans.

Bernard sat on the floor, his back against the wall, and looked around at all the quickly evaporating ectoplasm.

I spared him no more attention, instead focusing on the shadowy figure who'd appeared out of nowhere.

"Ayden," I said when he turned to look at me, a triumphant look on his face and a big old medical boot on his right foot. "What the hell are you doing here?"

"Isn't it obvious, M.J.? I'm saving your ass. And now, we're even!"

Chapter 18

Ayden sat in a chair next to my hospital gurney and kept playing with his crutches. They would clink against the metal leg of the chair he was sitting on, and he seemed to be amusing himself pulling the crutches away, then letting them clink to the metal again.

The sound was a little annoying, but my arm hurt so bad, I hardly cared. "That was a pretty smart move, magnetizing your crutches like that," I told him through clenched teeth.

"I'm a pretty genius guy," he said with a wink. "I rubbed them with magnets while I waited at the airport for the plane. I'm just glad there's enough metal in them to be magnetized. Pure aluminum doesn't hold much of a charge."

"Well, if I haven't told you how grateful I am for coming to my rescue, then I hope you know how much I appreciate it."

He stopped tapping the crutches and eyed me sweetly. "Least I could do," he said. "Plus, it got me out of surgery for a day or two." Ayden had arrived at our condo just as he saw us leaving. He'd been the one following us, actually.

"Doesn't look like I'll be so lucky," I said, wincing as I tried to shift myself on the gurney to a more comfortable position. I had a compound fracture and they were trying to decide how to fix it while not causing any harm to my baby. I'd been given the option of general anesthesia for the surgery necessary to repair the bone and close the wound, and I'd absolutely declined, which meant that I'd be given a local and something to bite on while they fixed my arm. I wasn't looking forward to it.

"How you doin', kid?" Ayden asked me after a moment.

"I've had better days," I told him. "You?"

He grinned. "Today was a better day than two days ago, so I'm good."

"Excellent," I said. "Any sign of my husband?"

Ayden leaned back and looked around the curtain. "Nope."

Heath had gone off in search of the orthopedist who would operate on me, because I'd been sitting on the gurney for more than an hour, waiting to be wheeled into the OR, and the pain was starting to make me crazy.

Gilley had tried to hang out with us, but he kept gagging at the sight of my arm, which I couldn't really see, thank God, because, well . . . *compound fracture,* right? Anyway, he'd gone off in search of something to ease his nausea. Probably chocolate.

"Hey," Chris said as she pulled the curtain aside and stepped into my area. "How're you feeling?"

"Like I wished everyone would stop asking me that," I grumbled. The pain was making me seriously snippy.

"What'd they say about the baby?" she asked anxiously.

I'd been seen by the resident gyno even before the orthopedic. "The baby's okay," I said, closing my eyes in relief. My poor sweet child. The size of a bean and already she'd been through way more than anyone should.

"Thank God," Chris said, coming over to sit on the edge of my bed. Ayden had the only chair in the area. "We booked Bernard and Angelica," she told me.

"Good," I said, taking some deep breaths. I'd been given a pain pill that was safe for pregnant women, which meant it was having little to no effect blocking the pain. To take my mind off my discomfort, I said, "Has Captain Comb-Over said anything?"

"No," she said with a smile. "But Angelica agreed to testify against him in exchange for a lighter sentence. She filled us in."

"Tell me," I said.

"Well, it's a lot like you guys guessed. She and Bernard were insanely jealous of you and Heath. They felt you guys stole their one shot of really making it, and that's how they first got together, actually. Misery loved company. They talked a lot about the *Haunted Possessions* show, and how, if they'd had a chance to sit in front of the dagger, nobody would've gotten murdered."

I snorted. "Sure," I said. "Nobody but them, probably."

"Yeah, well, they each seem to have a pretty high opinion of themselves. Anyway, Angelica said that over the years, their jealousy turned more toward obsession, but she claims that Bernard was far more obsessed than she was. She said that he watched every episode of *Ghoul Getters* and followed the updates on the fan site religiously. When he saw that there was a movie coming out featuring one of your busts, and that the studio was going to partner with a museum here in Boston to showcase items from your show, he saw an opportunity, especially when he learned that you and Heath were taking a vacation out of the country for three weeks."

"I knew that fan site was a bad idea," I said.

"You really should take it down," she agreed. "There's way too much personal information on there."

At that moment, Heath pulled back the curtain and offered me a pained expression. "I'm still trying to find this surgeon, Em."

"Okay, honey," I told him, and forced a smile onto my face. He'd been fussing over me since we got to the hospital, and it was driving me a little crazy. I liked that he'd gone in search of my surgeon. "Keep looking, will you?"

Heath nodded and headed off again, leaving Chris to get back to her story. "Anyway," she said, "Angelica told me that they'd met Gilley in San Francisco and found him to be a very gullible guy."

I sighed. "It's true. He is. Obvs."

"So, she and her husband hatched a plan. Bernard called Gilley, posing as one of the studio producers, and since he also knew that Gopher was away in the Himalayas, he figured he could drop Gopher's name as the source for hearing about the dagger without raising any suspicions in Gilley.

"Gilley took the bait and Bernard and Angelica waited for the dagger to be delivered to the museum. They then used some of the money Angelica had recently come into from an inheritance to bribe Sullivan and Murdock into allowing them access to the exhibit. Bernard had thought himself very clever when he'd used the name of Todd Tolliver to set up the accounts for the wire transfer. He was hoping that you'd figure out he'd been stalking Ayden too."

I looked at Ayden and said, "I bet you're regretting doing that news story. See what fame brings you? Nothing but misery."

"Hey, the reporter on that story was cute," he said. "I was unduly influenced."

Chris chuckled. "Yeah, well, all of this has convinced me to take down my Facebook page."

"Good idea," I said. "Now, tell me what Angelica said next so I don't think about my arm too much."

Chris got right back to her story. "Angelica said that once Sullivan and Murdock let them into the exhibit, it took them several hours to remove all the magnets at the display and replace them with duds. She said that Bernard also made a deal with Angelica's son—a loser thirty-year-old with a record of assault and battery— that if he could stake out Ayden and make sure that when the dagger was stolen that Ayden didn't get on a plane to come help you figure out who'd taken it, that Bernard would give Angelica's son the deed to their house when the two of them got their own TV gig."

"She was delusional to think she and Bernard were going to get a TV deal out of this whole thing," I said.

"Yeah, well, Bernard had her convinced that if he could get ahold of the dagger, unleash the demon into a crowd to cause a little mayhem, that he could be the big hero who put the genie back in its bottle."

"So we were right," I said. "They planned to sabotage the opening night of the exhibit."

"They did," Chris agreed. "But it backfired on them when you guys showed up and your gear wasn't the same gear that'd been tampered with. Bernard was there in disguise, but he lost his nerve to unleash the demon when you and Heath found your way in the dark to the display case and brought back the magnetic field around the dagger. He abandoned the effort when the lights came back on, but he went back later that night to steal the dagger from the museum.

"He had the access code for the back door, so he let himself in, but he wasn't expecting Sullivan to be working late, and as he'd promised but not delivered to the director a lot more money to look the other way when Bernard switched out all the exhibit's magnets, he and Sullivan got into it and Bernard killed him. He then found the computer with the security footage, stole the dagger, and went right over to your place to see what would happen when he opened the portal."

"So he was stalking us," I said, knowing my theory about the dagger needing to be close by when the various spooks from my past began showing up.

"He was," she said. "Anyway, Murdock knew that Bernard had killed Sullivan, and he too tried to blackmail Bernard into giving him more money, which Bernard did, but then Angelica said that Bernard killed Murdock after he led us straight to Ashworth Commons, where Bernard and Angelica were hiding. Murdock had been hoping that after he warned Bernard that we were onto the security guard's involvement, Higgins would protect him from us, but it turns out Murdock needed protecting from Bernard."

"Wait," I said. "They were hiding at Ashworth Commons this whole time?"

"Yeah," she said. "On the first floor. Apartment One-B."

"How'd they know about the Commons?" Ayden asked.

"It was on the fan site," Chris told him. "As your last active and not quite successful bust, Bernard hoped you might come back to clear out Gertie, and he'd be lying in wait for you."

"Gilley and that stupid fan site," I growled.

"Yeah," Chris said.

"He couldn't have known all this would come about from his posts," Ayden said in defense of Gil.

I sighed and nodded reluctantly. "True. Still, I'm

going to have to lecture him about it. And get him to take down the site and our Twitter page."

"Or become a little more circumspect, like Rick Lavinia," Chris said, with a slight smile.

"He didn't have anything to do with any of this, right?" I asked.

"Nope. Angelica admitted that she forwarded the photo of Ashworth Commons to Rick with a note that it was a location you guys were considering for one of your next shows. She said that Bernard hoped it would send us in the wrong direction, and if Rick actually happened to show up, he'd have the pleasure of taking him out with one of the spooks from the portal too."

"Wow," I said. "Bernard was way more bloodthirsty than I ever gave him credit for."

"His obsession to reclaim or ignite some fame overrode every other thought," Ayden observed. "When I worked homicide, I'd see extreme cases of sociopathic narcissism like this all the time."

Chris said, "Yep. He's a classic case, and Angelica had more than her fair share of the narcissism part."

"So now what?" I asked.

Chris got up and moved a few feet away from my gurney. "Now I leave you to go fill out some paperwork. Lots of paperwork. Some of it has to do with the fact that the murder weapon used to kill Charlie Murdock was not found on scene. I doubt we'll ever see it again, right, M.J.?"

"Not unless you go looking down a very deep hole, covered in cement," I told her. Heath had taken Oruç's dagger from me before the paramedics arrived to take me to the hospital. He smothered it in magnets, and he'd promised me that as soon as he knew I was all right, he, Gilley, and Ayden were going to drive out to the woods somewhere, spend an hour digging a hole, throw that dagger and as many magnets as they had on them in it, and cover the whole mess with concrete.

"Good," Chris said, with a wink at Ayden.

He grinned back.

After she'd gone, he leaned forward and said, "She's a looker. Any chance she's single?"

The next day, after being released from the hospital, I shuffled slowly and carefully around the condo, sore from head to toe, and with my upper arm feeling like it was on fire.

The doctor had ordered me to take it easy, but I needed something to take my mind off the discomfort, so I tidied up the condo a little, then looked around for something else to do.

Heath had taken Ayden back to the airport, and then he was heading to the grocery store for food and such; after that, he'd pick up Doc from Teeko's place.

I hadn't heard much from Gilley since I'd been back, and I decided to head downstairs to visit with him. As I approached the door I heard laughter from inside. Gil's distinctive laugh, and that of a woman.

I paused, wondering if I should intrude, but the thought of heading back upstairs and pacing the floor until Heath got back didn't appeal to me, so I knocked.

Gilley opened up almost right away. He was back in his flapper dress with full makeup, but now he had a tiara on his head. "M.J.!" he said warmly. "How you doin', sugar?"

"Bored," I admitted. "And my arm hurts."

"Aww, puddin'," Gil said, his southern accent thickening. Very, very carefully he leaned in to hug my good side. "Catherine-Cooper-Masters is here. Come on in!"

I walked into Gilley's condo and spied Cat perched demurely on the edge of one of Gilley's living room chairs. "M.J.!" she exclaimed, getting up to come over to me and take up my good hand. "Oh, Gilley has told me all about your harrowing experience. I've decided to send you to my spa for a day, as soon as you feel up to it, to be pampered head to toe!"

I forced a smile. "That's so nice of you, Cat, but I couldn't impose on you like that."

"No, no," she insisted. "It's no imposition." She gently tucked a stray strand of hair behind my ear and added, "And we can find someone there to do your makeup and hair. Make you look pretty."

Gilley was nodding like a bobblehead. I had a feeling they'd been conspiring against me.

Catherine squeezed my hand before moving back over to her chair. I then noticed that there were small white boxes with tissue paper all over Gil's living room.

"What's all this?" I asked, motioning to the boxes.

"Tiaras," Cat and Gilley said together.

My eyes widened as I looked around, and then at Gil. He took off the tiara on his head, put it back in its white box, and took out another, the size of a beauty pageant crown. When I stared at him in surprise, he shrugged and said, "What? She gets me."

I laughed, and it felt so good. "Got any green tea?" I asked him.

He moved over to stroke my cheek fondly and said, "Coming right up."

Cat and I made small talk for a bit, and as Gilley fussed with the tea and something to snack on in the kitchen, my cell rang. I looked at the display curiously, excused myself, and went to answer the call. "This is M.J.," I said.

"Oh, thank goodness I got you!" said a voice I didn't recognize. "M.J., my name is Diana Dahlmer. I got your name and number from Lucy Ashworth. She said you could help me. I've just purchased an old house in Swampscott, and there's some awful poltergeist scaring us half to death! We need you to come and get rid of it for us, and I'll pay whatever you're charging. I'm that desperate."

I didn't say anything for a moment—that instinctive urge to help someone in need was pulling at me. But then I turned and looked back at Gilley and Catherine sitting in his living room, gabbing like old school friends—like Gil and I had when we were young—and my next thought was to my child, and what friends she might grow up with. What I said next was actually far easier to say than I'd expected. "Diana, I'm so sorry that you haven't heard, but my husband and I are retired. We're no longer available to do any ghostbusting."

"Oh!" she cried. "Please, M.J.? Won't you please reconsider just this one time? As I said, I'm desperate!"

At that moment there was a knock on Gilley's front door, and a second later Heath's voice echoed out from the kitchen. I heard him say, "Hey, Gil, any chance that gorgeous wife of mine is here?" His voice sounded so happy and relaxed, and my heart filled with love for him.

"M.J.?" Diana said. "Are you there?"

"Yes, Diana, I'm here, but my answer to you is no. I won't reconsider, and I really am sorry. You might try Rick Lavinia, though. I hear he's always looking for work." With that, I hung up the phone and headed back out to my husband and my best friend . . . and the rest of my life, spook-free.

Read on for a look at the first book in
Victoria Laurie's *New York Times* bestselling
Psychic Eye mystery series,

ABBY COOPER, PSYCHIC EYE

Available now from Obsidian
wherever books and e-books are sold.

My basic philosophy is simple: People are like ice cream. Take me, for instance. You'd think that by my profession alone—professional psychic—I'd be a ringer for Nutty Coconut, but the reality is that I'm far more like vanilla—consistent, a little bland, missing some hot fudge.

The exception, of course, is my rather unique ability to predict the future. Okay, so maybe with that added in I'm at least a candidate for French vanilla.

Still, overall my life is sadly *that* boring. I'm single with no immediate prospects, I rarely go out (hence the no immediate prospects), I pay all my bills on time, I have very few vices and only two close friends.

See what I mean? Vanilla.

Now, I'm not saying my life is *all* bad. At the very least I'm privy to the richly flavorful lives of my clients. Take the Tooty-Fruity sitting in front of me, for example. Sharon is a pretty young woman in her mid-thirties, with short blond hair, too much makeup, a recent boob job and not a clue in sight. On her left hand dangles a rather opulent diamond wedding ring, and over the course of the last twenty minutes all I've been able to do is feel sorry for the poor schmuck who gave it to her.

"Okay, I'm getting the feeling that there's a triangle here . . . like there's someone else moving in on your marriage," I said.

"Yes."

"And it's someone *you're* romantically interested in."

"Yes."

"And they're telling me that you think this is true love . . ."

"Yes, but, uh, Abigail? Who are 'they'?" she asked, looking around nervously.

I get this question all the time, and you would think I would have learned by now to prepare my clients before beginning the session, but change was never my strong suit. "Oh, sorry. 'They' are my crew, or rather, my spirit guides. I believe that they talk to your spirit guides and it all gets communicated back to me."

"Really? Can they tell you their names?" she whispered, still looking around bug-eyed.

We were getting off track here. I pulled us back on course, afraid I would lose the train of thought flittering through my brain. "Uh, no, Sharon, I don't typically get names. I only get pictures and thoughts. So, as I was saying, we were talking about this love triangle, right?"

"Yes," she answered, leaning forward to hang on my every word.

"Okay, I'm just going to give it to you the way they're

giving it to me. . . . They're giving me the feeling that this other guy is saying all the right things, that he may say he's interested in you and that he wants to be with you but he's not telling you the whole story." Sharon's bug eyes squinted now as she looked at me critically. "Okay, does this other guy have blond hair?"

"Yes."

"And he works some sort of night job, like, he works at night. . . . Is he a bartender?"

"Oh my God . . . yes, he is!"

"And your husband, he's the guy with dark brown hair and a beard or facial hair, right?"

Sharon sucked in a breath of surprise and replied, "Yes, he's got a goatee."

"And your husband does something with computers, like he has something to do with making computers or something."

"He's a computer engineer . . ."

"Okay, Sharon, they're telling me that the blond is a liar, and that you may not think your husband is Mr. Don Juan but he loves you. They're saying if you leave your husband for this other guy with the blond hair that there won't be any going back. You won't be able to fix it once it's out in the open. And I get the feeling that if you continue to fool around on the side you're going to get caught. If you think you won't, then you're kidding yourself. They're saying there is already a woman—I think she's older than you—with red hair who's *very* nosy and she already suspects, and she wouldn't think twice about telling your husband. I think this is like a neighbor or something . . ."

"Oh my God! My neighbor, Mrs. O'Connor, has red hair, and she *would* tell my husband!"

"See? She's already very suspicious, and I get the feeling that if you don't rethink this whole thing you could end up divorced and alone. This bartender guy isn't going to marry a divorced woman with two kids. You have two, right? A boy and a girl?"

"Yes, but . . ." she squeaked.

"No," I said firmly. "No buts. You need to do some hard thinking here, 'cuz there will be no going back, and if you continue down this path I'm seeing nothing but heartache in your life. You won't really know what you've lost until it's gone."

At that moment I heard the blissful sound of my chime clock dinging and the tape in the cassette player clicked off. I instantly felt relieved. This woman wasn't picking up what I was laying down and it was pretty frustrating to me. I stood and said gently but firmly, "And that's all the time we have." I flipped open the cassette player and removed the tape, enclosed it in its plastic case and handed it to her along with a tissue. Sharon got up with me and walked with a bent head and a forced smile toward the door.

She thanked me for my time and was asking when she could come back when I said, "Actually, Sharon, I'd prefer it if you made an appointment with a friend of mine." I walked back toward my credenza and retrieved a card from a stack piled there. "This is Lori Sellers. She's a psychotherapist with an office over on Eleven Mile. She's very good and I think it would be a good thing for you to talk to her about the choices in front of you." I put the card in her outstretched hand. "If you want to come back and see me, I allow only two visits per year, and that's a good rule of thumb. You shouldn't get hooked on readers; remember that all of the answers are inside you. All you have to do is trust yourself and listen."

Sharon didn't look convinced, so I placed my hand on her arm and walked her gently to the door. "Now I want you to go home and replay the tape and consider everything I've said. You have the gift of free will, and it's a powerful force. You can change your own destiny if you put your mind to it. Just be careful, okay? I mean, you've been married for . . . what? Ten years?"

Another sucked-in breath of surprise. "Yes. How did you know that?"

I smiled and spread my hands in an "aha" gesture. "I'm psychic."

As I watched Sharon leave I couldn't help but consider for the billionth time how much that word "psychic" still caught in my throat. It's just too close to the word "psycho" for my taste. Typically, when asked what I do for a living I tack on a softer word, like "psychic *intuitive*" to lend a smidgen of legitimacy. I'd even had business cards made up reading, ABIGAIL COOPER, P.I. with teeny-weeny little letters underneath in parentheses spelling out PSYCHIC INTUITIVE. Most people think I'm trying to be clever. The truth is, I'm a chickenshit.

I never wanted to be a psychic, professional or otherwise. It's something that was more or less thrust upon me, and I've never really felt comfortable with it.

It isn't that I'm not proud of what I do; it's just that I've always been conscious of the fact that I'm *different*.

For instance, there are plenty of people out there who will engage me in casual conversation and might even find me amusing until they discover what I do for a living . . . and then they recede like a tide from the beach and I'm left in the sand feeling like I've got a big red X on my forehead. I've been a professional psychic for four years now, and I'm still waiting for the proverbial tide to come back in.

I was just about to close the door after Sharon when one of my regulars, Candice Fusco, came walking down the corridor, carrying a large manila envelope. "Hey, Candice," I called as she caught sight of me.

"Hi, Abby. I'm on time, right?" She glanced at her watch and hurried her step.

"Yup. I was just seeing my last client out." I stepped sideways, holding the door open and allowing her to enter. Candice was probably only an inch or two taller than me, but the three-inch heels I had never seen her go without made her tower over me. She was an elegant woman, with a fondness for expensive suits. Today she wore cream silk that flowed and rippled with the breeze of her movements and set off the tan of her skin and her light blond hair. Her femininity usually makes me a little self-conscious, but within a minute or two I'm over it, eased, I think, by her genuine nature. You would never guess by her dress and mannerisms that Candice is a private investigator, and a damn good one at that—although her most recent successes were helped a bit by yours truly.

"Would you like to sit here or in my reading room?" I asked, closing the door behind Candice.

"Here would be fine, Abby. This shouldn't take us too long," she replied, pulling the straps from her purse and shoulder bag off her shoulder.

"So how's Kalamazoo these days?" I asked, gesturing toward the two chairs in the office waiting room for us to sit in.

"Still there," she said, taking a seat. "I swear this drive takes longer every time."

"The way you drive? I doubt it. How long did it take you today?"

"An hour and forty-five minutes."

"New record?"

"Nah. I've done it in an hour and thirty-five before. Of course, I was doing ninety-five the whole time, but I've slowed it down a notch since you told me to."

"Yeah, not a good idea to ignore a warning like that when it comes up." I'd told Candice the last time we saw each other to watch her lead foot or she could end up with a hefty speeding ticket. "So, is that the stuff?" I asked, pointing to the manila envelope she still held.

"Yes, these are the three employees we've narrowed it down to," Candice said, extending the envelope toward me. I took it and opened the flap, extracting three pictures—two women and one man, all posing for mug shots of the employee-badge variety. I flipped quickly from photo to photo, then back through more slowly, taking my time to open my intuition to each person. Candice had called me the previous evening about a new case she was working on. A large company that handled mutual funds had discovered several thousand dollars missing from its clients' portfolios. The company had not made the discovery public yet and wanted Candice's help in identifying the embezzler.

"Okay—these two?" I said, holding up a photo of a man in his mid-forties, with droopy jowls and yellowed teeth, and another of a woman in her mid- to late twenties, with bangs poufed high above her head and gobby eyes coated with too much mascara. "There's something going on between them. I get the feeling that they have some sort of romantic connection. This guy"—I pointed to the photo of the man—"he's up to no good. I get the feeling that he's sneaky, and it's not just about fooling around with another employee. There's something more sinister here. Did he just buy a new boat?"

"He's made quite a few purchases lately, which is one of the reasons the company suspects him. And yes, one of his purchases was a boat."

"Okay, this is your guy. There's something about this boat, though. I get the feeling that he's covered his tracks pretty good, but there's evidence hidden on the boat. I'd start by snooping around on it and seeing what you turn up."

"What about the third photo?" Candice asked.

I looked at the third photo, an older woman roughly in her late fifties to early sixties, with washed-out gray hair, a prominent nose, and muddy eyes. I held the photo and felt around using my radar. "I get the feeling this woman has no clue about what's going on, that she's being used as a pawn or something. This guy may be using her in some way to cover his tracks, setting her up to take the blame for the crime."

"That makes a lot of sense," Candice said. "Most of the evidence is pointing to her right now, but she's been an exemplary employee at the company for almost thirty years. She's about to retire, and we couldn't figure out why, after all this time, she would start stealing from the company."

"Yeah, I agree with your instincts. It really feels to me like she's being set up. Look on the boat, Candice. There's something there."

Candice gave me a big smile as I put the photos back in the envelope. "Thanks, Abby. You've probably saved me a ton of legwork on this."

"No sweat, Candice. By the way, what's the deal with Ireland?"

Candice gave a startled laugh. "God! Does anything get by you? I'm going there next month for a six-week vacation."

"Wow," I said enviously. "Well, you're going to have a great time, but you'll need to pack warmer than you think."

"Thanks. I'll make sure I do. I'll be back in September, and I'm sure I'll be calling you for help on the next big case I get."

"Anytime," I said, standing up as she handed me a check and we walked to the door.

ALSO AVAILABLE FROM
NEW YORK TIMES BESTSELLING AUTHOR

VICTORIA LAURIE

NO GHOULS ALLOWED
A Ghost Hunter Mystery

On a trip to Georgia to see her father,
psychic medium M. J. Holliday finds herself
trapped in a haunted mansion...

<u>AVAILABLE IN THE SERIES</u>
What's a Ghoul to Do?
Demons Are a Ghoul's Best Friend
Ghouls Just Haunt to Have Fun
Ghouls Gone Wild
Ghouls, Ghouls, Ghouls
Ghoul Interrupted
What A Ghoul Wants
The Ghoul Next Door

Available wherever books are sold or
at penguin.com

om0134